ZELLIE'S WEAKNESS

'Please, Rodrigo,' she groaned.

'Please fuck me?'

'No . . .'

Boyish fingers slipped into the soft opening of Zellie's pussy. Her thighs opened of their own accord. She gave a long deep groan.

'Zellie always wants to fuck.'

She couldn't deny it. If he had said he wanted her doggy style, right then, she would have dropped to her knees and torn her panties open.

'So, I reckon I might as well fuck her,' Rodrigo concluded and he took her hand.

Her fingers closed around his. Her reason floated upwards. From a height, she saw her mildness, the wetness of her thighs, the still rucked-up skirt. She sighed. So many weaknesses. So delicious. Her head rested on his shoulder and, perhaps because he hadn't fucked her yet, he didn't shuck her off.

ZELLIE'S WEAKNESS

Jean Aveline

This book is a work of fiction.
In real life, make sure you practise safe, sane and consensual sex.

First published in 2007 by
Nexus
Thames Wharf Studios
Rainville Rd
London W6 9HA

A catalogue record for this book is available from the British Library.

www.nexus-books.com

Typeset by TW Typesetting, Plymouth, Devon
Printed and bound in Great Britain by CPI Bookmarque, Croydon CR0 4TD

The paper used in this book is a natural, recyclable product made from wood grown in sustainable forests. The manufacturing process conforms to the regulations of the country of origin.

ISBN 978 0 352 34160 0

Distributed in the USA by Holtzbrinck Publishers, LLC, 175 Fifth Avenue, New York, NY 10010, USA

1 3 5 7 9 10 8 6 4 2

Contents

Symbols key

 Corporal Punishment

 Female Domination

 Institution

 Medical

 Period Setting

 Restraint/Bondage

 Rubber/Leather

 Spanking

 Transvestism

 Underwear

 Uniforms

1

Aunt Shelby

Six months ago, at that time of the evening, Zellie would probably have been lazily sitting out in the back garden, thinking about nothing in particular. She might have been humming the words of a song or chatting on her mobile. She might have been trying out a new pen colour for her homework. A book might have held her attention for a few minutes. Time would have passed until her mother had finally told her it was too cold to stay outside.

Today, laziness was a thing of the past.

Clutching her school books to her bulging breasts, she had already walked hard for an hour and was not even home. She had slipped from her school by a hole in the fence as her friends had sauntered out of the front gates. She had cut through an area of scrub thick with midges. Brambles had torn at her stockings. She had trudged along beside a broad slow river where dragonflies dipped long red tails in soupy water. She had clambered over sun-hot rocks and soaked her shoes in a reeking marsh. She had cut through the car park of her local supermarket where men had stared (at her shoes, at her stockings, at her breasts). She had circled behind the fine stone-built church where once, long ago, she had been baptised in silk and holy water. She had crept along a urine-soaked alley beside a car repair shop, holding her breath and listening so intently for the sounds of boys that her ears had hurt.

And finally, after nearly an hour, she had almost made it home.

If she had taken the direct route, she could have walked it in ten lazy minutes. Even now, when she could see her house not fifty metres away, the ordeal was not over. Rodrigo would be sure to be looking out for her and Rodrigo was becoming more and more demanding. Worse, his cousin Eduardo was staying and, like boys everywhere, in pairs, they liked to show off. Yesterday, they had showed off so much that her pussy was still sore.

So, Zellie watched carefully from the dusty bushes next to the alley until she was sure no one lay in wait. Then she ran as fast as she could along the tree-lined street. From left and right, fine houses watched her long legs flash in the slanting sunlight. They saw her school skirt whip up. They saw the golden flesh of her slender arms and the goose bumps of anxiety there. If they'd had very good eyes, and were rude enough to stoop, they would have glimpsed the rounded behind, and the meagre white cotton beneath the nylon of her tights. If they had been male houses, their chimneys would have shot heavenwards.

She was twenty metres into her dash when a group of boys (younger boys, not the dangerous kind) shot out of a driveway right in front of her, their bicycles muddy and their faces shining with excitement. One of them shouted her name.

Zellie's nerves were not as good as they used to be. Startled, she felt her books and papers spill from her arms and scatter across the pavement. The boys laughed. They weren't bad boys – Zellie knew them all – but, just for a moment, they sounded like a pack of hyenas. Then Tom, the oldest and kindest, dropped his bike and asked if she needed a hand. She flashed a smile, then knelt and began scrabbling like a mad girl.

Still scanning the street for older boys – for the sort who would do more than just laugh at her – she scooped up the geography of America and grabbed the mathematics of ancient Greece. She reacquired the history of England from the long grass beneath a cherry tree and tucked Evolution into a dictionary of French, creasing the pages of both. Tom crouched down and rescued the animal kingdom from a muddy puddle. Flecks of mud stained her blouse as he dropped it into her arms. More mess! She thanked him as calmly as she could.

The boys watched her for a moment as she flicked through her stuff, making sure that everything was there, then suddenly they were gone. It was as if the air had parted and they had dived into the opening.

Zellie was alone. She needed to be quick. Just as she decided to run, a pen fell from an exercise book. It rolled across the pavement to hide itself under the overhanging branches of a bush. It was a special pen, a present from her mother before she had disappeared so suddenly and inexplicably. Her eyes swept the street again. A shadow moved in a window of the Prentice house, panicking her. It was boy-shaped. Will Prentice was growing by the day. I'll come back tonight, she thought. I'll bring a torch.

She ran off as fast as she could, her heart in her mouth. A man appeared in front of her and she gave a little shriek. But it was only Mr Angelo.

Kindly, ancient Mr Angelo, face scoured by smile lines, stiffened at the sound of the shriek and raised the watering can in his hand high, as a shield. Portia, his sleek retriever, made a play dart at her ankles. Zellie's legs, as athletic as they were long, as agile as they were golden, sidestepped them both adroitly.

By the time Mr Angelo started to smile a welcome, she was past him. Portia woofed.

'Is there a fire?' he called.

'Toilet!' she shouted over her shoulder, then blushed. How could she have shouted out 'toilet' in the street where she lived?

She ran on. Rodrigo's house was next. She refused to look. She blocked her ears with a thought. If he was on his balcony she wouldn't see him. If he called to her she would be deaf.

Only another twenty metres!

Still no Rodrigo. Still no Eduardo. God was good. God was as kind as Mr Angelo, who had always let her look through his telescope at the stars above. Her legs were tired now. At her groin, the muscles ached, but then they had ached all day. Eduardo had stretched her further than a girl should be stretched . . .

There were only two more houses now: the Henderson house and Jimmy's place.

Mrs Henderson was unloading her car. Ten or more white plastic bags filled the back of her four-by-four. She gave Zellie a pained look. Mrs Henderson was always pained and nothing anybody ever did or said seemed able to change that.

Zellie flashed a smile anyway. Zellie had been trained to smile beautifully in any situation. On another day, she would have offered to help. Helpfulness was one of Zellie's weaknesses. But this was not an evening to be helping. Guilt stabbed into her heart as she swept on by.

Jimmy's house seemed empty. Nothing leapt from the bushes that surrounded it. The clever topiary – swans, top hats, chessmen – did not come alive and grab her.

At last she was home. The deep shadows and still warm air of the driveway enfolded her. The old timber and brick house, wrapped in a bright wreath of gold and red ivy, smiled down. The flame bushes, where she had played hide and seek so many times with Jimmy, rattled their leaves in welcome.

Six months ago she would have been safe. Her mother would be waiting in the kitchen with crackers and cheese. Or she would be sunbathing on the patio with an empty lounger beside her and Zellie would collapse into it to tell her day, her *whole* day, in a long, sweet revelation. But everything had changed when her mother went away to work in a foreign land.

Now, Zellie was facing a more serious challenge than eating crackers and cheese. She needed to get to her room without being seen by the twins. She needed to change her torn stockings. She needed to dry and polish her shoes.

When she was younger, she would have climbed the big old tree if she had wanted to enter the house secretly. Now that she was a grown-up, it would not be dignified. Even so, she glanced at the thick strong branches of the cedar standing at the side of the house, branches that looped from the balcony of her bedroom all the way over to the balcony of Jimmy's bedroom in the house next door.

For a moment, she wondered if she should risk going out into the street again and asking if she could use that aerial highway. Jimmy was her friend. He would never say no. But he would have asked why, and Zellie could not have lied. It was another one of her weaknesses. She could never tell a lie. And she could never tell Jimmy about Rodrigo and the things he made her do.

So, it was more worry, more scrabbling to be safe. She thought of the front door with its creaking hinges. She thought of the side door that was usually locked. She realised that her only chance was to head for the patio door.

Her aunt would probably be resting in her room. The twins would probably be in the kitchen making a mess

– apple pie mess, popcorn mess, chocolate cake mess. With mess they were creative and this was the time of day for mess. Later, it would be the time of day for Zellie to clean up.

She passed under the tall cedar tree, pushed through the bushes that were supposed to keep out the burglars, slipped past the tool shed, skirted the fish pond and stepped out onto the open patio as nervously as a deer stepping out of its forest.

All was silent. All was still.

She walked as boldly as she could. If the twins or her aunt saw her, it was important that she did not look secretive. No one liked secrets. No one liked Zellie to have secrets.

The French windows were open and she stepped into the sitting room as carefully as an assassin. There was a smell of old flowers: her aunt liked pot pourri. Draped over the back of a chair was a half-completed piece of crochet – a tablecloth perhaps, a toilet roll concealer, a doily.

Her aunt liked pot pourri and crochet. She also liked the twins and religion. She did not like much else and she certainly did not like Zellie.

'The angels look out for good children,' she had said once. 'But whatever walks with you, my girl, scuttles on hard claws and smells of sulphur.' Alarmed, Zellie had rushed upstairs to the bathroom. She had scrubbed herself for an hour and then asked her aunt if she smelt any better. 'You are looking for a good hiding, girl!' her aunt had told her, and within half an hour Zellie had learnt not to cheek her elders and betters.

The crochet was a bad sign. Her aunt did not leave things lying around. Neatness was a virtue as was cleanliness and punctuality. Zellie had transgressed mightily in all these departments so her eyes scanned the room intently. It was mostly in shadow. The windows were covered by heavy drapes. Light was one of the things her aunt did not like. Not in excess.

There were half a dozen places where a person could sit and not be seen. It was the biggest room in the house and filled with sofas, sideboards, easy chairs, tables, chaise longues, screens, knickknacks and flummery from every corner of the world. Each piece was an heirloom, a hand-me-down, a container of family history.

This was the special heart of a special house. It had been her mother's favourite room because her mother had loved entertaining. Friends and family were lured to sit in the chairs with lovingly made food, the promise of an attentive listener, the siren sound of rich laughter from mother and daughter, and sometimes, when he wasn't buried away in his study, witty conversation from a clever but oversensitive and fragile father. The room had forgotten all that now, the memory driven away by the scent of dead flowers and the click of crochet needles. People were one of the things that Zellie's aunt did not like.

A tiny sound warned Zellie that trouble was coming – a wheeze, her aunt's dry, creaky, waking-up wheeze.

'Who is it?'

The voice was drowsy. Zellie looked at the door to the hallway. Hard parquet flooring lay like a minefield all around it. If she slipped off her shoes, if she was quick –

'Who's there?'

In the shadows of the sofa, a figure stirred. Two bright points of light told Zellie that she had been seen. Zellie had hesitated and was lost.

'It's me, Aunt Shelby.'

The woman rising from her bed of crochet materials – balls of purple and green, balls of grey and yellow – was neither an aunt nor a Shelby. Yet Zellie called her 'Aunt' because that was how she had been bidden and because compliance was one of Zellie's weaknesses.

7

Zellie *was* a Shelby, as was her father. In Acacia, Shelby was a name to be proud of. The school Zellie attended was the John Shelby Universal High School. The local newspaper was the *Shelby Herald*. The local hospital was a Shelby Hospital, one of many in that part of the world.

Zellie's grandfather had made his money with skill, hard work and luck in the area of personal communications. Towards the end of his life, he had viewed the mouldering piles of cash and stock with increasing suspicion and had disposed of it all in a fury of philanthropic endowments. Thus, instead of using it to make his children idle, vain and empty-headed, he had used it to spread his own good name far and wide – though some had said it was the fear of God, a camel and the eye of a needle. Either way his children, and their children after them, cut free, spread and prospered like hardy weeds, occupying every niche available to the quick and the clever.

The woman yawning and straightening her hair and bringing her face to a focus as sharp as a thistle was not a Shelby except by association, and the association was of such a dubious kind, no one of any authority had explained it to Zellie, as yet.

Jimmy said that he had heard from somebody, who had heard it from somebody else, that Aunt Shelby had been wild once. The same unknown source contended that Zellie's dark horse uncle – Uncle Hum – had ridden her carelessly, producing what Jimmy now called the evil twins.

'Come here, girl!'

Zellie felt her stomach sink through the floor. She approached the wiry form of her aunt, praying that the gloom would save her. It did not. Aunt Shelby sat upright, as thin and hard as a broomstick (a broomstick that the twins rode to Black Mass on moonless nights, if Jimmy was to be believed), and she subjected Zellie to a full examination with scorching eyes.

'What in heaven's name have you done to your stockings?' Aunt Shelby asked, her voice as dry and scratchy as an old gramophone recording.

This was not a voice that Zellie had heard before her mother had been kidnapped/murdered by terrorists, seduced by a dark lover, lost her mind, or any of the other rumours that had emerged from Tunisia, the last country anyone could be sure she had been alive in.

The Aunt Shelby that Zellie had known before she moved in and took over the running of Zellie's home and life had a voice as sweet as honey. She had a smile as wide as salvation. She had been virtually a saint and the perfect choice to plug the gap in Zellie's life. It hadn't been many weeks, however, before the honey became vinegar and the smile, brimstone.

Whatever the old woman had cooked for Zellie's father in her oven of fundamentalist zeal had rapidly driven him to drink, and a cold exit from hearth and home. In fact, Zellie's father had drunk himself into and out of rehab so many times he was no longer allowed within a hundred yards of Zellie or the house.

'Well?' Aunt Shelby bellowed. 'Answer my question!'

Zellie began a long description of the scrubland behind the school.

Her aunt cut her short. 'And what were you doing in the scrubland at the back of the school?' Her voice rose in pitch then fell with a sudden, flat certainty. 'No. Don't tell me. There is only one reason a girl waits in the bushes.'

'I wasn't waiting,' Zellie protested.

Aunt Shelby raised a bony hand. 'Shh. I am not going to let you mither me today.'

'Mithering' was only one of the words Aunt Shelby had taught Zellie since her arrival. Other words were nincompoop, fathead and slattern.

Aunt Shelby brushed a few stray pieces of hair back into the bun atop her head, trying, it seemed, to compose herself, trying not to let the girl in front of her destroy her precious peace of mind. It was a futile effort. Aunt Shelby's eyes had continued their examination of Zellie unbidden, and she found herself staring at wet muddy shoes and the trail they had left across the beautifully polished parquet floor.

'Your shoes!'

Zellie hastily stepped out of her shoes and tried to explain how marshy the land beside the river was.

'And I suppose you were by the river for the same reason you were in the bushes!'

Zellie didn't know what to say. It was impossible for her to lie but it was even more impossible to tell the simple – complicated – truth that her clitoris had grown lately. That not only had it grown physically, to an impressive extent, but that it had grown in its capacities. The pip of flesh that had for so long been so peaceful and so modest had lately elongated and thickened to become a *finger* of flesh.

Even more than that, it had become a sort of radio tower that could detect boys and their desires at a distance and it could transmit desire in return, drawing boys of all kinds like a magnet draws iron filings.

Neither of these things – finger nor magnet – was in Zellie's control.

Even less in her control were the feelings her clitoris produced if a sweet boy smiled at her or a badly intentioned boy touched her, whether it be ever so lightly or ever so clumsily or, most disturbingly of all, if a boy touched her ever so *knowingly*.

These were things that Aunt Shelby should not be told because they would be a burden and her aunt already had too many burdens ranging from mithering children to mysterious headaches and too many taxes.

10

So, Zellie shouldered the burden instead and was learning the pleasures and pains of adulthood without being a trouble to anyone.

Luckily, her aunt was never much interested in what Zellie had to say so Zellie was neither obliged to tell the truth or bite her tongue. It was Aunt Shelby's assumption that Zellie lied about everything and Aunt Shelby preferred to reach her own conclusions. For once, her assumptions were not too far wide of the mark, missing the point by only 180 degrees.

'Boys! You've been chasing boys again.'

'No aunt, not chasing –'

Aunt Shelby's eyes hardened further. Popped from her head, they could have been used to cut glass. She raised her hand and Zellie stifled her protests. She knew that from this point on anything she said would be in vain and her head slumped onto her chest. There was only one way forward from here, only one way to assuage her aunt's rage. A sacrifice was required, a sacrifice of live human flesh – the flesh of her behind.

'Don't argue, girl. Go and wait in the games room.'

'But, Aunt –'

'Every word will earn another swat!'

'Yes, Aunt.' With her shoes in her hand and her heart in her boots, Zellie trudged out of the sitting room.

The games room was a late addition to the house, built out into the garden and reached by a little corridor. It was surrounded on all sides by bushes and trees which had been allowed to grow so that the light inside was greenish and dim.

Like every other part of the house, it contained history. There were old dolls and balls that no girl had played with in years. There were party dresses Zellie wouldn't wear again unless she fell through a looking glass. There were saved birthday cards – some signed by hands that no longer lived and others by hands that had hardly learnt to write. In a corner there was the paddling pool where Zellie had first learnt that frogs liked water – yuk! It was deflated now and sad looking. There was a kayak – very small – in which Zellie had once followed her father down the broad slow river. The prow of her father's kayak, very large and very red, could still be seen jutting from the roof of the tool shed. The red was turning to green where algae grew. A length of frayed mooring rope dripped from its very tip and swung gently in the breeze.

For a moment, Zellie stood in the centre of the room, her hand resting on a half-sized ping pong table. A doll's house stood on its slate-grey surface. If she were in a better mood, she could have greeted its inhabitants by name. There were books. There was one complete wall of books. On the floor were boxfuls of books. There were books which told a history that Aunt Shelby didn't believe in. Books which described a geography Aunt Zellie wasn't interested in. Books which contained a poetry that Aunt Shelby despised. Books, books, books. Unread, they could never protect Zellie.

There were many things besides these items but only one that truly mattered. Brown and fly-blown, there was the cupboard. Coffin-sized and sombre, it had a character that Aunt Shelby did approve of. Aunt Shelby had filled it with canes and paddles.

Abandoning the table, Zellie waited dutifully beside the grave column. Her wide blue eyes gazed through the window and out onto the darkening patio. Shoeless, her feet were cold. Tights-less (tights were not allowed in this room), her calves were prey to a draught from beneath the garden door. She shivered. She eyed the door which betrayed her. She remembered her mother in its frame.

She waited and waited. Aunt Shelby had a sense of drama, undeveloped by books, but richly embroidered by experience. She knew that a good beating could only begin with a good overture. A sumptuous feast of silence. A poignant anticipation. A firing-up of the memory of former beatings. A certainty of future beatings.

When Aunt Shelby finally appeared, she was a new woman. All sleepiness was gone. She was brimful of vigour and a whirlwind of determination. Zellie turned towards her slowly, a soft column of misery, twisting slightly at the waist, pale fingers pulling gently at her skirt. For a moment, their eyes met. Zellie's were resigned, rounded, puzzled. Aunt Shelby's were star-bright and narrow, glittering in a face dark with anger. They gazed at each other like different species.

The more Aunt Shelby glared, the more puzzled Zellie became. How could a pair of torn stockings turn the veins in Aunt Shelby's forehead into high-pressure hoses? How could Zellie's damp shoes wear so badly on her aunt's pinched nerves? How could a few muddy footprints lead to this? It was a puzzle. Yet Zellie was not one for shirking responsibility. Something that she had done had prompted all of this. And since letting Aunt Shelby beat her was the only way her aunt could regain her ease, Zellie was resigned to allowing it.

Of course, her behind was not the thing that Zellie would have most liked to offer the older woman. If Aunt Shelby could have been soothed by a cuddle, Zellie would have given that more gladly. If Aunt Shelby could have been eased by a good listening to, Zellie would have opened her ears with a more enthusiastic heart. Unfortunately, none of these things could avail.

'You are the most incorrigible girl I have ever had to deal with,' her aunt declared.

'I'm sorry, Aunt Shelby.'

'I believe you have no shame.'

'I do, Aunt Shelby.' Zellie had more shame than she could ever describe to Aunt Shelby.

'You stare at me as if butter wouldn't melt in your mouth.'

'It would, Aunt Shelby.' Many things had melted in Zellie's mouth (many more things had wanted to).

'You stare at me as if you *pity* me.'

'I do pity you, Aunt Shelby.'

Zellie's pity, hopelessly broad, indiscriminate and, at that moment, as sensitive as sandpaper, deepened as the colour of Aunt Shelby's face deepened. In a second, the skull-stretched skin went from red to scarlet and Zellie groaned with guilt.

Whatever she had said wrong this time was very, very wrong. Her aunt didn't even reply. Instead, she threw open the door of the cupboard and seized her favourite paddle.

'Over the table!' she snapped.

Zellie approached the ping pong table like a sacrificial lamb, meek and mild, soft and round. She laid her torso across the grey-green surface and stretched out her arms until her fingertips came to rest against the neglected doll's house. Her bare feet stretched up on tiptoe. The finger between her legs twitched.

Before her aunt had arrived, before Aunt Shelby's distinctive brand had been laid across Zellie's behind, that finger had been a stub – simple and innocent, a fully integrated part of her body, like any other organ. Now, it was finding its own life.

It was a difficult birth.

As each stroke was applied, Zellie felt the finger quiver and stretch out. She wriggled. She squirmed. She parted her legs to ease the pressure on that treacherous digit. She tipped her pelvis back to give the heat a chance to dissipate. She thought of things that sex had never touched (finding only a few). She tried to concentrate on the pain. She leant into it, *hard*, but the bitterness was not enough. The finger grew, the finger wriggled.

'Keep still, girl!' The paddle rose. 'And think of your sins.' The paddle fell. 'The Devil will not dwell beneath my roof.' The paddle broke the air in two.

The lamb *tried* to think of her sins but the more her aunt tried to beat the wickedness out of her, the deeper the wickedness sank. The more Aunt Shelby struck at the head of the Devil, the more securely his cloven hooves wedged themselves in Zellie's pussy. The harder her aunt struck at the Devil's horns, the more his hooves kicked and slipped. The more he kicked, the more of Zellie's wholesome flesh was displaced; outwards into the finger; down into the finger; through into the finger.

If Aunt Shelby had tried to remove a nail from a wall with blow after blow from a hammer, she would have had more chance of success. A hundred more blows and Old Nick would be buried to his fur-skirted waist. Two hundred more and he would be living inside Zellie's womb.

A more clinical woman might have noticed the little gurgling sounds that came from the back of Zellie's throat. She might have smelt the sickly musk of sexual dysfunction. She might have connected the slow shuffling of Zellie's feet with the flicked-back whites of her eyes and the pumping of her pelvis and realised that Zellie, fucked by the Devil's hooves, was coming. But Aunt Shelby was a doer not a thinker. Her mother before her had been the same.

Had Aunt Shelby the time or inclination to read learned journals, she might have known that no laboratory rat had ever learnt a single behaviour from the application of electrical shocks (the preferred punishment of the scientific community). If she had shared her life with thinkers and ponderers, she might have noted that whilst a dog can be cowed by a lash, even broken, it could not be taught a single trick.

Perhaps Aunt Shelby was enjoying herself too much to risk a shaft of thought falling across her motives. The procedure offered so many satisfactions. She was able to revel in self-righteousness. She could cosy up to the idea that a good beating had never done *her* any harm (when the opposite realisation would have been so very painful). She could enjoy the support of the broomstick of authority as it lay firmly along her calcifying spine (a broomstick that also tweaked her ring of power, a ring that in normal circumstances pumped black gold only once in three days, but that after a good beating opened with blissful, sensual ease). She could enjoy other releases too. The adrenaline that coursed through her veins opened passageways in her brain that she rarely dared to tread. Boulder-sized feelings of inferiority were clubbed aside as she stood tall above the doubled-up flesh of the lamb. Sand grains of doubt were driven out by the certainties of the cane. The exercise brought a rosy glow to her cheeks. There was the warm sense of obligations fulfilled, guidance offered, love delivered, with each smarting blow.

The psalms that she sang worked on different tissues. Psalms were the only poetry that Aunt Shelby had ever admitted to her life. She had long underestimated their power. They not only bathed, they inflamed her starving creative organs. They opened her imaginative eye, sometimes sleepily, sometimes to such a width that towards the end of a good beating the air was filled with angels. Cherubs would pluck on tiny harps and count out the strokes. Muscular Seraphim would hold the lamb firmly down. The Archangel Michael himself sometimes appeared at the end and, as Aunt Shelby fell to her knees to thank the Lord for *His* strength in *her* purpose, the highest beside the Trinity would lay the gleaming sword of justice on her shoulder and a spark of the divine would leap into Aunt Shelby's chest. Yet, when silence returned there was no satisfying afterglow. When all songs had been sung, when all orgasms were concluded, when both holy spirit and girlish mucus flowed no more, it was a sad, flat games room to inhabit.

Aunt Shelby left at speed. Zellie was left to stand in a corner for the contemplation of her crime. She snivelled, she rubbed her behind (though rubbing was forbidden). She remembered times when communication had a wider conduit than a quarter-inch cane. She consoled herself with images of her mother. She struggled with herself. She struggled against nascent feelings of anger towards her aunt. She struggled against feelings of self-pity. She struggled against the desire to take away the pain of it all with exercise of finger and *finger*.

There were many sighs. Many tears were shed that were not shed for the pain of her beating. She worried how she would get home tomorrow, without muddy shoes and torn stockings. She worried how she would get home *any* day. She worried that the finger would get bigger and bigger. She worried that she would like it.

There were self-recriminations – how could she be so weak? How could her girlfriends regulate their lives, their feelings and their reputations, when she could regulate nothing? Her own reputation was so tarnished that no image of goodness would ever be reflected again. She went through the long conversations she'd had with her mother on the nature of love and sex. She reaffirmed in her mind that sex without love was a barren field filled with tares and stones (though the thrill of that field almost made her faint).

She offered herself hope that some day a boy would appear who would look beyond the finger of flesh and hear a deeper sound than her whimpers of arousal. She offered herself the hope of a boy who would take her to his *heart* when no other boy had even troubled to take her to his *bed*, preferring instead to fuck her where she stood, lay or sat, on discovery.

Half an hour passed in these thoughts, then the twins appeared. Her aunt had probably sent them to tell her it was time to go to her room, but the twins were in no hurry. They installed themselves on the sofa opposite the ping pong table and snickered and whispered. Zellie did her very best to remain still, to stifle her tears, to steel herself for what Jimmy would call their evil and what she called their playfulness.

'You can turn round if you want to,' Purity called.

Zellie preferred not to.

'I think it would be better if you did,' Charity added, an undertone of menace in her voice.

Reluctantly, Zellie turned. Now they could see her tear-stained face. Now they could see her shiny nose. Now the doubts and self-recriminations had as unsympathetic an audience as could ever have been assembled.

'Mama sure took her time today,' observed Purity.

'She needed to take her time,' averred Charity.

As the girls spoke, Zellie looked from one face to the other. Plain, pustuled and sexless (they could so easily have been boys), these were the faces of a new world for Zellie. It seemed less kind than her old one. It seemed to have no key. It left Zellie feeling that somehow she didn't really belong and that the place where she did belong had moved somewhere else.

'Zellie doesn't *deserve* so much attention,' objected Purity, continuing her theme.

'But Zellie *needs* all the attention she can get,' concluded Charity.

'Especially her *bottom*,' ejaculated Purity.

The two girls burst out laughing – bottom was probably the rudest word in their vocabulary, and even Aunt Shelby's girls liked to be rude – as long as Aunt Shelby was far away.

Their laughter went on for a long time. These girls had energy. They had volume. Their high-pitched voices twined around each other like air-raid sirens, their arms snaked out to hug each other's waists. They pinched and nudged, pushed and poked. They only just managed to stay on the sofa.

'Can I go to my room?' asked Zellie, sinking deeper into misery with each pitiless glance, with each nudge in the ribs.

'Has Mama said that you can go to your room?' asked Charity sharply.

'No,' Zellie groaned.

Aunt Shelby had sent harpies to torture her instead, harpies sprung implausibly from her own scrawny loins.

'Then you better stay right where you are,' Purity told her.

'I think I should,' Zellie agreed.

'You wouldn't want us to say you were disobedient, would you?' asked Charity.

'No, I wouldn't.'

'That would only make things worse,' intoned Purity.

'If anything can make things worse for Zellie.'

'Or if anything could make *Zellie* worse.'

The girls rose from the sofa as one. They were tall for their age and as thin and stringy as their mother. Plain, pustuled and sexless they may have been, but they were still prey to every vanity. Make-up was not allowed, of course, but clothes were required and clothes were in abundance in Zellie's house. Charity wore a cashmere sweater and plaid skirt, both items that had formerly been Zellie's. Purity wore a cotton sweatshirt and hula skirt from the same source. Clothes that had emphasised sweep and curve on Zellie had been laboriously tailored to display bone and point. They had lost their charm. No one caught in a lift with these girls would have wanted to get too close. Bony buttocks can shred, pointy breasts can spear.

'What was it this time?' asked Charity. 'Did you break something?'

'No I –'

For the sake of regularity, in the pursuit of perfection, both girls wore star-spangled braces of rhinestone and stainless steel. When they smiled, two galaxies, brimful of false jewels, opened to the world. Today they were in a smiling mood.

'Were you disrespectful?' Purity cut in.

'No, it –'

'Were you just too damn silly?'

'I don't know.'

The girls were circling. They were smiling. Rhinestones glittered. Stainless steel flashed. Zellie was getting a headache.

'You must have done something to deserve it.'

The girls were blurring together. She could hardly tell one from the other. 'I think –' she began.

'Zellie!' exclaimed Purity.

'Zellie, *you* don't think . . .' added Charity.

'Not that I ever noticed,' concluded Purity.

A hand snaked out and plucked at the hem of Zellie's skirt. Zellie grabbed it back and crouched.

'Stand up straight,' Purity told her.

'A girl without posture is a girl without poise,' intoned Charity.

Zellie stiffened. The hand returned. Zellie backed away. 'Please let me go.'

'Are you going to cry?'

'No.'

'I never knew a girl who cries so easily.'

'I'm not going to cry.'

'Stand still. How can we examine you if you won't stand still?'

'I don't want to be examined.'

'But we need to learn.'

'We need to read the lesson written on your ugly –'

'– fat –'

'– wobbly –'

'– bottom.'

More laughter.

'No!' Zellie cried, but it was too late.

Charity had seized the defending hands, Purity had pulled the grey school skirt high.

'Be careful. She wears knickers two days in a row,' said Purity.

'I don't!' exclaimed Zellie.

'She doesn't spend a lot of time in the bathroom, either.'

Zellie could only gasp at the injustice of it all. She could hardly get *near* the bathroom these days. It was their headquarters. It was their altar.

'There is a *smell*.'

'Maybe she's sick.'

'Are you sick?'

'No.' Zellie pressed her legs together. She felt wet down there. Cold, stiff-jointed fingers pushed Zellie's knickers into the crack of her behind.

'Wow!'

Charity let go of Zellie's hands and bent to look where Purity gazed. 'My!' she said.

'That was quite a session.'

'Red isn't the word.'

'I can feel the heat,' said Charity, holding out her hand.

'She used a paddle with holes!' exclaimed Purity.

'A paddle with holes,' echoed Charity.

There was a moment's silence. Perhaps the girls were remembering the time when *they* had been the targets of Aunt Shelby's wrath. The times before they had learnt to say nothing except what they were meant to say.

'That is going to hurt for a week,' said Purity.

They giggled in unison, banishing the past in a rush.

'We will have to make sure Zellie's friends know how bad she's been.'

'No! Please don't say anything!'

'If we don't warn them they might go the same sad and sorry way as Zellie.'

'She is a germ.'

'Contagious.'

'We should warn her classmates at least.'

'The people most at risk . . .'

'Please!' Zellie groaned. She was beginning to cry now.

Purity dropped the hem and stepped in front of Zellie. 'Or you could volunteer to do *all* the chores this week? And hand over the money for them.'

Zellie groaned, but surrendered. 'OK.'

In synch, the girls stepped back. They displayed their jewels. They glowed with satisfaction.

'I think you'd better go to the kitchen now,' Charity told her, 'and start cleaning.'

'And while you're there –'

'– you can think about whatever bad thing you did –'

'– which isn't of any interest to anyone –'

'– but sad and sorry Zellie.'

2

Rodrigo

The kitchen was a mess. It looked as if a vanload of
eight-year-olds had been asked to make pancakes. Zellie
spent an hour scrubbing and scraping. With the radio
on low and no interruptions, it was like being at home.
She was humming cheerfully long before she'd finished.
It was almost dark by the time the last of the dishes were
stashed away, dark enough to risk fetching her pen. The
twins had disappeared. Her aunt was in bed.

It was now or never.

She stole out of the kitchen door like an eloping lover.
The air was cool. Halfway down the driveway she
realised that her stockings were ... well, she didn't
know where her stockings were! It was too late to think
about them. She was past the garage. She peeped out
into the road.

The widely spaced streetlights made strange shapes of
the bushes. There were small sounds from all sorts of
directions: music, traffic, laughter. Most of the houses
had lights in them but the road seemed to be empty. She
crept along in the lee of the topiary that fronted Jimmy's
house. A ragged horse head looked at her, squint-eyed.

She noticed too late that she was wearing her school
shoes. The hard soles rattled on the stone pavement.
Sneakers would have been so much better! If she had
only thought ...

Not thinking was one of Zellie's weaknesses.

There was no hedge in front of Rodrigo's house. She had to make a break into the open to pass. She crouched and half-ran, half-tiptoed. Her shoes sounded off like a machine gun in the still air.

Once past the open space, she looked back at the house. She was looking for movement. She was looking for a door, opening. She was looking for pursuers.

The lights were on in the basement. That's where Rodrigo liked to hide away from his family. That's where he took Zellie (if he got the chance) to study *girl*.

There were no bad signs. She hoped that he was playing computer games. Computer games, beer and sex were the only things Rodrigo cared about.

She passed the Hendersons'. The four-by-four was gone. Mr Henderson was probably out having a good time. Jimmy said that any time away from Mrs Henderson had to be a good time. Jimmy could be heartless – but never as heartless as Rodrigo. Another fifty metres and she reached the cherry tree. Opposite it was a patch of absolute darkness. Luckily Zellie *had* thought about a torch. She studied the street again. There were shadows in the bedroom window of Mr Angelo's. His wife would be going to bed. Mr Angelo would soon be going up to the attic to gaze through his telescope.

A car pulled out of a driveway back near the car repair shop. She waited for it to go.

All was quiet, all was still. Zellie flicked on the torch. A narrow beam of light shot skywards. Even people in jumbo jets would know what she was doing! She quickly directed the beam into the bushes. There was a rush of anxiety. They looked different. There was a whole row of them. She didn't remember there being a whole row.

The finger was starting to thrum. She looked around quickly: perhaps it had detected *boy*. There was no one. She warned herself not to panic and crouched to look

24

closer at the overhanging foliage. Still nothing looked right! If it hadn't been a very special pen she would have run home again, right then.

Suddenly, she needed to pee. The finger liked the feeling. It liked any feeling *down there*. For a moment, she imagined herself losing control in the street. She saw water running from beneath her skirt. She saw herself rolling on the pavement while the finger tickled her until she screamed. 'Zellie!' she hissed. 'Grow up.' Growing up had stopped being easy for Zellie.

She crawled under the branches of the most likely looking bush. Grit dug into her bare knees. Cobwebs made her feel sneezy. The torch showed her things that she didn't want to see. There were dead insects, a half-sucked sweet, live ants, rotting leaves. She crawled a long way – right through the row of bushes. Things stuck in her hair. There was a smell of damp, dead things.

Then, just as she was feeling too panicky to carry on, a glint of gold caught her eyes. It was a miracle. Her pen! She seized it. Her heart filled. It was like taking her mother's hand. She almost started crying. Perhaps the twins were right. Perhaps there was no other girl in Acacia who cried so easily!

As she backed out of the bush, a branch caught the hem of her skirt. She felt it rucking up. Twigs scratched at her blistered bottom. The finger liked that feeling too. It popped out of its hood, rubbed itself against white cotton. Then she was out in the street again, on all fours, her bottom exposed and her heart pounding. She was about to stand up when a voice told her she looked cute.

She froze.

'Insane but cute,' the voice said. A shoe touched her behind, rubbed a little. 'And very fuckable.' It was Rodrigo's dry drawl.

She stood up slowly.

'Switch that torch off. Unless you want everyone in the street to see.'

Zellie switched it off in a hurry. She didn't want *anyone* to see. 'I dropped a pen.' She held up the pen. It glistened faintly in the streetlights.

'A pen?'

Rodrigo, darkly handsome, tall, muscular, moved closer.

'I dropped it on the way home from school earlier,' she told him. She knew by the way he gazed at her breasts, by the way he licked his lips, by the look in his eyes (darker than the sky above) that he didn't care. His hands were round her hips. The skirt was still rucked up. The cool air rippled against her behind. Her pussy flooded. The finger had certain knowledge of *boy*.

'Do you want to fuck?' he asked in a reasonable tone. He might have been asking her if she wanted a glass of water, except he slipped his hand under the front of her skirt as he spoke.

'No, not tonight, thank you.' Politeness was one of Zellie's weaknesses.

The back of Rodrigo's fingers started stroking her pussy. Her legs almost gave way. 'Come back anyhow,' he said. 'We'll just hang.'

Zellie groaned. Rodrigo's fingers were pulling her panties aside. She could feel his breath on her cheeks. The finger had full knowledge of *fuck-wanting* boy. It rolled out to its full extent. Without cotton to rub against, it was seeking flesh. It moulded itself to Rodrigo's thumb. Her belly expanded and fell into his hand like a full-term apple.

'That's it, girl,' Rodrigo murmured. 'Let it come.' His lips sucked in an ear lobe. His teeth nipped.

'Please, Rodrigo,' she groaned.

'Please fuck me?'

'No . . .'

Boyish fingers slipped into the soft opening of Zellie's pussy. Her thighs opened of their own accord. She gave a long deep groan.

'Zellie always wants to fuck.'

She couldn't deny it. If he had said he wanted her doggy style, right then, she would have dropped to her knees and torn her panties open.

'So, I reckon I might as well fuck her,' Rodrigo concluded and he took her hand.

Her fingers closed around his. Her reason floated upwards. From a height, she saw her mildness, the wetness of her thighs, the still rucked-up skirt. She sighed. So many weaknesses. So delicious. Her head rested on his shoulder and, perhaps because he hadn't fucked her yet, he didn't shuck her off.

The basement in Rodrigo's house smelt of rope and wood, cobwebs and hot electronics.

There was everything a boy could need down here: a sound system that at full volume could break open the floor of the sitting room above; a PC with a bucketload of porn; a fridge filled with drinks of every colour and, for bad days, ice cream; a long line of remotes on top of the TV.

Mostly, though, there was wood. It surrounded the sofa and chairs where Rodrigo played Nintendo with his friends. Piles of wood acted as tables for the electronics. Clusters of wood acted as hiding places for the illicit. There was old wood and new wood. There was wood as dark as chocolate. There was wood whiter than paper. There was wood impregnated with creosote. There was wood covered in chipped and flaking paint. All of it was wood that was being eaten to dust by insects. It was in the air. It made Zellie sneeze. It made her drowsy. Rodrigo's hands made her drowsy and excited at the same time.

In one corner stood the furnace that heated the water. When it came on, the floorboards above their heads shook. It was hot. When he told Zellie to take off her clothes, she was grateful. He helped her. He was a kind boy at heart. If it wasn't for the finger between her legs, he would have been respectful as well as kind. He would have asked her out to the movies. He would have brought her flowers. But that big old finger wasn't interested in flowers, and neither was Rodrigo once it pushed out and beckoned. After her first throaty groan, flowers, respect, movies, ice cream and conversation were forgotten. They were both of them slaves of the finger.

Soon, she was as naked as the day she was born. She stood in the centre of the room like Venus Rising (from wood dust not waves). Her golden hair gleamed in the light from an old standard lamp. Her lips were moist from nervous licking. Her eyes were liquid with lust.

'You have great nipples,' he told her. Rodrigo liked to talk. He believed in being direct. His fingers pinched up her nipples. They were the colour of strawberries – the pale inside of strawberries, after they had been bitten open. 'So hot!' he exclaimed. 'I wish I could keep them.'

An image of razor blades made Zellie jump. She hoped he didn't have a *collection*.

'But I reckon I can have them any time.' He kept on pinching. Her groans thickened. 'Was there ever a girl who wanted fucking more than Zellie in all of Acacia?'

'I don't know,' she said uncomfortably. She had been brought up to be pure of heart. Impurity of the body had ambushed her.

'So who have you been fucking since yesterday?'

'No one!'

'What! You got through a whole day at school without fucking anyone?'

'No one asked.'

It was a joke. He didn't laugh. 'You are so lame.'

Zellie's head hung down.

'Look at me,' he told her.

She looked up. She had the look of any girl who wants to be loved. Her eyes were large and plaintive, her lips begged to be kissed.

'That's better. Now I can see the mouth that I'm going to fuck.' He flicked at her nipples, first one then the other. Each stinging contact brought a thick gasp from her throat. Her neck stretched, her tongue whipped along her lips. He flicked at the undersides of her generous breasts. There was the same throaty reaction.

'Is there anywhere that I could touch you that *wouldn't* make you horny?'

Zellie couldn't think of anywhere.

'One time, I'll try to make you come just by twisting your nose,' he told her. His eyes narrowed. 'Maybe I should try that now.' He took hold of her nose and twisted. Water tumbled from her eyes.

Her hands came up reflexively. 'Please don't,' she groaned.

'Think of it as an experiment. You believe in science, don't you?'

Zellie was not a test tube, but sometimes Rodrigo made her feel like one.

He brushed her protecting hands away then returned to her nose. He was grinning in a bad way. 'Do you think it will work?'

'I don't think so.' Her voice was adenoidal.

He twisted a little harder. She gave a shriek. He eased the pressure off a fraction. 'I suppose you'd like it better if I pushed my hand up your cunt?' Pussy stuffing was one of the things Rodrigo liked to do. It was one reason why Zellie's pussy had been sore all day, why lately her pussy had been sore a *lot*.

29

'If you want to,' she said. Anything was better than having her nose twisted.

'Well, I guess we could try. I don't think it's as tight as it used to be.' There was a note of doubt in his voice. Zellie's pussy was a thing of mystery. He let go of her nose and reached between her legs. 'You need to do something about all this hair,' he told her. 'Get rid of it. Shave it, all of it. Do whatever girls do.'

'People would know.'

'What do you mean, people would know?'

'The girls at school would see. In the shower.'

'Duh!'

She flushed. 'I'd be embarrassed.'

'You'll let me put my hand up your cunt but you're embarrassed if a girl sees you with a shaved pussy?'

Zellie blushed.

'Every girl in your class must shave their pussies,' Rodrigo asserted.

'I don't think any shave *everything* off.'

Rodrigo's eyes glazed over. She saw that he was thinking of school showers. He was thinking of the hot spaces under school skirts.

'Who shaves off the most?' he asked suddenly.

'I don't know!' she cried. Zellie tried not to look at other girls' pussies. It was rude.

'I know for a fact that Lizzie Barret shaves her pussy,' he said.

'She just trims,' said Zellie.

'Trims like a lawn mower trims.' His fingers were teasing along the sides of her pussy. He wound a tuft of hair around a finger and pulled hard. She jumped. The gasping sound came from her throat again – half shock, half lust. 'Did that hurt?'

'Yes,' she moaned feebly.

'If you shaved I couldn't hurt you that way.'

He would find other ways.

30

'Anyhow, lie on the sofa. Let's see how that pussy's coming along.'

Stretching Zellie's pussy was a personal project. It was turning into a marathon. No matter how hard he worked, how deep he went, how many fingers he used, Zellie's pussy simply sprang back to what it had always been. It was no looser now than it had been a month ago. Zellie was *resilient*. Rodrigo didn't seem to mind. Sometimes it was the journey that mattered, not the arrival.

Zellie lay out on the lumpy, scuffed sofa. A haze of dust enveloped her. She sneezed.

'Get those legs wide.'

She opened them to their full extent, looping one calf over the backrest. Her pussy unzipped to reveal pink and red. The finger, blood-gorged, stood straight up, as big as a nipple.

'Wow. That clit of yours is mutant.'

Zellie flushed and buried her head in the sofa back. She was resilient but she was *sensitive*.

'What did I say?' He perched on the sofa and took her hand. 'I wasn't complaining. I like big clits. I mean it. I like big cunts and I like big clits.'

None of these declarations made Zellie feel any better.

'You better not cry,' he told her in an irritated voice.

She began to sob. It had been an emotional day.

'For God's sake!' he said in disgust. 'You're worse than Gina.'

Gina was his sister. Gina knew how to use tears. Tears were Gina's life jacket in the stormy seas of Rodrigo's household.

He stomped over to the refrigerator and threw open the door. 'You better not still be crying,' he called. He ate a frankfurter. He cooled his forehead with a piece of ice. When he came back he had a can of Coke.

31

Nothing had changed. She was still sobbing. Her legs were just as wide. Sitting at the bottom of the sofa, he gazed at her open pussy. He measured the height of the finger with dark eyes. He pulled a bottle of lube from under the sofa and blew off the dust. Squeezing a dollop onto his hand, he told her he was going to make it *all better*. He used the tone of voice he used to his sister when *she* started crying – and his dad was on the way.

He pushed a finger into her pussy, gently. Then another. She gave a huge, grateful groan. He finger-fucked her slowly, making her mew like a cat. She forgot the twins, she forgot her aunt, she forgot that Rodrigo was watching her with the same eyes he used to watch porno movies.

For fun, he rested the bottom of the ice-cold Coke on her clitoris. She yelped and half sat up. He pushed finger number three into her pussy. She grimaced.

'Sore?' he asked with that bad grin.

'Yes.'

'You're still so tight.'

'I'm sorry,' she groaned, bucking as his thumb grazed her clitoris.

'We need to make room for Mr Big.'

The fourth finger was always the difficult one. He pushed hard. Zellie slipped along the sofa. He pushed even harder.

'Fuck me,' she groaned. 'Please.'

The look in her eye, the need in her voice, was too much for Rodrigo. Suddenly he looked like a boy who couldn't wait any more. Zellie had seen that boy before. She liked that boy . . . Very much.

His hand pulled out and he stood. 'Kneel up. Show me how a good doggy gets fucked.'

Zellie shot him a hurt look.

'Forget the princess bit. You know what you want.'

Zellie sat up reluctantly. She turned over slowly. She knelt up magnificently. There was no shape in Acacia to compare with the shape of Zellie's behind. It was full. It was indented. It had lines no sports car could outrace. There were openings and closings. There were places to lose fingers, a cock, a mind. There were the marks of a puritan's cane.

'She never lets up,' Rodrigo said softly, examining those marks. He was almost sympathetic (if Jimmy had seen them he would have cried for her). 'She just hits you harder every time.'

Her head was pressed into her skirt where it lay on the sofa. She watched his face from behind her knee. She watched the sympathy fade, saw the scientist, the prodder, the poker, emerge.

'Does she know how much it turns you on?'

Zellie turned her head away. Even she thought there were issues best dealt with by denial. His fingers stroked along her stripes. It hurt when he pinched. It made the finger thrum. She groaned and pushed out her bottom for more.

'Shh,' he told her when she cried out.

Zellie buried her head deeper. He pinched his way along the stripes. She made sounds that women make in childbirth. She pushed her crumpled skirt into her mouth. He wanted to pinch her breasts.

'Let's see if *that* turns you on,' said the scientist.

She flipped onto her back. It turned her on – but not as much. He should write it in a book.

'Let's try those stripes again.'

She knelt up. He pinched. Only guilt stopped her from coming. Then he wanted to pinch her breasts again. She turned back.

He couldn't make up his mind which he enjoyed most.

She found a way to show him her breasts and behind at the same time. She lay on her back with her hands under her hips. Her glowing behind was lifted high in the air and he licked his lips. He pinched alternately, breast and behind. Her eyes closed. After a while it made no difference. It turned her on equally.

He moved on to a spanking – gentle but firm, the way she liked it. Sometimes he *was* a kind boy. She pushed the skirt deeper into her throat. She voided mucus like a snail. She bucked. She was coming.

'That's it,' he declared. 'Fuck the foreplay.'

His voice told her that every boy but the boy who couldn't wait had left the room. He stripped off his clothes while she rocked urgently from side to side. She was in the field of tares and stones. Her smile was golden. She was gazing into the eyes of the boy who couldn't wait. She was teasing him with mucus. She was calling him with little gasps.

He kept saying fuck.

She was a dream that had been made for boys to fall into. Rodrigo was anxious to jump.

'Fuck, Zellie. Fuck!' It was his way of saying that he liked her. 'Fuck, fuck, fuck!' His shirt was gone. The flat belly, where every muscle was a knot, gleamed. 'Play with yourself,' he told her.

'No, Rodrigo, please.'

'Do it.'

She touched herself and came. She went a little crazy. He watched with eyes that didn't care about porno movies.

'Fuck, fuck, fuck!'

In too much of a rush, he dropped his trousers on the floor. Clouds of wood dust rose up to surround them. Zellie was coming and sneezing at the same time. Mucus ran from her nose and her pussy.

'Jesus, you are a mess,' he told her. 'Kneel up again.'

She knelt up. She showed the cleft. She willed the openings to open. She wished she had a tail to wag.

He swung into position behind her. She saw his erection. It looked too fat. The skin looked too much stretched. She hoped that he wouldn't hurt himself. She hoped that he wouldn't rupture. He used his fingers – just for a moment. It was enough. She started to come again. This time it was for real. She needed the skirt but it had fallen on the floor. Her shrieks filled the room. Mrs Henderson would hear as she sat at home and wept. Mr Angelo would be turning his telescope earthwards, looking for a *beast*.

Rodrigo didn't even try to shut her up. He picked a remote off the floor and pointed it at the stereo. Gangsta rap made the room quake.

He was behind her again. His balls looked as big as oranges. Zellie wanted to drink juice. She wanted to suck zest.

He was inside her but only for a moment. As soon as his cock parted her pussy lips, she lost control. Her legs spasmed, her behind jerked upwards. He fell out. He was angry. She kept on coming. He pushed down on her back to keep her still and went into her again. It was no good. She bucked and threw him out again.

'I'm sorry, Rodrigo . . .'

He fetched rope.

He tied her up on her back with her elbows pressed into the joints of her knees. He wrapped the thick cobwebby hemp around elbows and knees, around calves and forearms, around wrists and ankles. She rocked from side to side on her back like an upended turtle. Her pussy pushed up. Her clitoris searched for hand or cock like a leech searching for blood.

He went into her again. She still couldn't keep still. He tried wedging her into the corner of the sofa. It was hopeless. Her back arched and threw him out again.

'I'm so, so, so sorry, Rodrigo. Please try again.'

35

In a fury, he spanked her stripes, raising his hand above his shoulder. He applied venom. It only made things worse. She writhed like a wounded cat. He fetched extra rope. He fetched wood. He untied the cobwebby hemp.

She sat on the settee with her arms around her knees trying to think of something to say that would not upset him. 'Let me suck you,' she offered. Little orgasms kept surprising her. Her words came out as if she was on a fairground ride.

He ignored her, his young, beautiful face as dark as thunder. He laid out a cross on the floor and made her lie on it. He wanted to tie her out like a sacrifice to the sun. It hurt her back, she got splinters. Worse, *she could still move.*

'Please don't be angry, Rodrigo.'

He stamped over to the furnace. Beside it was a cupboard. He threw open the door and dragged out a tool box. More dust. Now *he* was sneezing.

He brought an electric screwdriver, a saw, a plane, hammer, nails.

The screwdriver would not work.

'I am not a fucking handyman . . .' he muttered. 'All I want is a screw.'

'Oh, Rodrigo . . .'

'I'm calling Eduardo. He can hold you down.'

The very mention of Eduardo made her heart miss a beat.

'Don't! Please, we can find a way. If you tie me like this –'

She brought her knees up to her chest and wrapped her arms around her legs. Her pussy pushed out bulging but closed between compressed thighs. 'I can't move if you do it this way.'

'I want to fuck you properly.' He switched off the music and picked up his trousers. More dust. There was a mobile in the pocket.

Eduardo answered immediately. Zellie could hear him laughing, thin and high like an insect, as his cousin explained the problem.

'He's coming right over,' Rodrigo told her, as soon as the call finished.

Zellie was left in the basement while Rodrigo went upstairs to shower and calm down. He locked the door. Zellie started to cry. Eduardo was cruel and he was knowing. It was the knowing boys that Zellie most feared. It seemed to be a rule of life, in Acacia at least, that it was the very worst boys who had the most profound knowledge of how to touch a girl and it was the very worst boys who saw all of Zellie's weaknesses, from honesty to soft heartedness to carnality, in a glance.

Twenty minutes later, the door opened and there were footsteps on the stairs. Sound filled the basement. It sounded like a whole party of people were filing in. Zellie did not dare to look. She pressed her still naked legs together. The sounds grew even louder. Eduardo was capable of bringing a whole university of boys with him.

'Well . . .' said the first of the party, coming to stand over her.

It was Eduardo. He was as big as Rodrigo and older. His muscles were harder. His face looked more finished. His features had already settled into the cruel lines Rodrigo's might someday assume.

'Little Miss Muff,' he said. 'You've been screwing up my cousin's night.'

'No, I –'

Zellie glanced at the rest of the party. It wasn't as bad as she thought. There was only Rodrigo and a girl that she didn't know. The girl wore stiletto heels – the source of all the noise.

The girl had attitude. She smiled with narrowed, suspicious eyes. It was the smile that cats have in cartoons when they catch a mouse. Even so, Zellie couldn't help smiling back. Zellie had been trained to be nice. Niceness was one of Zellie's weaknesses.

'Come round and say hi,' Eduardo told the girl.

She skirted the sofa. She was dressed sluttishly in a slashed black satin skirt and black stockings. Closer to (closer to Eduardo perhaps) her eyes were milder, nervous even. Jimmy would have called her a tame punk.

'Tricia, Zellie. Zellie, Tricia.'

The girls managed a couple of muted greetings.

'You girls need to say hello properly,' Eduardo said. 'Sit down,' he told Tricia.

The girl sat. She looked up at Eduardo the way Portia looked up at Mr Angelo when she wanted a treat.

Eduardo stepped a little closer then reached for the zip in his trousers. He pulled it down and flicked out his cock. It was semi-hard, already big.

'You first,' he told Zellie.

She scooted to the front of the sofa. There was no point in arguing. Eduardo didn't like arguments. The only cut and thrust he liked was the cut and thrust of his cock. She took it right in.

Out of the corner of her eye, she saw Rodrigo come to perch on the sofa's armrest. He watched with porno eyes. She could feel the coolness against her cheek.

'Hey,' Eduardo told her. 'Pay attention.'

She looked up. She faked a look of lust.

'That's better. You are getting to be *trained*,' Eduardo cooed. 'Isn't she cute?' he asked Tricia.

The girl smiled. 'Like a puppy.'

'Yeah! Like a puppy.'

Without being asked, Zellie started to suck.

'That is *good*.'

Zellie sucked until he was hard. When Eduardo was hard he was also big – way too big to fit in her mouth. With only a third of a cock inside, he was butting against her tonsils.

Eduardo pulled out and moved over to Tricia. His cock was wet with Zellie's spittle. She sucked him in without hesitation.

'What better way for two girls to get acquainted?' Eduardo asked. 'Cock sharing is so *sisterly*.'

Rodrigo laughed.

'The more girls share, the less they bitch, right?'

'Right,' said Rodrigo.

'You,' he said to Zellie. 'Let me see what I'm going to be fucking tonight.'

Tricia was giving him a slow blowjob. She looked practised. She looked unmoved. She looked like a whore.

Zellie opened her legs and reached down.

'From behind.'

Zellie threw Rodrigo a plaintive look as she turned around. His heart had yet to turn to stone. He looked away guiltily.

She presented her behind with a delicate regret. Even Zellie knew she was too good for Eduardo.

'Somebody made a start,' Eduardo said, looking at the marks. He glanced at Rodrigo, appreciatively.

'Not me. Her aunt's a holy roller.'

Eduardo gave a low whistle then hissed, 'Twisted.' He told her to open up.

She reached around and used her fingers to pull apart her pussy lips.

'My, that looks tasty,' said Eduardo, eyeing the stretched flesh. 'Sell that by the ounce and no one would *ever* make a return.'

Rodrigo giggled.

'Come and take a look, *bro*.' Eduardo was mimicking the delivery of a rapper.

Rodrigo stood and examined the gaping fruit.

'She's dripping on your furniture,' Eduardo growled.

Rodrigo giggled again. 'That is *unhygienic*.' He picked up Zellie's skirt and slipped it between her wide-spread knees.

'Unhygienic or not,' Eduardo said, relenting, 'we need a picture of that.'

'Yeh.'

'For the album. Something to show the folks when they drop by.'

Another giggle from Rodrigo. He reached under the sofa and came up with a collection of CDs, a couple of empty cans, a hunting knife, a live bullet, a padlock and finally a digital camera.

'Don't hide, little girl. Look at the man,' Eduardo told her.

Zellie had buried her head in her shoulder. She had willed her hair to cover her face.

'That's it, look at the birdie,' Rodrigo told her. He was back to using his 'talking to little sister' voice.

There was no alternative. Zellie shook her head. There was a spray of golden hair. A sad face appeared. Moist eyes gazed over a round, tanned shoulder.

'C'mon, girl. Look like you're enjoying it! Happy, happy, happy!'

Zellie wanted to cry. Crying didn't work with Eduardo. She forced a smile.

There was a flash.

'Has that camera got red cunt correction?' asked Eduardo.

'It's got red eye.'

'Probably good enough. Get closer.'

Rodrigo knelt down.

'You need details for a *hot* album,' Eduardo told him. 'I have an aunt who *eats* photographs of pretty little girls in church dresses with bows and such like. She will love this.'

There was another flash.

'And now her face. That is such a pretty face. She could sit on top of a Christmas tree and even your mama would say coo-ee.'

Rodrigo knelt on the sofa. Tears filled Zellie's eyes. 'She's crying again,' he groaned boredly.

'Play with that dick between her legs.'

Rodrigo took Zellie's clitoris between finger and thumb. He squeezed and twisted. It was crude. It was brutal. It worked. Zellie began to moan.

'*Now* take the picture.'

'Open your eyes,' Rodrigo said.

She opened them. There was a flash.

'That is going to be some picture,' Rodrigo exclaimed. 'Put it up on the PC.'

Rodrigo flicked open the back of the camera and pulled out the memory card. In a few seconds Zellie's face filled the monitor. It was a face of rapture. A pure heart and an impure body made Zellie shine. The boys admired it. The boys decided she looked like Britney Spears on Viagra.

Zellie was still holding herself open. She was still dripping.

'Well, as pretty as that pussy is,' Eduardo drawled, 'it's not what I'm going to be fucking tonight. Pussy fucking is old. We need to get past that.' He let the implication sink in for a moment.

Zellie twisted to look at him. Her eyes grew wider.

'Show me the other place a guy can fuck a girl,' he told her.

She knew exactly what he meant. Eduardo liked porno. Eduardo liked Zellie to suck him while he watched porno. He watched porno so he could learn how to treat a girl *right*.

'Don't be shy,' he said, with the softness of a kiss. He looked down at Tricia. 'You aren't shy, are you, bitch?'

41

A thick 'uh-huh' came from Tricia's cock-filled mouth.

His attention returned to Zellie. 'So show me the hole I'm going to be fucking tonight.'

Zellie's fingers released the reddened lips of her pussy. They inched upwards. Rodrigo was watching her intently. He would probably have watched an animal die the same way.

The fingers halted. Zellie groaned in despair. She didn't want it *that* way.

'Open up for daddy.'

There was a note of warning in Eduardo's voice. She heeded it. Her fingers found the roundness of the well surrounding her anus. They dug in. They opened.

A secret place felt air, felt eyes, felt a future of invasion and pillage.

'You think she has room for us?'

Rodrigo's lips pulled out into a grimace. 'I don't want to fuck a dirty hole like that.'

Zellie shot him another hurt look. He hadn't needed to say *that*.

'It won't be dirty. We'll scrub it up. Inside and out.'

There was a gurgling sound. Eduardo was pushing hard into Tricia's mouth. More than half his cock had disappeared. Tricia's eyes were watering. Eduardo cupped the back of her head with his hand. He started to get a *rhythm*. His eyes never left Zellie's anus. He didn't see Tricia's fear. If he had he would probably have liked it.

'I don't want anal sex,' Zellie groaned. Her mouth tasted bad from just saying 'anal sex'.

'What doesn't kill you, makes you stronger,' Eduardo said. 'I like strong girls. I like girls who can take a serious fucking.' He was grunting as he thrust.

Rodrigo turned the music on again. His family didn't need to hear Eduardo come. It was the same gangsta as before. The homey was smokin' the same bitch.

42

'Put your finger inside,' Eduardo told Zellie in a thick voice. 'Now!'

Zellie ran her finger around the dark ring of muscle. She tested the opening.

'Help her,' Eduardo told his cousin.

Rodrigo started to press on Zellie's finger. He tried to force it through the constriction.

'No! Not like that. Play with her pussy.'

Rodrigo's fingers dived towards Zellie's pussy. Two slipped deep. They opened, they wriggled, they pinched.

Zellie flexed her back. She pushed onto the hand. She couldn't help herself. She wanted those fingers. She wanted more. She wanted a handful tugging on her womb. Her anus opened. Her finger slipped inside. She felt Rodrigo's fingers through the thin membrane as he rummaged inside her. Her mouth opened. Her tongue was a pink flower poking through wet lips.

'Look at me, bitch,' shouted Eduardo.

He was thrusting hard. On each down stroke, his cock was three quarters buried. Tricia's face was a sickly green.

Zellie turned her melting eyes to his. She read rage and lust. She was frightened and turned on. Rodrigo was pinching at her stripes. She was coming and it was good. She was coming and it was *bad*.

Eduardo started to come too. He grunted like a pig. He thrust deeper and deeper. Tricia began to struggle. Eduardo didn't even look at her. He slapped her though, once, twice. Her arms fell limp. He was looking from Zellie's anus to her eyes. He was sucking the goodness out of her with his gaze.

He gave a final thrust, arched his back, screamed 'Fuck!' and pulled out.

'Whoa! These bitches will kill me.' He staggered back to the armchair, collapsed.

Tricia was holding her throat and gasping for breath.

'Don't swallow,' Eduardo told her sleepily. 'If I give you something, you treat it with respect.'

She glared at him. The hatred in her eyes would have scratched steel.

'That's no way to look at me, honey pie . . .'

'Fuck you!' The mask of compliance had slipped. Her history spoke through her contempt. She had been born in a tough part of town. She should have been searched for a knife at the door.

Eduardo ran his tongue slowly along his teeth. The room was suddenly very quiet. Rodrigo's hand turned to stone. Zellie squeezed it out. Tricia had said the wrong thing. She had said it in the wrong way. They waited for something *bad*.

Eduardo rolled out of the chair. He didn't look sleepy any more. For a moment, his clenched fist hung in the air. Tricia crouched. She was ready to run or curl into a ball or maybe just scream.

Then Eduardo smiled. It didn't reassure but at least the fist opened.

'Did you swallow?' he asked.

She shook her head quickly. He stroked up his cock, which was hard again. Throat mucus made it gleam. One step forward and he was towering over her.

'Open up.'

Her lips parted.

'Catch me with a tooth and you'll lose them all,' he told her. He put his cock back into her mouth and pushed steadily. It bottomed out somewhere past her larynx.

She gave a look of surprise, as if she had been stabbed through the heart and had felt nothing.

He pulled out again. 'Now say thank you.'

'Thank you.' Her voice was catching on something.

'Now smile and say "do it again, *big boy*".'

She forced a smile. It trembled and broke without tightening. 'Do it again . . . big boy.' It sounded as if she had swallowed a sponge.

He grinned. 'I think I will.'

This time he pushed in at speed. She convulsed. Her shoulders wrapped themselves around her chest. He held the back of her head. She was coughing round his dick. He shook her head heartily.

'Now, look at me.'

Her eyes were bent. Only one looked at him. It had no focus.

'You look like something ran you over.' He laughed and pulled out slowly. Crouching down, he curled his fingers around her throat. 'Now work all that nice goo up into your mouth.'

Her throat rippled. She coughed. She made gurgling sounds.

He massaged her throat with the heel of his hand. 'That's it. Is it coming?'

She nodded quickly. She was eager to please now – too eager for Zellie to watch any more. She couldn't watch Eduardo either. There was a light in his eyes that would blind babies.

'Good girl. Show me what you've got.'

Tricia opened her mouth. It was full of white foam.

'I would say that was a pretty good load,' he declared. 'Play with it.'

She ran her tongue through it. She twirled. She sucked it through her teeth. There were bubbles. Her eyes were a void. Zellie felt nauseous.

'Now push it out. Push it out of your mouth.'

She pushed. It ran down her chin. It fell in gobbets onto her dress.

Eduardo stepped back. 'That's the kind of make-up I like to see on a girl,' he declared. 'She's prepped for a night on the town!' He looked from Rodrigo to Zellie.

45

They regarded him with degrees of horror. 'What?' he asked. 'Haven't you ever seen a girl getting fucked before?'

'Just don't kill anyone,' Rodrigo murmured.

'The fuck?' In one fluid movement, Eduardo had his hand around Rodrigo's face. 'Do you have something to say to me?'

Rodrigo looked scared. Zellie had never seen him look scared before. She was suddenly cold. A shiver ran through her naked body. The finger popped out of her anus.

'Nothing, I –'

Eduardo shook the boy's head from side to side, then pushed him down on the sofa. 'We're getting out of here,' he told Tricia.

She seemed too shocked to move.

Eduardo's eyes scoured the basement. Contempt drenched the broken-down furniture, the piles of lumber, the dusty floor, the finger-smeared TV.

'This place has a bad *vibe*.'

The CD finished. The gangsta had smoked enough.

There was a hammering on the door. Maybe, someone had been knocking for a long time. There was a voice, muffled but angry.

Rodrigo leapt to his feet. 'Shit, that's my dad,' he groaned. 'Get dressed!' he told Zellie.

'Your *dad*?' cried Eduardo. 'What am I doing here?' He grabbed Tricia's hand. 'This kindergarten's no place to be.' He pulled her towards the door.

'Her face!' cried Rodrigo.

Eduardo glanced at the dripping slime dismissively. 'Who gives a fuck?'

Rodrigo grabbed Zellie's shirt and ran after them. He caught Tricia at the bottom of the steps and wiped her face as if she was a baby. 'This is going to be bad,' he groaned. 'Just be polite, OK? Don't say anything. Let me do the explaining.'

Eduardo had watched the cleaning with a mixture of amusement and contempt. 'Explaining? He'll smell it. These bitches stink of fish.'

Rodrigo groaned again. 'Polite. Please. Polite!' He threw the shirt back to Zellie. She held up the come-heavy fabric between forefinger and thumb. 'Put it on!' he hissed.

With downturned lips, Zellie worked her arms through the sleeves. A puddle of come had soaked through the front. It cupped her breasts in cold sticky hands. The fabric became see-through.

Rodrigo groaned again. 'I'm fucked!' The hammering on the door was getting louder. He ran upstairs in near panic.

'Are you OK, Tricia?' Zellie called.

Tricia was still pale. Her face shone unhealthily. 'I need some air.'

Zellie smiled sympathetically as Tricia turned to climb the steps. She picked up the remote and switched on the TV. It was a movie with Brad Pitt and Angelina Jolie. Brad was trying to shoot Angelina. They looked sweet. Jimmy would have said it was a 'wrong' movie (he thought Brad was the pits) but Zellie sank deeper into the sofa and made herself comfortable. Brad's soft shaven head and fuzzy blue eyes made her want chocolate.

There were raised voices at the top of the stairs. She found the little arrow on the remote and raised the volume. Suddenly, everything was fine. Eduardo was gone. Brad Pitt was on TV. No one had done anything bad to her anus. She noticed her panties draped over a wood pile. She decided to leave them there. If Rodrigo's dad came downstairs they would take some explaining . . .

Jennifer Lopez was wearing futuristic sculpted leather. She was a 21st Century super-foxy biker chick.

Rodrigo's dad didn't come. Rodrigo didn't come either. They must be having a *serious* talk. Zellie gave a little gasp. Jennifer had fallen into a vat of radioactive waste. Now her breasts would be *atomic*.

When Rodrigo finally reappeared he looked sad. 'Eduardo's banned,' he said. 'He dropped the F-bomb.' His voice was hoarse from shouting.

'The F-bomb?'

'He said "fuck". Twice.'

Zellie looked upset on Rodrigo's behalf. Empathy was one of Zellie's weaknesses.

'You're banned too. My dad thinks you're a bad influence.'

Zellie frowned. 'Do you think I am?'

'Yeah.'

She sighed and looked around the basement. She knew for a fact that she wouldn't miss it. 'Can I watch the end of the movie?'

'No.'

3

The Hotel

Two days later, Eduardo turned up at the school. Zellie had no chance to sneak out the back way. He was waiting outside her classroom. The other girls flirted with him as they filed past. He was tall and strong. He was good looking and his daddy was rich. Everyone knew Eduardo had a credit card.

Zellie did not flirt. With a sinking heart she went over when he gestured.

'You aren't an easy girl to find,' he told her. 'I waited outside for you yesterday and the day before.'

'I must have missed you.'

'Well, I missed you, girl. We have some serious fucking to do.'

His voice was loud. One of the girls heard and turned with a big grin. As she walked away she whispered to her friends. Zellie's reputation was taking another downturn.

'Not tonight, Eduardo.'

'Well, I can't force you. That would be wrong.' He was smiling like a wolf. 'Take a walk with me, though,' he continued. 'Tell me why you don't want to fuck.' Eduardo's voice was even louder than before.

Zellie looked anxiously down the emptying corridor. She glanced back through the open door of the class-room. Mr Peres was sorting out his papers before the drive home. If he had heard, he was being polite. Then, he glanced up with a faint frown.

Suddenly, a walk seemed like a good idea. She wanted to get Eduardo out of her school. He was a menace.

'Let's walk, then.'

They started off down the corridor.

'That is a very sexy dress,' Eduardo told her. It was a short, pretty sundress. Zellie never dressed to be tough. Before she could stop him, he flicked up the back of her dress and revealed her bare buttocks.

'Sexy thong too.'

'Eduardo!'

'OK! Just checking,' he said with a grin.

Through the windows to the left, they could see a group of girls running round the school track. Further on, boys were playing football.

'Are you wearing a bra?' When she didn't answer, his hand snaked out and moulded itself to one of her breasts. She wasn't wearing a bra, her dress was backless. Straps would have ruined the look. She unpicked his fingers, blushing deeply. 'Braless and bare-assed. You are ready for action, girl.' He slapped her behind hard enough to sting.

'Ow!'

'Ow? That was not an "ow" slap, that was an "ooh" slap.'

'Ooh,' Zellie hissed, rubbing her behind despite herself.

He stepped in front of her. The long corridor was empty now but the row of big windows to the left allowed anyone outside to see them easily. She backed away but he quickly corralled her in a corner.

'Kiss me, then say you don't want to fuck,' he told her.

'Not here, Eduardo!'

He leant over and kissed her. She tried to turn her head away but he held her firmly in large powerful hands. He ran the tip of his tongue across her lips and they opened automatically. The tongue went inside. His pelvis pushed into hers. His hands went to her skirt and lifted it to her waist.

It was the beginning of the end. Just like Rodrigo, he knew her weakness. He knew what a kiss would do. He knew that exposing her behind when at any moment her teacher might walk into the corridor would have an impact. Just to be sure he brought up his knee and ran his thigh across her pussy. The finger poked out. It wanted boy flesh. It needed to be pulled and poked, squashed and mashed. She made a few more protests but soon he was dragging her to his car and she was hardly resisting.

In the car, he undid the front of her sundress and pulled out her breasts. He said he was unpacking the meat.

She told him not be rude.

He said he would make gravy of her pussy juice.

She tried to close her ears.

He told her he would spread it all over her and she would lick it off.

She groaned in despair.

As the car sprang away from the kerb, her breasts wobbled. He stared. 'Fuck, you are prime,' he cried.

The car was a bullet driven by a penis.

He took her to a hotel, a mile away. Before stepping into the street, he let her push her breasts into her blouse but he wouldn't let her button up. The desk clerk leered as she walked past. As soon as she was in the lift, he pulled her breasts out again. He bit and licked. By the time they reached the right floor, her nipples were red and sore and wet.

It was a relief to be in the room.

He took her into the en suite bathroom and made her sit open-legged on the toilet. He unzipped his flies and

51

she quickly pulled up her skirt. She knew what he was going to do. She was horrified and excited. He peed over her pussy. It was dirty and wrong. It turned her on. Her clitoris pushed out to bask in the hot fetid stream. He cleaned his dick on her lips. To her shame, that also turned her on.

'The prettiest, dirtiest slut in town,' Eduardo murmured. 'And all mine, no limits.'

She posed naked for him in front of the fifth-floor window while he ordered room service. Outside, the traffic swept by. Jimmy was missing a show.

She made herself come on the post of the double bed while he ate beefburgers and drank Coke. He watched her for half an hour. Every time she came – rubbing her pussy into the tubular steel, then slumping to the floor – he made her start again.

Her golden hair flew from side to side. She cupped her breasts for him. She licked her nipples. Guiltily, she enjoyed every slow grind of her pelvis. Guiltily, she enjoyed watching his eyes glued to her bare pussy and breasts.

She even talked dirty when he told her to: 'I want to do this to your cock. I want to make it hard and swallow it . . .' She became more frenzied. She was no longer herself. Eduardo had the power to take her away from who she was.

'I want that post wet from top to bottom,' he told her.

It soon was. He only let her stop when she was too exhausted to stand.

Then, he undressed and pulled her onto the bed. He laid her head on a pillow and helped himself to her mouth. He went deep, cutting off her breathing, making her feel dizzy. Finally, he decided it was time to fuck her.

'I hope your ass is clean,' he said in thick voice.

'Not that, Eduardo.'

'Let me smell it.'

'Eduardo, please.'

He made her kneel up with her behind in the air. His large muscular body leant over her. He took a deep sniff along the length of her pussy and anus. She was a mess from making herself come.

'You stink,' he said cruelly. His foot propelled her towards the bathroom. 'Get washed. You look like "little-miss-butter-wouldn't-melt-in-your-mouth" but you are the dirtiest bitch in all of Acacia.'

She was too tired to resist. Too upset by the things that he said. There were tears in her eyes when she entered the bathroom. All she ever wanted was to be good. Why was it so difficult?

The shower was a gleaming cube of polished granite and stainless steel – a tiny palace. Eduardo's credit card had not been wasted. She washed lazily, allowing the water to be as hot as it could be without burning. Already drained, her muscles became jelly. She slumped against the polished granite blocks. Slipping into a corner, she wedged herself there so that she did not fall.

He came in and sat on the toilet watching her as the water ran down her reddened flesh. He had a beer now. He was in no hurry. 'Is there anything that you won't do to get off? Is there any boy you would say no to?'

His words surrounded her. She fell into them. She was no longer able to resist his definitions. She was not pure. She was not wholesome. She remembered the orgasms as she had danced for him against the bed post. Her body remembered them and was hot inside, hotter than the water that steamed around her.

She wanted to come again. She was too lazy to touch herself. She wanted him to sink his fingers inside. Her head felt heavy and she allowed her eyes to close. Her neck bent back. Her back arched. She was offering her pelvis. He drank beer and laughed.

The last sane part of her mind was worried that she would slip and injure herself. The corner supported her badly. The polished granite held her badly. She was going to fall. Her head slumped forward. Her breathing was slow and deep. Her consciousness was insecure. She stopped caring if she fell.

She began to feel that Eduardo was in the shower with her. Her eyes flickered open and she saw his bare feet hazily in the steam. Then the water grew cold and she gasped. When she tried to straighten up, she found that there was a hand around her neck. He was telling her to stay still. The water got colder. It was hard to breathe. She struggled weakly and groaned. Tears flowed again.

He let her sob for a few minutes, then the water grew warm again. This time, her relaxation was total. All the strength had left her muscles. She slid down the wall until she was squatting, head down, legs wide, unable to resist at all. He turned the water back to cold. She gasped and groaned. When she started to shake uncontrollably, he switched the water to hot and left her. Water ran into her mouth and ears. She lost control of her bladder and a flood of urine turned the granite floor yellow.

When he came back and helped her to her feet, she babbled her thanks. She was feeling too vulnerable to be alone.

He led her to the toilet and bent her over it. Her head rested on the white plastic seat. He pushed lube into her anus. There was no resistance. She opened immediately. He fingered her for a long while and it felt as if his whole hand was inside her. She heard him murmur 'good' and again she wept. She wanted so much to be good. He left her like that. He told her to finish washing.

'Use this,' he said, dropping a coiled tube and a plastic bag on the toilet seat beside her head.

When she had the strength to stand, she realised it was an enema kit.

There was the sound of a TV from the bedroom. It would be porno. Eduardo liked to watch porno while he fucked a girl.

She recovered herself and washed her hair. She brushed her teeth. She read the instructions included with the enema kit and used it. She hoped he would not hurt her. She knew that if he could, he would.

Finally, she emerged from the steam and the scents of perfume and faeces. Her head was wrapped in a white towel. Her eyes were blinded by tears and hair and shampoo suds. She did not see him rise quickly from the bed. She did not see the hand arcing upwards towards her pussy. There was a sharp sound of flesh on flesh. She yelped as her pussy burnt.

He caught her as she began to fall and slapped her pussy again.

She began to howl. It was shock. It was over-stimulation. Her mind surrendered completely and tears were no longer enough. He told her she was way beyond a slut, that she was something else but no word had been invented for her yet. He lifted her onto the bed, laying her out on her back with a pillow below her pelvis. He pushed her ankles beside her ears and lubed her anus again. He told her to look at him as he pushed in.

She was still weeping. Between sobs, she groaned.

His dick went into her like a rod of hot brass. It burnt and she writhed.

He kept pushing in. 'You won't forget this,' he told her.

It felt as if she was being branded inside. So hot! 'It's burning me,' she groaned.

'Yeah, I've heard that before.' He was grunting with effort as he drove to the root. 'Every time a guy fucks

55

you like this in the future you are going to see my face. Your ass is mine forever.'

He began to pump. The pain did not ease. He went in from different angles. She was fighting him. It was futile. He was too big. He knew how to handle a girl, how to hold, how to control.

He pulled out all the way and then went back in, hard. More heat! She became limp. He arranged her body to suit himself. He took his time.

'You like this?' he asked.

She groaned a 'no'.

'Well, that's a first.'

'Please, no more.'

'We've only just started.' He started playing with her clitoris. 'Does that help?' he asked.

'No, it burns too much.'

He grinned and fucked harder.

Then, without warning, everything changed. A dam burst. She was washed away. Suddenly, it was good. It was better than good.

He saw straight away. 'Now you like it,' he told her, derisively.

She liked it beyond words. She liked it beyond bearing. She came in a way that she had never come before. It was a whole body come. Every nerve sang.

It was too much.

After a few minutes, she went limp. She must have passed out. She woke up to a series of slaps on her face and breasts. He was telling her not to die. He was telling her to open her eyes. She began to fight again but he was still on top and he was still stronger. She gave in. She started to come again.

She was swearing at him. Zellie never swore. She called him a cunt. It wasn't Zellie. Zellie would never use that word. She called him a cunt a hundred times.

When he finally came, she clung to him desperately.

'I'm going to stop calling sluts, sluts,' he declared. 'I'm going to start calling them Zellies.'

He rolled off her and told her to suck him.

They had only just begun.

4

The Daughters of Clean

It was two days before Zellie earned herself another beating. The twins had left the garage door open. They had blamed Zellie. Zellie earned the beating by not arguing. If she had argued she would have earned an even bigger beating.

Her aunt used a heavy, flat strap she had found on a church charity stall. 'The church never lets you down,' she said afterwards as Zellie hyperventilated and wept and moaned all in the same moment. The twins missed out on the aftermath of this beating. Aunt Shelby had sent them ice skating – wholesome exercise for girls.

After the customary half hour of crime contemplation, Aunt Shelby appeared and told Zellie to get upstairs and pray for her soul (if it wasn't already too late). Zellie climbed the stairs slowly. The up and down motion triggered nerves. The nerves were jittery. Jittery nerves lash out in surprising ways.

When she stepped into her room, she got a surprise. Jimmy was climbing in through her window. They gazed at each other for a moment. His eyes were wide and anxious. Zellie smiled a reassurance – Jimmy brought out the big sister in her.

'Close the door,' he hissed.

Zellie pushed it to.

'Lock it.'

'I can't.'

'Why not?'

'The twins . . .'

The twins had thought that she might be up to no good. Where the bolt had been there was just a series of holes. It defended their room now – from burglars, from Zellie, from the devil and all his cohorts.

Jimmy let himself down from the window sill as quietly as he could. He crossed the room quickly on tiptoe and picked up the chair from in front of Zellie's dressing table. He wedged it firmly under the door knob.

'That should do it.'

'I would say,' agreed Zellie, knowing how much it would enrage the twins if they found their entry blocked.

They gazed at each other. Old feeling flowed. Feeling that had no words.

They might have been looking through a smoky mirror. Their eyes searched and found, moved on, found again. An outsider might have taken them for brother and sister. They seemed to blend into each other. He was as blond as Zellie, as tall – but slighter (he lacked her breasts and hips and his shoulders had yet to fill out). He was as gentle. He was even more nervy.

In a moment, this exchange became too serious, somehow, for Jimmy. He grinned and ran a hand through his tangle of blond hair. Zellie sighed as any big sister would. A few years ago, before breasts and hormones, she would have given him a cuddle. Nowadays, things were more awkward.

He skipped over to the window and looked down into the street.

'I thought I heard someone,' he explained, then shrugged and laughed at himself.

'You will get me into trouble,' Zellie told him.

'I came the old way, across, not up,' he said, nodding towards the cedar tree. 'No one saw.'

'You haven't been over in a long time.'

'I didn't think you wanted me to. I thought that you were avoiding me.'

'No!' Zellie said quickly. 'You should know that I would never do that.'

He looked reproachful. 'You don't call round.'

'Aunt Shelby doesn't like me going out.'

Jimmy pulled a face. 'Aunt Shelby!' He hissed, then shuddered. 'If she were human we could kill her.'

'Jimmy!' Zellie looked at him in alarm. 'It's wrong to even joke like that.'

Jimmy sat down on the bed. He sighed. He gazed out of the window. His fine blond eyelashes quivered with emotion. '*Someone* should be killed.'

Zellie laughed, despite her bottom, despite the twins. Jimmy always thought that someone should be killed. He thought his teachers should be killed (for being stupid), he thought his father should be killed (for being his father), he thought any number of kids should be killed (for laughter, for pushing, for wearing Radiohead T-shirts, for liking 'wrong' movies). Zellie knew him though, and knew that killing wasn't one of his strengths. She sat on the bed beside him.

'You've been crying,' he said, without looking at her.

'It's not important.'

His eyebrows crept upwards. 'Some things *are* important.'

'What was important enough to climb over here for?'

He still wasn't looking at her. She had the time to examine him minutely. She could linger over the details of his ears, the whorls, the flourishes, the dark insides. She could trace the veins in his hands. She could examine the freckles on his cheeks as if each were a smudgy world. She could be eight years old again and hiding in the tool shed while it rained outside and the whole grown-up world dissolved.

'I've been hearing stories about you,' he said. This time, he looked. His expression was very serious. There was hurt, as if she had broken something between them. There was something else too, something curled up deep inside that she had never seen in Jimmy before, something very, very boyish.

Zellie stiffened. 'What kind of stories?' This was perhaps as close as Zellie had ever got to a lie. She knew exactly what kind of stories.

'That you've been having sex with a whole gang.'

'A gang?' She was squirming. The tears were close by.

'With Rodrigo and Eduardo. With some guys who live out near the lake. With –'

He stopped speaking abruptly and waved his hand in the air. Then he stopped that too and slumped back on the bed.

'I'm sorry, Jimmy.'

'Is it true?'

She wished that the bed would open and take her inside. She wished for invisibility. She wished that a giant hand would come through the window and pull her skyward. None of her wishes were fulfilled. There was only the truth. 'I couldn't help it.'

This had him sitting up again. 'What do you mean, you couldn't help it!'

Zellie was wringing her hands. The tears flowed.

He was staring at her with shocked eyes. 'I remember you saying that you were going to wait until absolutely the right guy came along,' he exclaimed.

'I tried.'

'And then Rodrigo! I mean Rodrigo, he is *Neanderthal* . . . and other guys . . .'

Zellie was gazing at him with cow-round eyes. There was contempt in his voice when he said 'Rodrigo'. There was a look in his eye.

61

'Something comes over me.'

'Something that doesn't come over you when you see me . . .'

The boyish thing was unwinding. Zellie felt herself becoming wary.

'Jimmy . . .'

'What does that mean? Jimmy . . .'

She had never seen him so angry. He *never* got angry, not even when he thought multitudes should be killed.

'Do you know how many times I looked out of my window and waited for a glimpse of you?' he asked abruptly.

This surprised her. 'You watched me?'

'I watched your window.'

She felt oddly hurt. He had violated a trust. He had kept a secret.

'Did you see anything?'

'Sometimes I saw a bare arm. Sometimes I saw you wrapped in a towel before you closed the curtain.'

'I thought we were friends.'

'We are friends.'

Friendship seemed to mean something different now.

'I didn't think you wanted anything else.'

'I didn't want *you* if *you* didn't want *me*,' he said bitterly.

Zellie was getting confused. She was tired. This would all need thinking about. 'Does everybody know about these stories?' she asked, changing the subject.

'Not at our school. I heard it from a girl at Lonsdale.'

Lonsdale was Eduardo's school. Eduardo was a rat. He didn't even deserve to be thought about. She changed the subject again. Subject-changing kept their friendship fresh.

'You know a girl at Lonsdale?'

'Just a friend.'

That was Jimmy's problem. He was *too* good at getting girls as friends. Rodrigo never troubled with girls as friends.

'Is she nice?'

'Not as nice as you.'

There was silence.

'I don't know what to say,' Zellie murmured after a moment.

'Leave the curtain open. At night.'

'What?'

Jimmy wouldn't look at her. He was looking at his house. Perhaps he was hoping his mother would call. Perhaps he was hoping they would be saved.

'You want me to leave the curtain open at night?'

'Everybody else has seen you naked. It's the least you can do.'

'Jimmy!'

He uncurled from the bed and headed for the window. He still wouldn't look at her. In a moment, he was jumping down onto the balcony at the far end of the branch. He slipped through the window of his room. He was gone.

5

The Square of Darkness

After the evening chores, after cleaning and scrubbing
the kitchen, after picking up popcorn from behind the
fridge, Zellie was sitting in front of her dressing table,
combing out her hair. From time to time she eyed the
square of darkness in the mirror. Once it had simply
been a window. Once it had been as innocent as
daylight. Now, curtainless and huge, it stared.

She had combed her hair for longer than usual. It had
soothed her less than usual. Her spirits were low. There
had been a lot of disappointments that day. Jimmy had
disappointed her, especially. She was almost angry with
him. She was disappointed in herself too. She hadn't
noticed what was happening with Jimmy. She was
supposed to be his friend. They were supposed to be
close.

Her eyes kept returning to the square of darkness. It
disturbed her. It was like an eye. *It* watched her as she
watched *it*. Now and then the wind blew a tree branch
and the movement made her jump.

She had undressed and slipped on her nightdress
(especially white that day, especially virginal) in the little
space between her wardrobe and the wall.

It was the only place that the eye couldn't see into.
Hiding had produced a strange stab of guilt. Jimmy
would have wanted to watch her undress. He would

have wanted even more to watch her dress. The nightgown was long and narrow, a tube of cotton. She needed to lift her arms above her head and draw it down. Her breasts were squashed into new shapes. Her nipples had sprung up.

The new Jimmy, the one that was forming in her mind as she ruthlessly combed her hair, would *certainly* have liked to see *that*.

She wondered if he had ever seen more than just a bare arm. She wondered if she had ever forgotten about the eye – just for a moment – and let it see *everything*. She wanted to go the window and call him (she was sure he was watching). She wanted to ask if he watched a lot. She wanted to know how long ago he had started watching. She wanted to know if he was proud.

She was almost annoyed. Her hand was moving faster than it should. Static was building up in her hair. It crackled. It clicked and flicked at her scalp.

Set against this anger (this almost-anger), there was the recurring thought that she had let Jimmy down. She had never even thought of him as – well, as a boy. That was somehow rude (she would be upset if someone forgot that she was a girl), but they had grown up together and the realisation had grown so slowly, she had never really noticed. Or perhaps she *had* noticed but it was so long ago that she had forgotten.

She tried to think of him as a boy now. She tried to remember boyish things about him. She had certainly noticed his lips. They were thicker than most and redder. He could have pouted to effect if he were a girl. She had never wanted to kiss them though. Except to say thank you. She had seen his behind a thousand times. It was as round as a pumpkin and far sweeter but she had never wanted to seize it the way that she seized Rodrigo's when she came. She had certainly never wanted to bury her tongue in the divide and . . . Her

65

hand came down especially sharply. The comb scraped her scalp. The offending tongue hid itself more deeply in her mouth.

As for Jimmy's penis, well, that was a thing of mystery, unseen and unimagined.

Finally, she laid the hair brush down. An unusual energy seized her. She stood abruptly and walked over to the dark eye. It was the sash kind and heavy. She hardly ever opened it. She was afraid it would fall and cut through her wrists. At that moment though, anger gave her strength and it opened with a grinding rush of sound.

Zellie thrust her head out into the darkness. Only the branches of the cedar could be seen, twisting away into darkness. Jimmy's house was no more than an absence of stars, a dark bulk. The window was invisible.

She was just about to call out when the bedroom door opened with a squeak. Zellie turned quickly, so quickly that she hit her head on the bottom sash.

'Ouch!'

For a moment, Zellie felt faint. She caught a glimpse of a tall marshmallow with a cherry on top, then sat on the side of her bed and put her head between her knees. She took a deep breath. Then another.

When she looked up, she saw Charity staring at her, open-mouthed. She was wearing a big fluffy dressing gown of pink and cream. The cherry was her head wrapped in a red towel.

'Were you trying to run away?' Charity asked. There was a thrill in her voice.

'No.'

'Wait there.'

The marshmallow disappeared as if the wind had caught it.

Still feeling woozy, Zellie gazed out into the darkness. She wondered if Jimmy was laughing. She frowned as hard as she could. She hoped that he would see her *disappointment*.

Cool evening air was creeping into the room. She shivered. She felt too weak to stand up and stop it.

The eye was big where she sat. It made her feel small.

If she had been stronger she would have pulled the eyelids to. Jimmy had seen enough for tonight. Besides, the curtain was pretty. Gold and shiny like the sun.

Her eyes searched the darkness. They edged along the branches. She hoped he would be too embarrassed to tell his friends that she had hit her head and almost fainted. The cool air reached her breasts. She felt her nipples stiffen. Was Jimmy close enough to see?

She felt a sudden shock. Was he doing *boyish* things, right then? Was Jimmy ... Her mind bumped into a wall. She couldn't imagine his penis. How could she imagine him playing with it?

No boys were trustworthy, she reminded herself.

Her head was spinning. She wished she was in the tool shed again and it was raining outside. She wished Jimmy was holding her hand.

The bedroom door opened again. There were two marshmallows this time.

'Running away were you?'

It was Purity. She seemed even more excited than Charity had been.

'No –' Zellie began.

'She was climbing out of the window.'

'In her nightie?'

'We should call Mama.'

'It's *very* serious.'

'I wasn't running away.'

They were standing over her.

'Perhaps she was just hot.'

'I don't think so.'

'If she was just hot we could cool her down.'

'You mean –'

'Take her hand.'

Zellie found her hands being taken. Purity seized one, Charity the other. She was pulled upright. She was marched by giggling girls across the room. She was taken down the floor-creaky hall like a toddler between grown-ups. The bathroom door was open. It was still steamy inside from the twins' baths. It smelt of toothpaste and soap.

'In!' Charity said, indicating the bathtub.

Zellie eyed it doubtfully. It looked slippery. There was a scum line. The twins liked cleaning themselves. They didn't like cleaning anything else.

Charity started to take off her dressing gown. 'I think Zellie will splash,' she explained.

Purity murmured an agreement. She unwrapped the towelling belt around her waist.

Zellie was astonished to see that they were still wearing their skating outfits. Long pale legs that she had never seen before emerged. They were better formed than she would have guessed, more shapely, but they were still terribly thin.

Purity had a pale blue spandex top and a flouncy skirt of black, tiered polyester. Charity wore a skirt that was very, very short. Her bare legs ended at a crotch of shiny pink viscose. The material which enclosed her pointed breasts was as thin as cigarette paper. Across them a rabbit was picked out in pink sequins. The rabbit shot out light beams in every direction.

Zellie shrank back. There was something unhealthy in all this.

'I don't think she likes water,' Charity decided.

'No one can remember the last time she had a shower.'

'I wait until you go to bed,' cried Zellie. (This was the only time she could get near the bathroom.)

'She tells such stories!'

Purity stood on tiptoe and did a shaky pirouette. The ruffles of her dress flew up to reveal a narrow behind torn open by shaped, lime-green lycra. Zellie was almost shocked. Had Purity discovered boys?

'Come on. Water won't bite.'

Zellie stepped into the bath, reluctantly. She wasn't expecting this to be a good experience. There was a shower attachment on the taps. Charity lifted the chrome head and turned the water on. Cold water splashed against Zellie's ankles. She danced.

Purity mimicked her steps, casting up toothpick arms like a dying swan. 'She is such a baby!'

A moment later, colder water splashed across Zellie's back. She shrieked.

'I think we used all the hot water earlier,' Purity declared gleefully.

'Well, we can't stop. This must be the first shower she's had all week,' Charity said with relish.

'That is not true!' Cold water hit the back of Zellie's neck. She tried to get out.

Purity laughed cruelly. Charity pushed her back. She was stern. 'If you don't want Mama to come and see what all the fuss is about, you had better be good.'

'Mama gets *very* angry if she has to get out of bed,' Charity reminded her.

Zellie clenched her teeth to stop herself from screaming. The water had soaked through her nightdress. It coursed down her breasts. It ran in rivulets across her belly. It was cold as Charity's eyes. It was sharper than the sequins on Purity's breast.

A stream dived between Zellie's legs. She stopped breathing. Her heart stopped too. The finger – shocked – burrowed deep into its hood. The hood betrayed it and shrank to nothing. Exposed and frozen, the finger shrieked in anguish. Zellie clenched her teeth harder.

'Get the back scrubber. We'll give her a hand,' said Charity.

Purity picked up the long-handled brush and used it on Zellie's back. The bristles felt sharper than wire. Purity worked with a will. Zellie was so cold, the brush seemed to burn.

'Don't forget her bottom.'

Purity scrubbed. Aunt Shelby's holy fire was reignited. The lumps and bumps of the paddling grew. With all the giggling and scrubbing, freezing and burning, Zellie almost collapsed.

'And don't forget the smell,' Charity said.

'I don't smell,' Zellie managed to say through chattering teeth.

It made no difference. Purity thrust the brush into the opening at the bottom of the nightdress. She scrubbed at bare calf. Zellie danced again. If it had been sharp through the cotton fabric it was twice as bad now. Zellie was snuffling. Her nose was blocked.

'Open your legs.'

'No!' Zellie cried. Her tone was almost adamant.

'Open your legs or we'll take off your nightdress and start all over again.'

Zellie knew there was no escape. There were two of them. Behind them was the spectre of Aunt Shelby. She edged her legs apart, but only by a fraction.

'Wider.'

'Come on, Zellie,' Charity's voice was sweetness and reason, a postcard from Buddha. 'The quicker you open your legs, the quicker I can scrub all the bad things away and the quicker we can all get some sleep.'

Purity was less charitable. 'I think she likes to smell.'

Zellie groaned a protest. Charity lost her patience.

'Zellie, open your legs now!'

Sweet reason had vanished. She sounded so much like Aunt Shelby that it made Zellie's stomach do a slow, puky roll. 'I think I might be sick,' she said.

'She will do and say anything just to stay filthy.'

'Pretending that she's going to be sick!'

Zellie's stomach rolled again. 'I mean it,' she groaned.

'Open your legs.'

'You can be sick afterwards. In your own time.'

Zellie surrendered. Her legs opened. The brush soared upwards like a jet into heaven. It swooped and strafed. It dug deep. It scratched thigh and pubis. It scoured pussy and anus.

Purity hummed one of her favourite songs.

'Whistle while you work . . .'

Zellie retched and clutched her stomach.

'Bad acting,' Charity declared.

The brush flushed out the finger. The bristles had it at their mercy. They slapped it around. They poked and spiked.

There was a sea change. Zellie's body rearranged itself automatically. Now, she was pressed against the wall. Her breasts were flattened against the cold tiles. Her legs were parted. Her bottom was thrust out.

She started to moan. Nausea and cold were forgotten. The finger was as stiff as a little penis. It danced with the bristles. It poked back. Delicious, wicked feelings coursed through her thighs and belly.

Suddenly, the brushing stopped. Everything stopped. Zellie remembered where she was. She noticed how she was standing. She realised that it was not dignified – not in any way. Still breathing heavily, she glanced nervously over her shoulder. The twins were looking at her in horror.

'You are the weirdest –'

'Sickest –'

'Most –'

There were no more words. Zellie had stepped outside of the describable.

Charity put the brush down firmly. Purity turned off the taps as if she were strangling chickens. The twins weren't looking at each other any more. They weren't talking. They definitely weren't having fun.

Charity threw Zellie a towel (the oldest and thinnest). Zellie dried herself through her nightdress as best she could.

The twins watched her as if she were an animal in a zoo. The transformation of wholesome pain into sick pleasure seemed too much to comprehend. Layers of numbness would be obliged to rest over blocks of denial. Soon they would forget what they had seen and then they would forget that they had forgotten. Everything would be as it was. Everything would be sound and solid and they could get back to having some *fun*.

This was not an instantaneous process however. So they avoided each other's eyes and watched Zellie instead. Their eyes were narrowed, their lips turned down. As soon as she had stopped dripping, they marched her wordlessly down the hallway and into her bedroom.

'We should put a bolt on the *outside* of that door,' Charity declared darkly.

Purity was still unable to speak. Instead, she pulled out the chair from Zellie's dressing table, then, taking the wet, cold and miserable girl by the arm, obliged her to stand on it. Perhaps she thought that if Zellie was isolated, the contagion couldn't spread.

'Stay there,' she managed to say in a thick voice.

'We'll be back to check,' said her sister in an ominous voice.

Then they were gone.

Zellie was left to gaze at the dark square of window. After a moment, something caught her eye. Her heart

72

fluttered. There was a tiny pinprick of light. It moved occasionally, as quick as a firefly. She stared. She needed to be sure. The light grew brighter for a moment. It would be Jimmy. He liked to smoke sometimes – when he wanted to forget.

She looked down the length of her body, trying to see what he could see. The white material clung to her. It clung to thighs and belly. Flesh turned the whiteness pink. Her navel was a dark funnel in a sea of pink. The cold made her nipples stand up – more pink.

When she glanced at the window again, she realised that the fire was gone. Perhaps Jimmy had seen enough. Perhaps he had gone to sleep. She glanced resignedly at her empty bed, then at the dressing table with the comb that her hair desperately needed again. She saw a sweater lying over the front of a chest of drawers – how much she would have liked that!

When she looked out of the window once more, her heart leapt into her mouth. The firefly was back. It was at the window. It was glowing as bright as a star in Mr Angelo's telescope. There was a smell of smoke.

She stared. She wanted to jump from the chair. 'Is that you, Jimmy?' she called as softly as she could. There was no reply. The finger began to thrum. There was boy. She groaned at the hopelessness of her situation. Then, her mind turned a somersault.

What if it wasn't Jimmy? What if it was a house-breaker? What if it was Jimmy's father? What if it was a policeman investigating teenage perversion? What if she was just going mad?

The firefly glowed brighter. There was a faint outline of a face. A plume of smoke entered the window.

'Please say something.'

'Lift up your nightdress.' The voice was thick. It might have been Jimmy's. It might not.

Her heart began to pound. 'Go away,' she hissed. Her legs felt weak. It had been a difficult day. She needed to sleep. She needed to scream. The firefly moved abruptly.

'Lift it!'

She knew that she should step from the chair right then. She should fetch her aunt ... Her aunt ... The image made her shudder. Whichever way things went, it would mean a trip to the games room. And Jimmy would get in such trouble.

There was a feeling that this was all her fault. Why hadn't she just said no, earlier? Why had she left the curtains open at all?

'Lift it up.' The voice seemed even closer but still she couldn't identify it. It sounded muffled. Perhaps it was Jimmy and he was talking through something – a scarf, a –

'Show me your legs.'

The finger was burning. It pushed against the wetness of her nightdress. The cold helped. But not very much.

'Will you go away if I show you my legs?'

'I won't if you don't.'

The voice sounded less and less like Jimmy's. For a moment, she was scared.

'Do it!'

She reached for the hem of her nightdress and lifted it slowly. She prayed that it was Jimmy. Her goose-bumped legs appeared.

'Higher.'

Feelings were spreading from the finger. Her belly felt loose. Her breathing was getting deeper.

'You're turned on.' The voice could see into her.

'I'm cold.'

It was true and untrue. Inside, she was hot.

'Take off that wet dress, then.'

'No!'

The hem was only an inch or two below her pussy.

'If you tell me that it's you,' she said, 'I'll lift it higher.'

'It's me.' The voice was mocking her.

'Jimmy, please!' she groaned.

'It's Jimmy.'

The words were empty. She couldn't trust them. She let the hem fall.

'Do you want me to come in?' The voice asked sharply.

'No!'

'Lift it higher then.'

She looked at the door to the hallway. What would the twins say if they found her with her nightdress around her waist?

'I'm coming in,' said the voice.

'No!'

She lifted the nightdress. The air licked at her damp pussy. There was no cooling. Exposed, it burned. Her pussy was as treacherous as the voice.

'Stand on one leg.'

'This is mad!'

'Stand on one leg. I can't see anything.'

He wanted *details*. She laughed. It was the stress. It was the absurdity of her position.

Giggling, she stretched out a leg. He still wouldn't be able to see much. There was a pleasure in teasing him.

'OK?' she asked.

'Good enough.'

She laughed again. 'Are you playing with yourself?' she asked, emboldened.

The voice didn't want to say. She let the leg down.

'I want to see your tits.'

The words cut through her laughter. She felt cold again. It couldn't be Jimmy. He would never say 'tits'. The firefly glowed bright as he took a deep draw. She saw dark eye-pits in a white face. She started to let the nightdress down.

'I can't do this,' she groaned.

'I have a camera. You want me to take pictures?'

'No.' That was something she did not want.

'Lift it all the way.'

Suddenly the voice *did* sound like Jimmy. Or perhaps she imagined that it did.

She still didn't want to lift her dress. It frightened her – it might turn her on, *too much*.

'Lift it.'

'All right!' She lifted it in a single, angry movement. It didn't turn her on. Her breasts bobbed like apples in a barrel of water. 'Are you happy?' she hissed.

'Keep it up.'

The voice was urgent.

She groaned in dismay.

'And turn around.'

'No!'

'Quickly.'

There was something in the voice that Zellie couldn't refuse. It was a need that she understood. It made her feel dizzy. Now, she *was* turned on. She turned slowly. Whoever was at the window could see her dark-striped behind. Her head hung in shame.

'I'm not so very bad,' she said softly.

There was a long silence.

'Hold yourself open,' the voice said, finally.

For a moment she thought it must be Eduardo, but Eduardo would have just climbed in and fucked her whether she wanted it or not.

'Please.' The voice was suddenly *polite*. 'One minute and I'll go.' The voice was making *promises*.

Even so, a minute is a long time to show an invisible boy your pussy and anus. With a sigh of resignation, she reached round and pulled open her behind.

'Look at me.'

She flashed an almost angry face at the square of darkness.

There was stifled groaning – staccato, urgent. It was the sound of someone coming. A guilty arousal flared in Zellie's belly.

She hoped it had been Jimmy. She hoped *someone* had got what they wanted that night.

'Thanks,' the voice called.

She managed not to say, 'You're welcome.'

The next morning Zellie waited uneasily near the garage door. She needed to confront Jimmy but she needed to make it look like an accident – it was a delicate subject. It was a subject that couldn't be left. School books weighed down her arms. She kept flashing nervous glances back towards her house. She didn't want the twins to see her. They would want to know why she was *loitering*.

As soon as she heard footsteps in the drive next door, she hurried into the road. It was Jimmy's father.

'Oh, hello, Mr Cricket.'

'Hi, Zellie. Going to school?'

'Yeah . . . Er . . . No. I forgot something.' She scooted back into the driveway.

Mr Cricket watched her go with a puzzled smile then swung himself into his car.

Zellie hid between the side of the garage and the Crickets' hedge.

It was dark but not dark enough. Mr Cricket waved as he drove past the Shelby driveway. 'Hope you find it,' he called through the side window. Bad hiding was one of Zellie's weaknesses. She flashed an embarrassed smile and stepped deeper into the gloom.

The next set of footsteps *was* Jimmy's. She hurried into the road again and fell into step beside him. He smiled sleepily. It took a long time for Jimmy to wake up. Sometimes he didn't wake up for the whole day.

'Late night?' she asked.

'Command and Conquer'.

She guessed it was a computer game.

'I left the curtains open,' she said.

'I saw.'

'Did you watch?'

'That's a secret.'

'A secret. How can it be a secret?'

There was a *look* in his eye. 'If we talk about it, it won't work.'

'If we talk about what?'

'Our arrangement.'

'It wasn't an arrangement.'

'Then why did you leave your curtains open?'

'I was confused.'

'That's why we shouldn't talk about it.'

She remembered the look in his eye when he had said that Rodrigo was a Neanderthal. It was the same look. He was punishing her.

'But *was* it you last night?' she asked in exasperation. She needed to know, badly.

'Watching?'

'Yes!'

'You want to take the fun out of it?'

'So it was fun!'

'Did *you* have fun?'

'No. It was creepy.'

They had reached the corner of the road. Lonsdale was left. Shelby Universal was right.

He skipped across the road. 'Call round tonight,' he shouted. 'We'll talk about it. Or are you seeing *Eduardo* again?'

Jimmy had certainly been watching something. Or he had spies.

A group of boys was calling to him. He had to hurry.

Zellie turned right. She was sure it had been Jimmy at the window. He wouldn't say because he was angry that she was having sex with Rodrigo. He had become possessive.

Twenty yards further on she was sure that it hadn't been Jimmy. Jimmy would have looked *guilty*. Jimmy knew *shame*.

6

Dolores

At a base just outside of town, Colonel Martin Philips was slowly and painfully reaching a conclusion. He cut a fine figure as he stood at the window looking out over the rows of trucks and piles of crates that filled the base from end to end. His shoulders were as wide as a jeep, his legs as thick as the barrel of a howitzer.

He stood as a colossus protecting our world, but a colossus troubled. Lines of concern cut deep fissures in his rough-hewn, bronzed face. The hands, held behind his back, clasped and unclasped spasmodically. The conclusion was disturbing. The consequences would be painful, for a man that he valued and for an army that he loved.

There was no alternative. He should communicate his conclusions to a higher authority immediately. There would be an investigation. Officers would descend from headquarters. Every document, every computer on the base would be seized. Abuses of all kinds would be uncovered. No one would come out of it smelling of roses.

He would not come out of it smelling of roses.

A shudder passed through his powerful frame. His promotions had been on the battlefield, not in the corridors of power. He could face an enemy with a gun without flinching but an enemy with a memo . . .

He returned to his desk. There lay the evidence, piled high: bills of lading, invoices, account books, spread-sheets. An unavoidable and ugly collection of facts. Jealous rivals had despatched him to this godforsaken nowhere. This would bury him forever – a massive fraud, begun under his drunken whoring predecessor but continued during his own unhappy tenure of six months, when his only consolation had been playing golf and the despatch of poisonous letters under a false name to army journals that he, personally, never read.

It was a fraud of such clumsy execution that only a commanding officer derelict in his duty could have failed to notice it immediately. That was the rub. Nature had not equipped Colonel Martin Philips for penpushing but a general – and he wanted very much to be a general – needed to know a Biro from a Parker.

His rivals would praise him in public and then bury him here, far from the action, in a memo-lined coffin.

So, he had vacillated. So, he had paced back and forth in front of the crate-filled window all day and well into the evening. And so at the point when he should have rung headquarters and asked for Criminal Investi-gations, he decided instead to confront the suspect in the vain hope that he was somehow wrong.

'God help me,' he groaned as he reached for the phone to demand a car.

Half an hour later, the colonel's jeep pulled up outside one of the grandest houses in Acacia. The noise and dust of the street were far behind. The long tree-lined driveway with glimpses of Greek statuary and broad ponds provided time for a man to forget the travails of life, allowed a man to prepare himself for rest and recreation of a kind the army rarely offered.

Captain Astor had clearly not wasted the army's money on vain pursuits. He had not gambled away the hundreds of thousand of dollars that he had embezzled, he had not drunk it, he had not buried it in a remote location. He had invested in bricks and mortar, high electric gates, closed-circuit surveillance cameras and a row of very fine motor vehicles. Captain Astor's spending was as conspicuous as his crime, for anyone who cared to look.

It was only when the colonel rang the doorbell and was received by Mrs Astor that he realised just how well the captain had spent his money. Mrs Astor stood clad in bikini and silk wrap, a perfect forty, her skin as smooth as a teenager's, her belly as flat as a new dollar bill, her face as refined as any renaissance rendering of an angel.

The colonel, who had grown used to rougher women in the bars of Acacia, found the anger draining from him and the rat of envy sharpening its teeth on his ribs. This was a woman to fight a war for! This was a face to launch a thousand ships and, most probably, a pussy to sink ten thousand more.

Mrs Astor smiled broadly and looked the colonel over in a leisurely way. She did not say, 'oh my' but she might as well have. There was chemistry. There was the heat that comes from dropping raw calcium into receptive water. There was steam clouding the inside of the colonel's eyes before he had even spoken a word.

'Colonel Philips!' Mrs Astor exclaimed after that slow examination. 'I am so pleased to meet you. I have told George a hundred times that he must invite you over. I assume that you are Colonel Philips, after all there couldn't be many colonels in sleepy old Acacia.' She held out her hand and the colonel took it in his muscular paw with the reverence he usually reserved for rocket launchers or combat knives. 'My husband is playing golf. But you must come in.'

'Golf?' the colonel said in surprise. 'I didn't know the captain played golf.'

'He's there all the time. And I am here. All alone.'

Mrs Astor rested her hand on her ample bosom and for a moment seemed a tragic figure.

The colonel noted the bosoms, and his heart went out to them, but the other occupant of his chest, the rat, demanded information. 'Where does he play?'

'The country club.'

Now there was the rat, a longing heart and pure rage contending for space. For six months, the colonel had been obliged to hack around the local pay-per-round course with its worn-out greens and uncut fairways! He had been hurried along by the sergeants of industry and had been slowed down by lame drunks. He had lost balls in the swamp of the 12th and a bag of clubs from the back of his jeep in an unmonitored and very public car park. And during all that time, Captain Astor had been treated with the respect of a sheik in the very private environs of Acacia Country Club, a facility the colonel had only seen through the eyes of a dreamer.

The colonel cut his thoughts short. There would be time to deal with the captain later. For the moment he could allow his mind to drift in other directions, over the fairways and bunkers of the soft flesh before him.

'But I haven't even introduced myself. I am Dolores Enfield Astor.'

'Dolores,' the colonel repeated back in a way that told the drift of his mind as clearly as an erection jumping from his uniform might have done.

Dolores giggled nervously, suddenly aware, perhaps, of what was happening. She pressed her hand to her bosom again and this time it seemed like a genuine attempt to stop her heart from leaping from her chest. 'Well, we can't, um, talk out here, colonel.'

'No, ma'am,' the colonel agreed.

'Let's sit out by the pool.'

'The pool?'

The colonel should have known there would be a pool but it did not stop the rat in his chest from growing restive again. He stepped into the marbled hallway. An air-conditioned breeze cooled his brow and, for a moment, he relaxed. Then he thought of his own cramped and stuffy apartment. There, the scents were of boot polish and starch. Here, there was the perfume of fresh flowers standing on a large mahogany table inlaid with ivory. The rat twitched again.

Dolores closed the door and then stood for a moment with her back pressed against the ornate frame. No longer the fireproof hostess, a delicious confusion opened her face. She looked like a woman who was intending to make a confession, a *cri de coeur* perhaps or a *mea culpa*. The colonel felt contending impulses. His arms wanted to protect her, his pelvis to impale.

Dolores collected herself. 'It is so nice to have a man in the house!' she said abruptly. 'My husband invites so few people. I sometimes think that he is embarrassed of us.'

'Or has something to hide?' the colonel snapped, using the opportunity to dig a little, to catch her off guard perhaps.

If Dolores had a guilty conscience, it certainly didn't show. 'Something to hide?' she said with a puzzled smile. 'I don't think my husband has anything exciting like that in his life.' She sauntered past him, confessions of all kinds off the agenda.

'A man might want to hide you for a lot of reasons,' said the colonel in a softer voice.

Sensing the compliment, Dolores looked at the colonel mischievously. 'Me? Really? You must come out to the pool and tell me.'

The colonel watched her walk down the long wide hallway for a moment. The sun, low in the east, sent shafts of amber light through the tall windows, bathing Dolores's bare legs in the same gold that had filmed Zellie's. Here, though, there was no school skirt to meddle with a viewer's gaze. Here, the onlooker could enjoy not just ankle and calf, but thigh and behind as well. Dolores was a follower of fashion – high-cut silk showed a broad expanse of firm, tanned buttock.

'A drink, colonel?' she asked, looking over her shoulder. 'George won't be long.' She didn't seem at all put out by the location of his gaze. 'We can have something cool or we can have something hot.' As she spoke, she reached behind and rearranged the band of silk that concealed – barely – the cleft of her behind, an apparently unconscious gesture that left the colonel wanting something hot, something very, very hot. 'We have beer, we have coffee,' she said in a playful sing-song voice. 'We have spirits and we have juices. Or if you would like to poke around in the cellar you could probably find a wine that you liked.'

The only cellar that the colonel was interested in disappeared from view as Dolores turned a corner. He hurried after her, not wanting to miss a moment. The house that opened out in front of him was a cross between the Alhambra and the Paris Hilton.

'This is some place,' he said.

'I know. It's too much really, for the two of us, but, well . . .' She looked around at the pillars and the arched ceiling glittering with gold and silver. 'It is gorgeous. George would have quit the army long ago if we hadn't inherited this place and then decided we couldn't let it go.'

The colonel finally understood why Captain Astor had passed up every opportunity of promotion in the

85

last ten years. This was his treasure chest buried in full view.

The colonel had stopped at an ornate display case filled with what seemed to be Ming dynasty china. 'Are these original?' he asked.

'Probably.' She gave a little laugh. 'My husband comes from a large wealthy family who suddenly stopped having children. My son and daughter are the only part of the line that will go into the next generation. The more of them that die, the more *objets* we inherit.'

The colonel realised that the captain might not be able to fool an audit but he had certainly fooled his wife.

The expression that Dolores had worn at the door returned. 'Sometimes I feel like I live in a mausoleum.' She pulled her silk slip tighter, as if caught by a sudden chill. The narrowness of her waist and the breadth of her hips were accentuated. The hem of the slip, rising, came to rest on a pubis of kitten-like dimensions.

The colonel stared. His gaze seared the thin white cotton of her bikini. It searched the deep cleft, it measured the dark axis, it calculated arcs and angles. It came to a profound conclusion. This was perhaps the biggest cunt he had ever seen *and* the most perfect. The colonel looked from the tragic eyes to the bulging cotton, hardly able to control his breathing. Pelvis and arms contended again.

Dolores let her arms fall to her sides. The slip fell. The colonel, deprived of something he wanted very profoundly, gave a deep sigh and almost fainted.

'I need something cold,' he said. 'Beer.'

She looked at him with concern. 'You do look very hot.' She walked to his side and took his arm. 'You must come out to the pool and sit down.' Her soft touch made the colonel feel even weaker. He allowed himself to be led away like a lamb.

The pool was shaded at that time of day, and so a little gloomy. Dolores flicked a switch and the pool lamps came up. A pattern of aqua lights played across her wrap. Now, she was a siren.

'Would you like to swim, colonel?' she asked.

The water looked invitingly cool but the colonel needed to be strong. He needed to stick to his purpose. He shook his head.

'Well, I *must* swim, I have a programme.' She glanced at her watch. 'And my programme says half an hour in the pool.'

The colonel respected schedules. He respected good habits.

'You go ahead.'

'We have fresh swim suits. It would be better to join me than to watch.'

Watching was good but she was right, joining would be better.

Dolores took off her wrap. An acre of flesh appeared. It was a field for a soldier to conquer. It was a land to seize.

The colonel allowed himself to be persuaded that the pool was the place to be. Five minutes later, he emerged from the poolside changing room. His shorts hardly concealed his interest in the woman who was already scything a path through the water. He stopped to admire her. He stopped to let her admire him. He thrust his well-hung pelvis forward.

She smiled and gestured for him to join her. Her chest was angled towards him. Her breasts were as bold and full as her smile.

The colonel dived in. Soon he would dive into her. It would take a very long while for him to hit bottom. It would take even longer for him to feel the need to come up for air. They raced. The colonel was more of a running man but he was strong and he had been trained (in this, as in everything). Dolores was practised. She knew exactly how to shape her hands. She knew when to kick and when to feather.

So they kept pace and water left the pool in sheets as two such powerful creatures ploughed through it. The exercise powered up the colonel's heart. The increased blood flow found its way into his groin.

'My, we have made a mess,' Dolores said as she hauled herself up the stainless-steel ladder and surveyed the flooded tiles.

The colonel was watching her behind. The silk strap of her bikini bottom had done its duty. It had hidden itself deep in the fold. The perfect beach for an amphibious assault lay open. The colonel was a landing craft cut loose from the fleet. He lunged.

Dolores stepped from the pool as the colonel's fingers wrapped around her ankle. She slipped free and turned to look back. The colonel gazed at her with burning eyes. Dolores was panting. Perhaps it was the exercise, perhaps it was anticipation. It did not matter to the colonel. Those heaving breasts captivated him completely. A steel mesh net could not have held him more securely.

This was a woman in her prime. As she towered over him, hands on hips, legs parted, the colonel could see deep into wet silk. Imagination was unneeded. The stray strands of pubic hair told him she was unshaven (the colonel liked the wildness of deep brush). The undersides of her breasts (huge, self-supporting) told him there was shelter there for all. The open smile told him there were lips to be kissed. He pulled himself up the ladder with a mighty heave. More water flooded from the pool.

Dolores stepped back. There was a look in her eye. It deepened when she saw the size of the colonel's erection tenting out his swimsuit. 'Is that for me?' she asked.

The colonel nodded.

'Christmas can come any day,' she murmured. 'Let me unwrap it.'

The colonel denied her the pleasure. He was in a hurry. He slipped his own suit down. Now she could see the biggest penis in Acacia. It was eyeing her, it was hunting. What woman could fail to be flattered? What girl could fail to respond?

'The bedroom's upstairs,' she told him.

'Get that damn bikini off,' the colonel growled.

She managed to blush as she unpeeled the silk. She managed a moment of looking virginal. It was fetching. It earned her the first fucking on a sofa not far away.

She earned her second fucking on the landing of the stairs. Her behind, as it climbed, was too much for the colonel. He pushed her against the wall and nailed her pussy to the plaster work like a scalp.

It was only during the third fucking that language began to re-emerge.

'You are the finest woman I have ever had the pleasure of knowing carnally,' the colonel declared.

Dolores cooed with pleasure.

After she had groaned with lust again, screamed in orgasm one more time and smothered the colonel in grateful thanks for the tenth, the awkwardness of language returned in full force: the colonel was obliged to tell her the reason for his visit.

Dolores didn't even try to deny the allegations on her husband's behalf. In her heart, she must have known for a long time that something was wrong. She slipped from the bed immediately.

'Will this mean a court martial?' she asked.

'I'm sorry. I would rather have met you in any other way.'

In a daze, she drifted over to the window. She gazed at the line of expensive cars. She examined the pool and the summer house. 'My life will be ruined,' she said in shock.

'Mine will be too,' he told her. 'I am guilty of neglect. I missed every sign for six long months. Two hours ago, I was almost past caring. Then I saw you.'

She looked at him distrustfully.

'Is this some kind of revenge?' She pointed at the semen running down the inside of her thigh.

'On my honour, you are the most desirable woman I have ever met. When it emerges that I had sex with you, things will go hard for me. The army can be moralising in ways no civilian can understand.'

'Then we shouldn't let it happen.'

She returned to the bed. The colonel was sitting up against the head board. She took his penis in her warm soft hand. 'I want this. And after I've had it, I will want it again.' She squeezed and the colonel was hard for the fourth time in an hour. She straddled him and guided the missile of flesh inside. Lust flooded her face. 'We will find a way to make my husband pay. I will sell everything in this house and return the money. I will sentence my husband to twenty years of house arrest. I will do whatever a military court will do, but I will keep *this*.' She lifted her pelvis until he almost fell out, then squeezed the crown of his penis with her internal muscles. Looking deep into his eyes, she descended in a beguiling, corkscrew motion. 'Neither of us should suffer for my husband's crimes.'

The colonel was almost convinced at the beginning of the slow descent. He was sold by the time Dolores's vagina hit bottom and spread its mouth across his pubic bone.

* * *

The captain was drunk enough to struggle with parking the Merc. He liked his cars to line up neatly. He liked the back of the Mercedes to align with the back of the Ferrari. It hadn't happened. He was irritated when he struggled into the house. It was a little after midnight. At that time of day his wife was usually asleep.

Today, he found her dressed in a sheer nightdress, her breasts clearly visible, and sitting on the colonel's lap. The colonel's feet were bare beneath his chinos. His shirt sleeves were rolled up. He looked as if he were relaxing at home.

The captain's face fell open. Then closed tight like a fist.

'What the hell is this!'

'Your future,' Dolores declared.

She slid from the colonel's lap.

The colonel stood. He towered above the captain. He was inviting an attack with his eyes.

'Sit down, George. We've been talking about embezzlement. We've been talking about courts martial,' Dolores told him, sharply.

The captain blanched. 'Embezzlement? What has that got to do with me?'

'Shut up, Astor. You hid your tracks like a dog hides its shit.'

'It's strange you should mention dogs, darling,' Dolores told the colonel. 'He has the same taste in sex as a dog. The same wandering eye, the same sensitive touch.'

'I have traced every fake invoice and every fake despatch note for the last ten years,' the colonel declared. 'You were clumsy. You might as well have left a signed confession with each.'

'We've been talking about your filthy perversions too,' Dolores told him. 'We've been thinking of a programme.'

The twin-track approach seemed to freeze the captain's brain. He looked from the colonel to his wife with speechless horror.

'You have lost everything, dear,' Dolores told him. 'Tonight you will sleep in the guest house. And the colonel will sleep with me.' As she said this, she lifted the colonel's hand and laid it on her belly. Her legs opened a little so that the captain could see she was wearing no underwear. The colonel allowed his fingers to wander downwards. He took the liberty of masturbating the captain's wife while the captain watched. The wife took it well. She was already glowing with health after the marathon of lust earlier in the evening. She began to glow even more.

'We have been mulling over your crimes and deciding on your punishments,' the colonel told him, after a few indiscreet manipulations had raised Dolores's clitoris to a condition of prominence.

'We have already decided that you will sell those cars out there in the morning,' Dolores declared, shifting a little to accommodate the colonel's fingers as they slid down and into her pussy.

'You will undertake an audit at the base and find ways to reintroduce the money,' the colonel continued, pulling mucus from the well-fucked pussy and spreading it around the proud clitoris.

'You will sell everything else over a period of six months. I am ashamed to live in a home built on crime. If you behave, I might simply divorce you once the house is sold and get you out of our life. If you don't, we will keep you as a pet.'

The captain sat heavily. He had never been an articulate man. He had never been burdened with intelligence or imagination. A change in fortune had obviously never been anticipated. There were no contingency plans to fall back on. There was no response available – either to the accusations or to the very obvious evidence of his wife's adultery.

'This isn't possible,' was all he could say.

'I found a chain,' Dolores told him. She picked up a dog chain.

That was too much for the captain. In a blind rage, he threw himself at the colonel. The colonel exploded into action. He sent the captain sprawling with a blow to the head then administered a few kicks to the captain's arms – enough to render them useless.

'Try that again and I'll have some real fun,' the colonel declared. He looked up at Dolores and smiled. Seeing that he wasn't rattled in any way, encouraged her.

'Stand up, George,' she said in a calm voice.

The captain stood unsteadily and the dog lead was presented again. This time when Dolores told him to hold up his hands, he complied meekly.

There was a collar attached to the lead. Dolores walked over to the bewildered man and, taking his hands, slipped the leather round his wrists. When he showed signs of renewed struggling the colonel stepped forward and boxed his ears. Dolores completed the buckling with a grim smile.

'Your wife is now your superior officer,' the colonel said. 'Disobey her and you will answer to me. Is that clear?'

The captain nodded slowly.

'I'll take him to his new kennel, darling.'

'Will you need me?'

'No, I think he knows his place, now.' She tugged on the chain.

The captain took a reluctant pace. 'Please . . .' he protested.

Dolores looked at the still grim-faced colonel. 'Tell him I don't want a word, a whimper or a woof for the rest of the night, dear,' she said.

'Zip it, Astor.'

The colonel was a master of lexical economy.

'I won't be long,' Dolores murmured.

'Hurry back. I have another Christmas coming.'

Dolores glanced at the colonel's crotch. His chinos had that sculpted look.

'I have a five times a night man,' she told her husband with a grin.

7

Jimmy's New Playground

The night after her scrubbing by the daughters of clean, the night after her mystery visitor, Zellie was lying on her bed in shiny silky pyjamas and reading a magazine. It was important to know who was sleeping with whom in celebrity land. It was important to know whose love child was missing his daddy. It was important to do things which had no importance at all.

From time to time, she glanced nervously at the unguarded curtain-less window. If the pervert came tonight, she was determined to be strong. She would demand to be treated with respect. She wouldn't be showing her pussy to an anonymous voice again.

Then the window slid up with a grating sound, loud enough to make her jump to her feet. It was Jimmy. He swung his legs over the sill and flopped clumsily into the room.

Shock changed to irritation.

'Tell me one thing,' she demanded. 'Tell me it was you last night.'

Jimmy looked sheepish. 'Yeah. It was me.'

Zellie took an aggressive stance, feet wide, hands on hips. 'How could you be so cruel!' she demanded to know.

Jimmy jumped onto the bed and lay down. He always seemed happier lying down. 'I was angry.'

'What about?

He looked her up and down in a boyish way. Her pyjamas were thin. His eyes lingered at the places where the fabric was stretched: across her breasts, across the dome of her pubis. 'You know why I was angry. I was angry because we had always been friends. I was angry because you were fucking everyone but me. I wanted to punish you.'

Zellie brought her legs together. She had become aware that her pussy was making a bulge. Jimmy's eyes had told her. A moment later, she folded her arms across her breasts, protecting those bulges from prying eyes too.

'I was really frightened,' she said.

'You looked turned on to me.'

Zellie stamped her foot. 'I was not turned on.'

'Your face was red.'

'I was embarrassed!'

'And your pussy was shiny. Like it was wet.'

'It's always wet!'

Jimmy laughed.

'I mean . . .' Zellie's voice trailed off. She hadn't meant to say that.

'Always?' Jimmy asked.

'No!'

'What about now?'

'No!'

'Show me.' He was staring at the gathered material at her groin.

'I will not!'

'It's not like I haven't seen it before.'

She couldn't deny that.

'You bullied me,' she said in a hurt voice.

'And the other kids don't?'

'No.'

'What, they just ask and you drop your panties and spread your legs?'

'No!'

The conversation was going badly.

'So what should I do if I want to see your pussy?'

'Jimmy!'

'Well, tell me because I *really* want to see it right now. I mean really, really, *really*.'

Zellie sat on the corner of the bed, keeping her legs tight together and her pussy well away from adolescent eyes. 'Jimmy, if we are really friends you won't do this.'

'What?'

'You're forcing me again.'

Jimmy sat up and leant forward. He took Zellie's hand in his. He was looking very sincere.

'I would never force you. But I have to see your pussy. It's all I've been thinking about all day.'

There was a sound from the hallway. Zellie's eyes darted towards the door. There was a bang from close by. The twins were about.

'You have to go.'

'Show me your pussy!'

'No!'

'I won't touch it. I just want to see how it joins onto your legs.'

'How it joins onto my legs?' Zellie asked in amazement. 'Haven't you ever seen a girl's pussy before?'

'Not a real one. Not close up.'

'Oh, Jimmy!' He had managed to make her feel like a big sister again. She wanted to ruffle his hair. Even so, she did not want to show her pussy.

'And I want to see inside,' Jimmy continued, undeterred by Zellie's pity. 'Real close up.'

'Can't you find a girlfriend?'

'I want you as my girlfriend.'

'But we are just friends!' Zellie said in despair.

'Just show me as a friend then.'

She was beginning to feel dizzy.

'Friends don't show each other their . . . their private bits.'

'I don't mind showing you my cock.'

'What!'

'Don't you want to see my cock?' He seemed hurt.

'I think your cock is probably very nice but no! I don't want to see it.'

'I still want to see your pussy.'

'For heaven's sake!' Zellie jumped up in a rush of exasperation and pulled down her pyjamas. Her panties followed, so that soon she was naked below the waist. She turned to face him and showed the space between her legs. She was shaved now. Rodrigo had insisted. Jimmy's face burnt and his eyes bulged.

'Wow,' he murmured. 'What is that big thing?'

Zellie glanced down. Her clitoris had swollen up and was poking out of its hood. Betrayed once more, she groaned in dismay.

'Is that your clit?' he asked.

'Yes,' she groaned.

He leant forward to see it better.

'I've seen pictures. Other girls aren't like that!'

'Well, I am.' Zellie was starting to feel feisty.

'Is it always that big?'

'Mostly.'

'Wow.'

Zellie glanced at the door again. If one of the twins came in and found her showing herself like this it would mean punishments on a scale that she couldn't imagine.

'Where does the pee come out of?'

'Jimmy, there isn't time.'

'I want to see.' He scooted closer on the bed so that his nose was only a few inches from her pussy.

She was starting to get turned on. His breath on the inside of her thighs made her feel even more turned on.

In a hurry to get rid of him, Zellie took hold of her pussy lips and pulled them open. She tugged and squeezed until the opening of her urethra was visible. 'It's just a little hole.'

Jimmy's eyes scoured the pink flesh. There was a physical sensation from the fire of his gaze. Little currents were stirring in her belly. Soon, currents of mucus would be flowing from her pussy.

'I can't see!' Jimmy declared in a despairing voice.

'Just under my clitoris.'

'Move your clit.'

Zellie used her thumb to pull the clitoris upwards. 'Can you see now?'

'Wait!' He leant over the bed and picked up the little table lamp. Pulling on the lead, he brought it between her open legs. Now her pussy was fully illuminated. 'I still can't see.'

'Oh, Jimmy! The twins might come in any time!'

'Pee a little. I'll see where it comes from.'

'I can't pee on the floor.'

Jimmy set the light down and cupped his hand. 'Just a dribble,' he said. 'I'll catch it.'

Zellie groaned. Feeling that she had fallen into a mad dream, she tried to pee. 'It won't come.'

'Relax.'

'How can I relax?'

Jimmy grinned. 'Close your eyes. Imagine you're in a hot bath.'

'A hot bath! Why a hot bath?'

'Try it.'

Zellie closed her eyes.

'Think of steam,' Jimmy suggested.

Suddenly a jet of water sprayed out. She groaned again. She was getting *very* aroused– peeing into a boy's hand was something new.

'That's enough,' she said, cutting off the flow before it could really begin, before she lost all control.

'One more time, I didn't really see.'

'What were you looking at, then!' she cried in exasperation.

'It was too quick!'

'If I do it one more time, you'll go then?'

'Of course I will.'

Zellie neither believed nor disbelieved. In mad dreams, things were neither true nor untrue. She tried again. This time the urine came in a great flood. She couldn't stop. It felt too good. The water ran and ran. A great heat flared in her belly. Without being able to help herself, her forefinger flicked rapidly across her clitoris. Three quick flicks and she came, arching her back, opening her mouth wide and groaning loudly.

When she opened her eyes there was a spreading stain of urine on the carpet. Even worse, Jimmy was staring at her with a look of shock. She had crossed a line.

'Now I know why they call you a slut,' he breathed.

Zellie had been called 'slut' too many times to take it hard.

'I'm not a slut. I just like sex,' she said breathlessly.

'There is come running down your leg.'

'Girl's don't come, Jimmy.'

'What's that then?'

He pointed to the sticky wetness seeping down the inside of her thighs.

She groaned in embarrassment and snatched her panties from the bed. Squatting, she wiped herself. Jimmy watched in awe.

'You look fantastic even when you're wiping gunk out of your pussy,' he told her. He did not usually give compliments. She should have been flattered.

'You have to go, Jimmy.'

'Only if you promise to show your pussy whenever I ask.'

'I can't do that.'

'Promise,' he said resolutely.

The sound of a door opening made her jump. Luckily, it wasn't her door.

'OK, I promise. But you have to go.'

Jimmy jumped from the bed and headed for the window. 'Next time, I'll show you my cock,' he declared.

Zellie groaned and followed him. As soon as he was through the window, she slammed it shut. Jimmy was about to jump onto the aerial highway of the cedar tree when he stopped. Turning, he called: 'Don't close the curtains. I want to watch you while I jack off.'

Another groan of despair escaped Zellie's lips. What was happening to Jimmy? Once he had been nice! She watched him slip into his bedroom then very deliberately pulled her curtains to. He waved his arms frantically to try and stop her but this time Zellie was strong. He would have to masturbate to a memory. Then there was only the mess on the carpet to deal with and the ache in her belly – one come was never enough.

Later that evening, after Zellie had showered and combed her hair and was lying in bed ready for sleep, there was a grinding sound from the window yet again. She quickly flicked on the bedside lamp and watched with astonished eyes as the lower sash was carefully raised. Earlier, in the heat of the moment, she must have forgotten to slip the catch!

She felt as if she had fallen into a slasher movie where the monster will never die – it just kept coming back. Perhaps Jimmy was losing his mind. Perhaps Jimmy was becoming a monster. She watched in horror as a hand pushed aside the curtains and introduced a little block of wood to hold up the window. He might be losing his mind and he might be a monster but he was well prepared, she couldn't deny him that.

As soon as the block was in place, the hand withdrew.

A moment later, the curtains parted again. This time the flesh that entered was unequivocally boy. A large curving penis, genuinely impressive (even to Zellie who had seen many boyish members), slowly entered her bedroom, jutting in like the branch of a fallen tree.

A hand appeared and began to manipulate the column of flesh.

Part of Zellie felt like screaming. Another part felt like rushing down to the kitchen and fetching a knife (to sever all connections). The final and dominant part was simply stunned.

With the bedclothes pulled up to her neck and an expression half of horror and half of fascination, she watched as the fingers manipulated the penis and it grew even longer and fatter. Disembodied, it developed a personality of its own. The bulbous head seemed to examine the room, as if searching for a place to be. The mouth opened and closed. It dribbled and drooled. It smiled and frowned. Zellie half expected the creature to escape from the controlling fingers, slither down the wall and rush her bed. A tiny tingle of interest between her legs told her she might welcome it.

In only a few minutes, there was a crisis. The fingers moved with the speed of lightning and semen jetted from the broad mouth. It flew in every direction. Sticky wetness flecked her wall. Gobbets of come landed on her bed. There were more stains on the carpet.

Then it was all over and the intruder slowly withdrew, pausing only to wipe itself on her curtain.

'Next time leave the curtain open,' said a low voice.

Zellie was too shocked to respond.

8

The Captain's New Regime

In the days that followed the chaining of the captain, many things changed in the Astor house. The captain was confined to the guest house every evening after duties ended, for one thing. For another, the colonel took possession of his prize with military efficiency, mopping up any resistance with a relentlessly hard dick.

The prize never demurred. She wanted to be mopped up. She wanted all doubts grubbed out of their hiding places. She wanted all guilt flame-throwered to carbon by the colonel's boundless passion. The colonel obliged with gusto.

By the end of that first week she was his completely and, so as not to disappear irrevocably into dribbling slutdom, at the beginning of the second week she launched a counter attack with hot pussy and the heavy artillery of bouncing breasts.

By the end of the second week he was as much hers as she was his.

The captain could only listen from his chains as these two titans of lust clashed by night and day, on and in assets he had once owned (if obtained by illegal means).

This was only the first of many blows for the captain. His invitations to social occasions plummeted when his wife calmly said he was bored with the niceties of cocktail parties and golf parties. On the base, the colonel never missed an opportunity to upbraid him. Contempt spreads. Soon his subordinates no longer consulted him when making decisions. The captain's once square shoulders were now permanently slumped.

In the middle of the second week, whilst making an inventory of the house's goods, the colonel found a collection of video tapes. These were tapes that Dolores had never mentioned. They showed her receiving the captain's sexual attentions and for the first time the colonel understood why she had denounced him as a pervert on that first evening.

The captain had a predilection for humiliation. He liked drunken sex that involved obliging his wife to drink fluids no woman would have volunteered to drink. He liked to force his wife to crawl on all fours. He liked her to bark like a dog and lap water from a bowl. Apparently, when he was sober, he denied that all these things had ever happened.

Dolores had endured a lot for the sake of keeping a roof over her children's heads. Now the children were grown and gone, now the captain was revealed for the criminal dunderhead he had always been, the colonel was of a mind to exact revenge on the man who had once degraded his new-found love. Thus at the beginning of the third week a new operation began. It was an operation aimed at the heart and mind of the captain. It was designed to break both.

Dolores loved that special time of day when night comes with a blanket of stars then pauses, just for a moment, before falling across the earth. That evening, the first of the captain's new regime, the pause was finer than most. A sapphire light was bouncing from the sea to the south. The moon, almost full, was low on the horizon. Its attendant clouds were ruby and ginger. Everything seemed to stop. The wind slowed, the birds became quiet.

Dolores, too, paused and looked across the beds of passionflower and violet towards the last of the sun. Her dressing gown of royal-blue silk was fading to black. Her mind was slipping into the night and into the time of dreams. Then her back stiffened. She had a mission and she must not be deflected. Glancing back at the house, she could feel the gaze of the colonel. He would be watching from their bedroom window. She could feel his love. She could almost touch his strength.

A week ago, she might have waved. Today there was no need, no need to even search for his distant form. The bond between them grew stronger every day. Gestures and words had less and less importance. So, as night finally fell and darkness engulfed all but the pathway and its row of earth-pinned lights, Dolores deepened her resolve and walked on. In her left hand was a vanity case, in her right a key.

At the guest house, she let herself in quietly. There was the sound of a television from upstairs. The colonel had been kind. George had not been obliged to stare at a wall all evening as he sometimes was. The stairs creaked as she ascended. There was a note of doom in the sound but Dolores was not afraid. Tonight she was avenging wrongs done, tonight she *was* doom.

George was sitting up on the bed, his face coloured by the images from the TV. He looked at her nervously, half-smiled, glanced at the bag in her hand, tried even harder to smile.

'Hi, Angel,' he said in a strained voice.

Dolores smiled back. Her smile was comfortable. She was resolved in her mind about what needed to be done. The colonel had assuaged her concerns. The colonel had helped her pack the bag.

'I'm so pleased that you're here. I wanted to talk to you ... About a lot of things,' George began in a plaintive voice. 'I thought –'

'You sound sad. It's not nice to sit at home and wait, is it, darling?' she replied, cutting him short, running her fingers through his hair. So often, she had waited for George on the bed in the big house, the TV a useless distraction. So often she had greeted his arrival with conflicted feelings. Relief, expectation, trepidation. So often *she* had tried to talk to *him*. 'Don't worry, baby,' she said. 'It won't hurt. Unless you fight me.' She picked up the TV remote and switched it off with an air of finality.

George's thin face paled. His lips ceased trying to smile. It was what he had always said to her before . . . Well before many things that *had* hurt.

Dolores laid the vanity case on the dressing table. 'Now. I want you to behave,' she said. 'I don't want to have to tell the colonel that you were bad.' She looked at him steadily. 'Most of all I don't want to have to call the colonel down here. I don't want him to be upset.'

George shifted uncomfortably. He certainly did not want her to call the colonel down here. He had learnt that a colonel who was upset was a colonel to be afraid of.

'So when I take those cuffs off, I want you to do exactly as I tell you. I don't want any arguments. I don't want any cheek. OK?'

George nodded.

She opened the bag and took out a video camera. There was a tripod beside the bed. She took her time setting it up while George watched with increasing restlessness.

'We don't want to miss anything, do we?' she asked with a matronly smile, turning the lens, allowing it to measure George with a glassy eye. Her smile did not reassure.

Finished, she returned to the case and took out a familiar key. George held up his hands. The thin chain that ran to the wall tinkled softly. A lovely sound on a lovely evening, Dolores thought. She smiled warmly at her husband as she undid the handcuffs.

'I bet that feels better, doesn't it?'

'Yes, dear.'

'And one more thing. There is something that the colonel was very insistent about. From now on you will call me "Momma".'

'Momma?'

'I know that it sounds a little strange but the colonel thinks that it will help you.'

'Momma?' the captain repeated with dawning horror.

'Exactly. If I ask a question you will answer it and call me Momma. If I tell you to do something, you will say "Yes Momma", brightly, cheerfully. If you don't understand, you will say "Sorry Momma, can you please explain".'

The captain looked as if his world was collapsing.

'And when you speak to the colonel you address him as Poppa. Isn't that nice? We have decided to adopt you.'

'No,' said the captain. 'I can't –'

She pressed her finger to her lips. 'Shh. "No" is a word that you will never use, neither with me nor with Poppa.'

'It's impossible –'

'Nothing is impossible. Twenty years in a military prison is not impossible. Loss of TV rights is not impossible. Bed without supper is not impossible.'

The captain looked distraught. Dolores felt a moment of weakness. She had the impulse to throw her arms around her husband. She felt a stab of the love she had borne him as they walked down the aisle together. Then she remembered the colonel.

She remembered the love that she felt for him now. She also remembered her children. She remembered how the captain had endangered them with his greed and his criminality. Her heart hardened.

'You should think very carefully, George. You should realise that there is no alternative.'

An edge had crept into her voice. George's head fell.

'OK,' he moaned.

'OK, *Momma*.'

He groaned.

'Say it!' she told him. 'It will please me so much. You do want to please me, don't you?'

He threw her a defeated glance. 'OK . . . Momma.' His voice sounded strangled. There were strange swallowing noises in his throat.

'Good, now we can get on. I don't want this to take all night.' Dolores held out her hand. Her smile had returned. It was as big and comfortable as an old armchair.

George took the hand and let himself be pulled upright.

'First off, you need to undress,' she told him.

'Please . . .'

'Please, Momma.'

George seemed to decide that it was better to undress than it was to say the dreaded word. His crisp uniform came away in layers. The masculine cut, the masculine colours fell to the floor.

'There is one more thing that you should know,' Dolores said softly. 'The colonel has always had a hankering for a daughter.' She reached into the case and pulled out a bundle of soft hair. She shook it out to reveal a long blonde wig.

'No!' George cried in horror.

'Remember what we agreed about the "No" word,' Dolores told him. The crispness in her voice somehow replaced the starch of his uniform. He stiffened into unwanted compliance. She stepped in front of his naked frame and pulled the wig into place. Then, stepping back, she examined the crestfallen man critically. 'I'm not sure that blonde really works for you,' she said. 'But maybe with the right make-up.'

'Make-up!' he cried.

'Make-up, Momma!'

'Oh for God's sake!'

'God is not involved here, George. There is only George and his Momma.'

'Momma . . .' George repeated, as if the word contained every horror that man had known or invented.

'Perhaps I should call you Georgie from now on. Yes, Georgie is a lovely name. And of course you need make-up, Georgie. Nobody wants a girl who isn't pretty. But first –' She reached into the bag again and pulled out a skirt. 'Let's see if this is your size.'

George was obliged to step into the skimpy skirt. It showed his hairy but well-formed legs from ankle to mid-thigh.

'A little too tarty perhaps. And those legs are going to need shaving.' Dolores was beginning to enjoy herself. Her eyes were shining with glee. 'We will have some fun out here! Just you and me.'

The captain must have seen a different future. His knees buckled and for a moment he seemed in danger of fainting.

'We won't shave them tonight, though,' Dolores decided. 'The colonel is waiting.'

She pulled a bra from the case and obliged him to slip his arms through the openings. After clipping it at the back, she slipped a couple of falsies into the front. A tight blouse followed. 'I think that you will have to rely on your personality more than most girls, Georgie.' There was a note of disappointment in her voice. 'But as you grow into your new role things will improve.' Dolores always tried to look on the bright side.

She sat him in front of the mirror and considered his face from every angle. He stared morosely at the table top, resisting sullenly when she tried to turn his face to the light.

'You don't know how many times I sat in front of the mirror trying to make myself beautiful for you,' she hissed. 'Now, will you cooperate or will I call Poppa?'

He allowed her to turn his face this way and that but still refused to look at his reflection. She worked quickly and diligently, trying various colour combinations before achieving the look that she wanted.

'Now look,' she said, when she was finished. 'Look how sweet you are.'

The captain forced himself to face the mirror. The face that confronted him was very different from the one that he wore to work. This face was not authoritative. It was not a face to inspire fear in the lower ranks. It was sad and it was sweet. It was the sweetness which probably shocked him the most. It certainly surprised Dolores.

'Perhaps you won't need that personality after all,' she decided.

The captain's eyes were scouring the mirror. Perhaps he was looking for the man that he used to be.

'I think there was always a girl in there trying to get out. What do you think, Georgie?'

Broken, George agreed in a low voice. 'Yes, Momma.'

Dolores beamed. 'You said the word! And it didn't hurt at all. Did it? Now look in the camera and tell Poppa thank you for revealing a side that you never knew you had.'

George did as he was bid, uttering the words mournfully and with a shifty gaze.

'You need to work on your smile and you need to work on your self-confidence,' Dolores told him. 'But really apart from that I think you will be fine.'

She stood him up and led him to the bed. He held out his hands when she told him to and she slipped the cuffs back into place. He seemed to think that it was all over. His eye returned to the sanctuary of the TV, still flickering mindlessly at the foot of the bed.

Dolores had another agenda. She took a pillow and laid it out in the middle of the mattress. 'Lie down,' she told him. 'On your stomach.'

In a daze, George did as he was told. His pelvis lay on the pillow so that his bottom was pushed up. Dolores quickly slipped cuffs onto his ankles and, before he could react, he was securely spread-eagled.

'Now we come to the bit that I think you will like,' Dolores said with a wicked laugh.

She pushed another pillow under his hips so that his bottom was even higher, then flicked up his skirt, revealing bare flesh. She dug around between his legs until she found his penis. She pulled it back so that it was fully visible against the white of the pillows. She worked it until he was hard. It didn't take long. He hadn't come for at least a week.

'I said that you would enjoy this part. One little thing, though. I don't want you making too much noise.' She opened the case again and pulled out a red ball gag. He struggled a little but as soon as she pinched his nose, his mouth opened and the gag slipped inside. She buckled it behind his neck then skipped over to the camera. She relocated it to the head end of the bed so that the captain's face was captured.

'If you move your head, I am going to be cruel, OK? I'll find some way to tie it into place. It will probably hurt – so don't make me.'

She slipped off her dressing gown. Beneath the dark silk was a leopard-skin leotard. At her groin was a strap-on dildo. She stepped in front of him so that he could see it.

He began to struggle.

Dolores shook her head in disapproval. 'I know that you want it. So don't be silly.'

George struggled even more violently.

She sighed and sat on the bed looking very serious, even stern. 'Now remember. I always wanted yours. Even if I had a headache. Even if it was late and I was asleep. Even if you were drunk.'

He struggled even more violently. She stroked his hair.

'I'll be gentle,' she told him. 'I'll make it good for you.' She reached between his legs and started to play with his dick and balls. 'My! You are hard. You shake your head but you're as hard as iron.'

Dolores abandoned his balls and went over to the case again. She plucked out a bottle of lubricant and squeezed a goodly amount into the parting of his buttocks. 'I bet that's nice,' she said, massaging the lubricant over testes and perineum, allowing her fingers to dip into his anus just a fraction.

The captain was roaring into the gag and struggling wildly.

Dolores took hold of his head. The look in her eyes was still kindly but the message was firm. 'We can do this two ways,' she told him. 'I can take my time. I can open up that bottom slowly and gently and I can give you a nice fuck until you come. Or I can be cruel, get straight in there and screw you till you bleed.'

He screamed at her through the ball gag and she dropped his head.

'I want you to think about it. Just think of all those men all over the world getting a big fat cock up their ass right now. Almost all of them enjoying it. Almost all of them coming buckets. And remember if you go to a military prison it won't be *me* fucking you in the ass.'

The change of language seemed to surprise him. Perhaps he heard an echo of the colonel. Perhaps that was what quietened him. He watched intently as she stood up and slipped on her dressing gown.

'In the meantime, I am going to ring Poppa and tell him that you are being a very bad girl.'

Dolores went downstairs and used the phone in the hall. She had left the bedroom door slightly open so that the captain could hear what was said. She told the colonel about the success of the transformation. She told him what a sweet girl they had upstairs. Then she told him how uncooperative Georgie had become as soon as Dolores had mentioned anal sex.

For a while, Dolores simply listened to the colonel's reply. Then she began to protest. Then she began to plead. 'No, darling, please don't come all this way. I know how upset you get . . . Let me try again.'

The conversation went on and on. George would have heard them discuss all of the various options from outright rape to cruel punishments of his behind and his testicles to force co-operation. He would have heard Dolores accept the assertion that George was not necessarily supposed to enjoy this. He would have heard her say that it would turn her on more if he did.

Ten minutes later, she returned to the bedroom. George was a sorry-looking mess. His skirt was still around his waist, his make-up was smeared where he had rubbed his face into the bedclothes, there was mucus leaking from the corner of the ball gag. Interestingly, he was still hard.

Dolores sat beside him and lifted his head again. Her smile was at its most beautiful. 'Poppa says to give you another chance to be good. He says that it's natural for you to take a little time to adjust to all this. So I am going to take off your gag and ask you nicely if you will co-operate.'

George had a look in his eyes that bears have after long years of captivity.

She unbuckled the belt, and the gag – slobber-sticky, lint-coated – popped from his mouth. 'Now look at me and say, please Momma fuck my ass.'

Without warning, the captain started to cry. Sobs shook his lean frame from head to toe. Dolores was genuinely shocked. She had never seen as much as moisture in the captain's eye before.

'My! I didn't expect you to get this upset!' She cradled his head. There were muffled words. She raised the head again.

'I'm . . .' The captain's voice trailed away.

'You're what, darling?'

'I'm sorry. For embezzling funds, for being thoughtless. For . . .'

The voice trailed away again.

'I think you truly are,' cooed Dolores. 'And that is a very fine start.'

'Don't . . .'

'Don't make you into a sex-pet?'

The captain groaned.

'This punishment is far more lenient than you would have to endure in prison, my darling. You might have to service a whole gang.'

'You are my wife!'

'And you were my husband whilst you were stealing hundreds of thousands. You were my husband whilst you strutted and preened at the Country Club and I waited at home.'

The captain gave a mighty groan and buried his head in her lap.

Dolores stroked his hair. 'It will only hurt if you resist, Georgie. Accept what is going to happen and *enjoy*.' Her hand went back to his balls. He groaned. His penis twitched hugely. 'You see,' she said. 'You really

114

do want it.' She stroked his hair and whispered sweet reassurance. She used her other hand to gently work around the opening of his anus. Her fingers dipped and slipped. Finally, she lifted his head and looked deep into his tear-filled eyes. 'Don't disappoint me,' she told him. 'When I ask you if you are going to let me fuck your ass I want you to say, "Yes Momma". Nothing else. OK?'

Utterly defeated, he nodded and she kissed the top of his head.

She asked the question and waited. His eyes searched her face. Perhaps he was looking for a sign that this was just a bad joke. Perhaps he hoped to find a hint of weakness in his wife's determination. There was none. Finally, he answered in a small, shaky voice.

'Yes, Momma.'

A brilliant smile split Dolores's face. She told him how brave he was to accept his punishment and his pleasure in one nine-inch package. 'I will make it so good for you, baby,' she whispered. 'I will make you come and come.'

Half an hour later, the captain did come. It was loud and it was violent. His wife's long waist provided plenty of power. She had fucked him gently, she had fucked him with slow corkscrew motions and, at the end, she had pistoned into him as if she were an experienced whore. He broke like a schoolboy being beaten and wept.

Dolores swung her legs off the bed and her hand dived between his legs. She scooped up great gobbets of come and sniffed them. 'Concentrated girl come,' she said appreciatively. She took the captain's chin in her clean hand and looked into his tear-streaked face. 'We *really* are going to have fun,' she murmured, then told him to open his mouth like a good girl. Her come-soaked fingers slipped into his mouth and ran around cheek and tongue as he sniffled. Only when he had cleaned her fingers completely did she let go of his chin.

After she had undone his bonds and removed the pillows, she surveyed his long lean body. He was still hard and, for a moment, she had the urge to straddle him and help herself to the bulging cock. Then she thought of the colonel and her desire increased to a wholly new level. 'I won't tie your hands tonight,' she told him. 'You can masturbate while you think about what I did to you.'

She turned on her heel and hurried out of the room, carrying her flooded pussy to the colonel.

9

Dr Benlay

Dolores and the captain were sitting in the waiting room at Doctor Benlay's. The captain was fidgeting with the crease of his trousers. He looked bored and slightly constipated. Dolores was alternately reading *Homes and Gardens* and scolding her husband in a soft patient tone. He didn't appear to hear.

When the receptionist finally called their names, the captain stood smartly and marched into the office with a look of weary gloom. Dolores followed more slowly, swaying on her black high heels.

Doctor Benlay was stuffing some papers into the drawer of his desk. He was a stocky man of fifty or so, unhurried in his movements, apparently imperturbable. His head was a pink fleshy cube and almost but not quite naked. Close-cropped ginger hair protected the modesty of his scalp – barely; a thin ginger beard ran around his chin like a short straggly hula skirt.

The captain halted for a moment and surveyed the room like a field position. Dolores arrived a moment later with a broad but businesslike smile.

'Don't run off like that, Georgie,' she said smoothly. The captain huffed.

Stepping from behind his desk, Benlay thrust a square well-manicured hand in the captain's direction. Dolores intercepted the hand and shook it firmly.

The captain helped himself to a seat facing the window. The rubber plant that stood beside it was the only non-functional item in the room. The captain gazed at it impassively.

Benlay sat, a puzzled expression forming on his face. 'You are new to this practice?' he murmured, gazing from one party to the other. His voice was soft – unexpected from such a square bunker of a head. His eyes too were soft, blinking more than was needed, expressing at that moment an interest that bordered on curiosity.

'That's correct, doctor. I am Dolores Enfield Astor and this is my husband George,' Dolores told him.

'Good,' replied the doctor.

'How can a thing like that be either good or bad?' the captain asked brusquely. 'A name is a name.'

Dolores reached over and tapped the captain reprovingly on his knee. The next time the doctor glanced in the captain's direction, the captain refused to meet his eye.

'So what is the problem?'

'My husband has been having trouble ejaculating lately.'

The doctor looked at the captain sympathetically.

'Ahh. When your wife says lately, um, ah. How would it be best to address you?'

'Captain Astor.'

'I don't think we need that level of formality. I call him Georgie. I think that is much easier.'

'Georgie?'

'Yes.'

The captain's face remained impassive.

'OK, Georgie, exactly how long has it been since you last had a satisfactory orgasm?'

The captain continued his leisurely examination of the rubber plant. He made no sign of offering a reply.

'He was very reluctant to come,' Dolores told the doctor.

'Well, it is a sensitive subject.'

'For both of us.'

'I'm sure.'

'Are you planning on making notes?' the captain growled when Benlay picked up a pencil and reached for a pad.

'Would that disturb you?'

'Damn right it would.'

'Georgie . . .' Dolores's voice was not unkind but it was insistent.

'It would help me if I could . . .' Benlay murmured.

'Then you take notes,' Dolores told him.

If the muscles of the captain's jaws had tightened any further he would have crushed his own teeth. There was an audible sound of grinding.

Benlay set the pencil aside. 'Not today, perhaps.'

'Don't be intimidated by my husband, doctor. He growls a great deal but his bite is no worse than a flea's.' The reassurance was offered in a warm sultry tone and drenched in a sugar-sweet smile.

Benlay scrutinised Dolores for a moment. His eyes wandered across her large breasts as they breathed hard against her tight lycra top. They circumnavigated her broad hips, kept casually in a dark wrap-around skirt emblazoned with creamy columbine. For a long soulful moment, he gazed at her high heels and then at the puffed-up volume of her auburn hair. He picked up the pencil again and sank his teeth into it. 'Have you considered marriage counselling?' he suggested. 'I sense issues of an interpersonal nature here.'

'Issues of an interpersonal nature?' replied Dolores slowly. 'If a man doesn't come when his wife fucks his ass with love and tenacity that most certainly is an issue of an interpersonal nature,' Dolores agreed, 'but

119

there may also be issues of a medical nature, wouldn't you say?'

Benlay bit clean through his pencil. The sharpened tip fell onto the desk, rolled clean across it and fell into the captain's lap. The captain brushed it away with an irritated flick of his wrist. His face remained inscrutable.

'Have you tried any alternatives to anal sex?' Benlay managed to ask after a moment.

'I have tried a lubricant gel and a latex glove.'

Benlay gulped despite himself and carefully crossed his legs. 'And that didn't work?'

'No,' said Dolores, shaking her head regretfully. 'And it gave Georgie a blister.'

'Have you thought about vaginal sex?'

'The captain doesn't have a vagina, doctor.'

Benlay's eyebrows shot upwards for a moment then he suddenly grinned and relaxed, settling lower in his chair. He looked like a man who had finally got the joke. 'And neither, I assume, do you?'

'Oh, I have a vagina, doctor.'

Benlay sat upright again, abruptly.

'Forgive me, I thought you were a . . .'

'A cross-dressing queer? I'm not the pervert here, doctor.'

Benlay began to chew on the stub of his pencil. Dolores glanced at her watch.

'Forgive me, doctor, but my girlfriends are due for afternoon tea soon . . .'

'Tea . . .' Benlay murmured.

'I would like you to examine my husband and see if you can find the problem. It is probably something *so* obvious to a trained eye.'

'An examination. Of course, if he wishes me to.'

'He does, don't you, Georgie?'

The captain growled.

'There, he does,' Dolores declared and rose from her chair.

Benlay's eyes opened a little wider as her height and breadth filled his office. When Dolores parted her legs to stand at ease, Benlay took a deep, appreciative, pheromone-laced breath then exhaled slowly. He was beginning to look intoxicated. He was perspiring.

'Do you use this as an examination room?' Dolores asked.

'Of course.'

'Stand up then, Georgie, and get that uniform off.'

The captain stood stiffly and reached for the buttons of his shirt. There was a redness in his eye. His nostrils flared. He flashed a 'one day I will kill you look' at Dolores.

'I'm sure the doctor has seen all this before,' she told him. 'So don't be silly.'

She reached out and stroked his chin. Her gaze was pure momma love.

The captain unbuttoned his shirt and shucked it off.

'And the trousers, Georgie. The doctor can't examine your anus if you're wearing army chinos.'

'I'm not sure I need to examine the captain's anus just yet,' Benlay said quickly.

'There you are, Georgie. The doctor might not even need to explore that sore little bottom of yours.'

The captain stepped out of his trousers and slipped down his shorts.

'Good heavens!' Benlay exclaimed.

The captain was sporting an impressive erection.

'Oh, he has no problem getting a hard-on, doctor. That is one reason why it is so puzzling. I mean poor Georgie needs to come *so* much. And when he does . . . Well, I've been spreading out the towels *two* deep all week.'

The captain was gazing impassively at the rubber plant again. The huge puce and glowing blimp of a penis was gently bobbing. Benlay seemed poised between fascination and horror.

121

Dolores stepped forward gracefully. A deft flick of the wrist removed her skirt. The strap-on – more Zeppelin than blimp – broke free immediately.

'Bend over the desk, George. Let Momma see the wood for the trees.' She stepped behind the bending figure and grasped his hips firmly.

Benlay pushed his chair back from the desk and watched open-mouthed.

'I should call security or I should leave,' he declared.

'Leave?' cried Dolores. 'You have to help us, doctor. Poor Georgie hasn't come in a fortnight.'

The captain turned to Benlay and gave him one of the most curious looks one man has ever given another. There was a sense of hurt, a sense of humiliation, a sense of feral excitement in his eyes. There was a passivity, a patience, a greed in the up-tucked behind. There was a languid openness in his parted lips. There was depravity in the spittle that oozed from the corner of those lips. More than anything else, the captain looked like a tethered bull waiting for the relieving hands of a semen collector.

'I think I need a coffee,' the doctor declared.

'Aren't you going to take a sample of something?' Dolores asked. 'Aren't you going to palpate his prostate gland?'

Benlay was gone before her despairing plea had concluded.

Ten minutes later, the patients in Benlay's waiting room leapt from their seats as one. The bellow of a large male beast filled the air. The sound rattled the flowers on the receptionist's desk. It crashed down the adjoining corridor like a stampede and brought Doctor Benlay hurrying from the practice's rest room.

He found the frightened receptionist inclining her head to the door of his room. She stepped back guiltily as Benlay strode in. 'Nothing to worry about,' Benlay declared, smiling nervously.

122

When further bellows followed, a woman in a blue sun dress let out a cry of indignation and, folding the hand of her sulky charge in her own, led the child away.

'I'm not taking my daughter to a veterinarian,' she declared.

A few minutes later, Dolores and the captain stepped out of the consulting room. Dolores was smiling brilliantly. The captain looked less constipated. 'Problem solved,' she declared. 'It just needed a change of venue, doctor.'

Benlay was gazing at the bulge in Dolores's wrap-around.

'Good,' he managed to stammer.

'How much do we owe you?'

The doctor named his usual fee and the captain wrote a cheque.

Dolores took the captain's wallet and pulled out a few small notes. 'For the cleaners,' she whispered with a smile, and pressed the notes into Benlay's hand.

'Don't hesitate to *not* come again,' Benlay called after them as they left.

Dolores treated the doctor to a beautiful smile over a broad, tanned shoulder and squeezed the captain's buttock with a loving hand.

10

Runaway

It was a Monday morning.

Zellie was standing in the wood behind her school looking out along the river bank. Behind her classes had just begun. In front of her was escape.

Zellie had had enough of aunts and twins and canes and holiness and boys' basements and boys who climbed balconies and boys who had credit cards. She was, in fact, tired of *all* boys and most girls.

It was time to leave.

The decision had been sudden, a conviction on waking that nothing could be worse than staying where she was. The direction had chosen itself. She was heading south, to the sea. There, she would find her cousin, Amelie. Amelie had liked hiding games when they were little. Amelie would hide her now (Zellie was almost convinced).

She had packed a bag with a change of clothes, she had gathered every last note and coin, she had saved her favourite music to her iPod and she had struck into the woods behind her school as everyone else had headed into lessons.

No one would look for her out here. Only a mad girl would run this way: it was wet, it was marshy, it was wild.

It was also beautiful and, as she stepped from the wood onto the bank of the wide slow waterway, her heart sang. Here there was the blue of sky and water. Here was the sound of brook and birdsong. Here was an absence of eyes and hands, here a desert of penis and tongue.

She set off downstream in high expectations of nothing.

Half an hour of traipsing through low scrub and high grass brought her to her first target – a reed bed. She shucked off shoes and jeans and stowed them away in her small bag. Then, wading out into the cool water, her feet sinking into coarse sand, she worked her way along the outside of the reed bed.

Once, walking home from school (avoiding boy), she had seen an old aluminium boat wedged into this bed – almost certainly lost by its owners – but apparently in perfect condition. Even as she had examined it that first time, she had imagined herself being carried seaward like the Lady of Shallot.

Now, though, it was a challenge to find the rowing boat. The bed had grown in the last year. The reeds stood tall and dense like a hedge.

The current increased as she waded further out. The water rose. Soon it was scouring the inside of her thighs. After ten fruitless minutes of searching she decided that someone else must have found it. Then, she saw a glint of silver amongst the green stems. She worked her way into the tangle of plants and there it was!

It looked like the kind of boat that the men who maintained the weirs and dams used. Its shallow draught was perfect for skimming over the shallows and sandbanks. The aluminium construction meant that rocks would dent rather than pierce it.

She threw in her bag and began to haul on a nylon rope still attached to the prow. It was a struggle but Zellie was surprisingly strong for her age. Soon, the rowing boat was floating free and Zellie hauled herself up and into the broad bottom. Immediately, she felt the tug of the river's current and soon the boat was moving, drifting out from the bank.

A single oar wedged under the seat gave her a rudder if she needed one. At that moment though, Zellie was content to simply drift.

Looking back, she could see the wood behind her school. It shrank with each passing moment. Soon it would be gone.

Looking forward, she saw a soft river in a soft valley and she allowed herself to slump into the bottom of the boat. It was exquisitely comfortable: the cool, contoured metal pressed into her hot curves, her bag offered itself as a cushion, the sky smiled down, the boat revolved slowly as it drifted, the river rocked and carried like a mother.

For an hour, the boat bobbed along very sweetly. Once, it had nearly become snagged under a tree on the outside of a slow broad bend. Once, Zellie had to get out and push it off a sandbank. On the whole, though, it was as easy a ride as anyone could ask for, as gentle as a pussy cat and the paddle was hardly needed. The easy passage lulled her.

Soon, she was paying no more attention to her journey than she would have paid on a train or a bus. Instead of thinking about sandbanks or weirs, she was thinking about the sea. She was thinking about her cousin Amelie, and Amelie's boyfriend and Amelie's boyfriend's boat.

The boyfriend was cute. The boat was cool. Zellie was needing an adventure. Zellie's behind was needing some breathing space. Mostly, Zellie was needing time to herself – time without anyone trying to get into her pussy. These thoughts, running round and round inside her mind, were plenty loud enough to drown out the sound of the rapids until it was too late.

The moment that Zellie realised what was happening, was also the moment that it was too late to do anything about it. The current plucked at the boat like a wind plucking at a soap bubble. It shot forward and began to spin. Zellie sat up with a start.

Looking around herself, she realised that the river had become a different beast. It was no longer a pussy cat. It was a fierce creature with stony teeth jutting from a foaming maw. It looked as if it wanted to kill her.

Zellie gave a shriek and lunged for the paddle. No sooner had she picked it up than the boat hit a rock. There was a ringing sound from the contact. Zellie was thrown forward and the paddle flew from her hand. She could only watch as it raced ahead of the boat then wedged itself in the V of a pair of rocks. She tried to grab it as the boat hurtled by but it was out of reach.

Zellie gave another little shriek as the boat rounded a corner. Ahead of her was something she had never imagined. The banks of the river were growing steeper and steeper and the water was rushing faster and faster. She was entering a canyon.

There was nothing to do but hang on. For ten or fifteen minutes, Zellie had the ride of her life. More than once the boat crashed into the steep rock-strewn banks. More than once it was swamped by great sheets of water.

Then, quite suddenly, it was over. The river widened and the current eased. Soon she was drifting slowly across a mirror-smooth surface and there were dragon-flies and kingfishers to keep her company.

She made the mistake of relaxing again. She was just congratulating herself on a lucky escape when the boat tipped over a weir. It slid a full five metres before it hit the lower pool and tipped Zellie out. The boat sank. Her bag disappeared.

It was all Zellie could do to struggle ashore, wet and cold and lost. Her feet had barely touched dry ground when a voice rang out.

'Halt, who goes there!'

It was a friendly enough voice but Zellie's heart missed a beat.

A soldier appeared from the trees. A broad grin split his face.

'Did you come down the rapids?' he asked.

Zellie nodded.

'Where's your boat?'

'It sank.'

The soldier was examining Zellie with great interest. He held out his hand. 'I'm Sergeant Troy.'

Zellie shook the proferred hand reluctantly. 'I'm Zellie.'

Her life of solitude had lasted two full hours. Abruptly, she was back with creatures who stared and lusted. In a moment, she realised that her capacity to react had not been lost. Against her will, her clitoris was erect, ready for boy, boy and more boy.

'Well, I suppose you had better come with me,' the sergeant told her. He led Zellie through a screen of trees and into a large smoky clearing. There was a collection of tents around a single fire. Soldiers were washing clothes, preparing food, idly smoking cigarettes.

There was a loud roar when Zellie appeared.

'Don't worry,' the sergeant told Zellie, 'I'll beat them off if I have to.'

'My wife would have something to say if you beat *me* off, sarge,' came a distant voice.

There was a roar of laughter. The sergeant flushed and ignored the remark. He had found a seat for Zellie near the fire.

'Do you know how far away you are from the nearest road?' he asked, his voice displaying concern.

128

Zellie shook her head.

'A long way. And without a compass you would never find it. You could have been food for foxes.'

Zellie's heart missed another beat. To be eaten by a fox seemed a slow and painful way to go.

Sergeant Troy wrapped a blanket around her shoulders and shouted at one of the other men to make some soup. 'I'll try to find some clothes that will fit you,' he told her. 'Don't expect to be home tonight, we aren't due to head back until midnight.'

'I don't want to go home,' Zellie said solemnly.

'She can come home with me,' a voice piped up from behind.

'Cut it!' the sergeant boomed. He examined Zellie one more time. Zellie examined him in return. The finger was suddenly interested – so many young men, so much muscle, so many hormones. It was difficult for a girl to resist. It was impossible for Zellie. Her tongue flicked across her lower lip. It was not planned or even deliberate – it was a sort of nervous tic but it conveyed a meaning.

The sergeant seemed to have had his share of chance encounters. He seemed to know that the iron must be struck whilst it is hot. Leaning over, he whispered in her ear.

'If you want a fuck, follow me into the tent.'

It was the most brutal of invitations but delivered in a velvety voice and Zellie's belly turned a somersault. She looked around the camp and saw in every eye a variety of lust. Her isolation, her vulnerability hit her like a train. She found herself struggling for air. Waves of arousal washed through her belly. It felt as if she was at the top of a roller coaster. At any moment the ride would begin, and there was nothing she could do to stop it.

When the sergeant walked towards one of the nearby tents, Zellie had to follow. Inside the tent there was just enough light to see a camp bed and the sergeant making himself comfortable.

'I have a problem,' she said softly.

The sergeant looked her up and down.

'I'm very loud,' she confided, flushing as she continued, 'and you might need to tie me up. Or get someone to hold me down.'

The sergeant gave a low whistle.

'That is a problem.'

Zellie nodded as she pulled off her wet clothes.

As soon as her breasts were exposed, the sergeant stood and ran his hands across them. Zellie immediately reached for his groin. He was already hard.

'Are you always this greedy?' the sergeant asked.

'I can't help it.'

It was true, Zellie could not. There were so many boys – so many penises calling, such a great chorus of lust, an irresistible clamour.

She undid his flies and dropped to her knees. A moment later, his cock was knocking against the back of her throat. As soon as she swallowed him, the sergeant gave a cry as if he was going to come, then doubled up and pulled away.

'Hey, slow down,' he told her.

'Sorry,' she panted.

'Just get undressed.'

Half an hour later, Zellie's problems were drawing attention. Her groans had pulled a crowd. Her struggles had almost destroyed the tent.

Inside, the sergeant was trying to spend long enough inside Zellie's pussy to come. It was not working. Zellie was a strong girl. When she convulsed, the sergeant was bucked off like a cowboy by a bull.

In the struggle, they rolled out of the tent.

Ten or fifteen pairs of eyes watched the sergeant drive into her one more time. The same number watched

Zellie's mouth open in a howl of pleasure and saw her pelvis thrust and buck until the sergeant was repulsed again.

'Hold her,' the sergeant groaned.

Hands appeared from every direction. Zellie was pinched and probed as much as she was caressed and held. Even with so much help, it was difficult for the sergeant but eventually he came and rolled aside with a deep sigh.

Now there were only the privates for Zellie to deal with.

With her eyes closed, her hands snaked out. The finger of flesh told her that there was boy flesh in every direction. In a moment, she had found enough to suck into her mouth. A moment later her pussy was also being filled.

It was a long afternoon. Young men like seconds. Many like thirds.

Zellie had never been so well fucked.

It was a disorganised and ill-disciplined rabble that finally struck camp and started the hike back to the road. Most of them wanted to go AWOL – in Zellie's pussy and behind. The sergeant was obliged to pull a gun.

They trekked off in a crocodile of cursing.

Zellie walked like a penguin. Everything ached or was sore.

At the road, they threw her in the back of one of the lorries. Some of them wanted fourths. Zellie was beyond caring. It had been a busy day and she slept like a baby. It was only when they arrived inside the base that anyone bothered to wake her. Even then, she was only upright long enough to walk into the barracks. Here, they found a bunk for her and drew lots for her company. She was a popular girl all night.

131

It was Zellie's continuing enthusiasm that finally got her caught. She exhausted the boys to the point that they could not drag themselves to reveille. A military policeman was despatched. He helped himself to the pussy that was offered and the sultry smile that accompanied it but then with regret took her into custody.

Soon, she found herself being interviewed by Colonel Philips. As with every other soldier that she had come across so far, she found herself taken with the colonel. The colonel, perhaps because he was entirely satisfied with the sexual attentions of Dolores, was the first military man to respectfully refuse her pussy (despite the politeness and sincerity of her offer).

He was businesslike, courteous, and as soon as she told him that she was a Shelby he halted proceedings and telephoned Dolores – Aunt Dolores as far as Zellie was concerned. This is how Zellie came to be sitting self-consciously in the outer office of the commanding officer whilst every passing soldier tried to steal a glance at her through the doorway.

She had been waiting for perhaps an hour when Dolores appeared in a cloud of expensive perfume and feminine compassion.

'So you are Zellie, Diana's girl!' Dolores exclaimed as soon as she saw Zellie. 'You look as if you need a hug.'

Something about Dolores's tone had an immediate impact on Zellie. She stood up and wrapped her arms around Dolores's neck and burst into tears.

'There, there. You're safe now.'

The very word 'safe' made Zellie cry even more uncontrollably.

'You need to tell me everything, dear. Everything. OK?'

Zellie snuffled and sobbed a yes. 'Don't send me home,' she groaned.

'We won't decide anything until we have had a long talk. OK?'

Zellie pulled back a little and nodded.

'Well, let's go and see the colonel.' Dolores was about to lead the way when she noticed the wetness on Zellie's seat. She leant over, sniffed and looked more closely.

'Is that what I think it is?' the older woman asked.

Zellie nodded. The barrack-room boys had said goodbye in style that morning: sperm had been running out of Zellie's pussy ever since. Honesty compelled Zellie to confess.

'Were they invited?' her aunt asked.

Zellie blushed and nodded again.

'All of them?'

Zellie blushed even more deeply and nodded a third time.

'Well, you certainly aren't a shrinking violet,' Dolores declared.

'No, Aunt.'

Inside the colonel's office again, a full investigation began. Zellie's honesty was put to the test once more. Dolores was especially thorough in her questioning and soon knew everything about Rodrigo and Eduardo and every other boy.

When the colonel asked why she did not want to go home, the issue of the canings came out into the open. Before he could stop her, Zellie showed the colonel her behind.

He winced when he saw the stripes.

'You aren't going back to that hideous woman,' Dolores declared. The colonel agreed.

'I think there are more problems here than simply your aunt, though,' Dolores decided. 'Girls of your age should not be having sex with battalions of young soldiers.'

'I try not to.'

'Well, you definitely don't succeed.'

'No, Aunt.'

'I think we need a professional opinion,' the colonel suggested tentatively.

'Doctor Benlay, perhaps?' Dolores asked.

'Or a shrink.'

'I don't think Zellie is mad,' Dolores said softly.

'I have a very large clitoris,' Zellie declared in her own defence.

Dolores looked her up and down.

'I'm sure you do, dear.'

'Very large,' Zellie repeated, injecting a note of the surprise that she felt whenever she saw her own clitoris, erect and unconfined.

Dolores smiled. 'I'll call the doctor now.' She plucked a mobile from her handbag.

'Exactly how big *is* it?' the colonel asked.

'Darling!' Dolores cried. 'That is strictly girls' talk.'

The colonel tactfully found some paperwork to be getting on with. Dolores made the appointment.

11

The Exercise Bicycle

After an embarrassing examination at the hands of Doctor Benlay, Dolores had driven Zellie home. 'This is your life from now on,' Dolores said, showing Zellie around the villa and its grounds. By evening time, Zellie had already decided that she would like this new life – especially when it involved sitting out by the pool.

At that moment, she was eating an ice cream and watching the sunset reflect from the ripples. The colonel was sitting opposite her in a cane recliner reading the *Acacia Times*. His shorts were still wet from a previous dip. Dolores was curled up on a sun lounger.

'Sex is such a big thing,' Dolores declared, setting aside her magazine. 'Such a very, very, very big thing.' Her eyes wandered to the bulge in the colonel's swimsuit. Zellie's eyes followed.

The colonel's legs were open in a comfortable and relaxed attitude. His penis was soft but angled upwards. It was an object of veneration for Dolores. It was becoming a symbol of safety for Zellie.

The colonel accepted the twin gazes with equanimity, even shifting a little in his seat so that the two ladies could see better.

'What brought that on, my dear?' he asked, after due reverence had been shown.

'I was thinking of Zellie's predicament.'

The colonel looked sympathetic.

'I should call Benlay,' Dolores declared. 'He must have an opinion by now.'

'His office will be closed.'

'If he is disturbed at home, it will serve him right for not calling back sooner.'

A mobile sat on the little table beside her. She picked it up and dialled.

Zellie leant forward a little. This was the phone conversation she had not wanted to think about all afternoon.

The examination earlier in the day had been discouraging. The doctor had never encountered anything like Zellie's clitoris before. He had seemed impressed but perplexed.

'Doctor Benlay. I am so glad that you picked up. How did I get your number? My husband is a captain in the army. The signal corp still has a role . . .'

Dolores was thoughtfully allowing Zellie to catch both sides of the conversation. Dolores was a firm believer in full disclosure. 'I think you can guess why I am calling . . . Yes, it's about Zellie . . . Well, even your first thoughts are worth hearing, doctor . . . Surgery! Good heavens! *Merely* a reduction in nervous tissue . . . Merely! As far as I am concerned reduction is not much better than castration.'

The colonel crossed his legs at the sound of the word.

'Have you had the blood tests yet? All normal. Well, that is good news. Not good? It is bad because it gives you nowhere to start from? Well, we all need somewhere to start from.' Dolores flicked a fly away from her face. 'It is a puzzle of course. But every puzzle has a solution, doctor. You will get back to me? Well, have a nice shower. You've finished your shower now? Then have a nice towelling.'

Dolores switched off the phone. Her face showed a mixture of disgust and disappointment.

'The man's a stitcher and setter,' declared the colonel.

'Meaning, dear?'

'He can a stitch a wound and set a bone. After that you're on your own. Army's full of them.'

'He is supposed to be the best physician in Acacia.'

'Then we'll look further afield.'

Dolores nodded in agreement.

'But there must be something we can do *now*,' she murmured.

She was gazing at Zellie with concerned eyes.

'Prioritise, source, act,' the colonel declared. A puzzled glance from Dolores persuaded him to expand. 'Decide where you want to get. Uncover what lies in your way. Discover what resources you can bring to bear. Apply them with maximum force.'

'Zellie is not an enemy bunker,' Dolores reminded him.

The colonel allowed his eyes to wander across Zellie's curves and bumps. He was forced to agree. 'But the dictum has a universal applicability,' he insisted.

Dolores turned to Zellie. 'What do you think, dear?'

Zellie shifted uncomfortably in her seat. She looked into Dolores's eyes with a mixture of sadness and alarm. 'Did the doctor really think I should have it cut off?'

'Reduced.'

The colonel tossed his paper to the ground. 'That is not even a starting position. No one in this household has their sexual organs reduced. Not even the captain – who probably deserves to.' He looked Zellie straight in the eye. 'I realise that this is a woman thing,' he said briskly, 'so don't be embarrassed if I ask an awkward question. Answer as best you can. If you feel that you can't answer at all just run to your room in tears. OK?'

'OK, sir.'

'Zellie!' interjected Dolores.

'I mean colonel.'

Dolores had already warned Zellie not to fall too far under the colonel's spell. She was finding it difficult. The colonel was kind and he was big and he always seemed to know what should be done.

'What is the worst thing about such a large and overactive clitoris?' he asked.

Zellie felt no shyness with the colonel. The more direct the question he put to her, the more direct the answer she would give. 'Cravings,' she said. 'I have constant cravings. And then boys take advantage of them.'

'Can't you fight them?'

'I try.'

'I think that you should try a little harder.'

'Colonel, if I were to say that to you . . .' Dolores began.

The colonel understood her drift immediately. His own cravings *never* went unsatisfied.

'I would be very, very disappointed. Quite right. Absolutely useless advice.'

The colonel picked up the paper again. He seemed to have given up on the counselling role, but after only a moment's silence he found a second wind. 'One thing that *is* useful with lustful young men and women is exercise. Wear a man out and he loses interest in everything but food and rest.'

'Exercise might help. In the short term,' Dolores agreed.

'I could arrange a programme,' the colonel offered. 'What do you think, Zellie?'

'I could try.'

Later that evening, the colonel led Zellie into the gymnasium. He directed her to the exercise bicycle. 'This might be all you need,' he told her. 'If you get frustrated by the boredom of cycling you can take it out on the punch bag. OK?'

Zellie, clad in a cream leotard and blue tights, nodded and thanked him, though she doubted that the punch bag was for her.

'I'll come back in twenty minutes. By then I expect you to have made twenty kilometres.' He set the counter in the middle of the handlebars to zero.

Zellie swung herself up onto the saddle.

'I won't give you too much resistance, this time,' the colonel told her. He crouched and set the friction control to low. 'OK?'

Zellie beamed. The kindness of the colonel was a dream after Aunt Shelby's harsh regime. 'Thanks.'

He marched out. 'Remember, twenty kilometres!' he called over his shoulder. 'And no slacking.'

Dolores was in the conservatory. The captain was learning needlework under her careful eyes. He had successfully embroidered the words 'Glad to be' across the front of a fetching pink top in a shiny silver thread. Dolores still wasn't sure whether he should finish with 'of service' or simply 'serviced'.

She wanted him to finish the task tonight. Later, she would expect him to don his lovely top and ride himself to a satisfactory conclusion on a new and unusually large pole that was already strapped to her groin.

That night, he might have an audience. Zellie had learnt of the captain's condition with sympathy and interest. She had volunteered to help in any way that she could. Dolores was still running the offer around in her mind.

The colonel marched in with an optimistic smile.

'A healthy body is a healthy mind,' he declared, obviously still thinking of Zellie.

'Quite so,' Dolores agreed. 'I hope you have made sure that she can't hurt herself. Zellie is an enthusiast.'

'I've only let her use the exercise bicycle, today.'

A cloud passed across Dolores's face.

139

'Is that a problem, my love?' the colonel asked.

Dolores smiled. 'I hope not, my darling.'

The colonel sat. 'And what are you up to, Georgie?' he asked.

The captain looked up from his work with a pained smile. 'Embroidery, Poppa.'

The military clip had disappeared from his voice. He had learnt the virtue of finishing his words. He had also learnt the pleasures of acceptance and surrender.

The colonel leant forward and gazed at the half-finished work. He tried to look interested. 'Never could sew,' he declared.

'Georgie is doing a very fine job. But he is a little slow.'

'Put your back into it, girl,' the colonel growled.

'Yes, Poppa.'

'Tonight is fun night for Georgie.'

'Lucky Georgie.'

'And tonight I am excepting full abasement.'

This remark was directed at the captain as much as the colonel.

'If she gives you any trouble, just let me know.'

'Georgie understands what I want. Don't you, Georgie?'

'Yes, Momma.'

'And I think she's quite excited.'

'Are you excited, Georgie?' asked the colonel.

'Yes, Poppa.'

Dolores smiled. 'Lift up your skirt, Georgie. Show the colonel just how excited you are.'

The captain laid out his top on the table beside him.

The colonel sighed. 'Is it absolutely necessary for me to see?'

'It is important to monitor his condition, dear. And I think you should take a role.'

'Very well.'

140

The captain pulled his skirt to his waist. He wore no underwear.

'There!' cooed Dolores. 'I knew the needlework would do the trick!'

The captain's penis was hard and tall. A pulsing vein made it twitch spasmodically.

The colonel examined the captain's groin, dutifully.

'Very impressive, dear.'

Dolores smiled modestly.

'It's as much your work as mine,' she declared. 'The more Poppa shows an interest in his girl, the more she blossoms.'

'As long as it is a hands-off approach, I will show as much interest as you wish.'

'Thank you, darling.' She turned to the captain. A note of warning entered her voice. 'I am expecting you to fill the cup tonight,' she told him. 'You know what will happen if you come up short?'

The captain knew. An anxious cloud crossed his face. Whatever dark imaginings the threat had conjured in his mind were interrupted by an impassioned female cry.

'What was that?' asked Dolores in alarm.

There was a deep-throated moan.

'It can only be Zellie,' replied the colonel.

The colonel and Dolores rose as one. They marched in step towards the gymnasium. There were more cries and more moans before they got there.

'I think the exercise bicycle was a mistake,' Dolores murmured.

She was right. When they arrived at the open door of the gymnasium they were greeted by a sight of Dionysian debauchery. Zellie was grinding her groin into the saddle of the bicycle with the kind of abandonment Dolores always sought from the captain. Her face was a tableau of joys, her throat a sound box of ecstasies.

When Dolores stepped forward to intervene, the colonel rested his hand on her elbow. 'Let her work it out of her system.'

Dolores watched the writhing girl with wide eyes. The colonel, too, watched transfixed. Zellie's pelvis was a blur as it sawed across the leather seat. Sweat poured down her lovely face.

'That is straight female,' he declared. 'Undiluted, single malt, no ice.'

'I feel envy,' Dolores confessed.

'The young have every advantage in these things, dear.'

Zellie's eyes turned to the couple at the door. There was a hint of regret. A hint of apology. It did not slow her pelvis. In fact, the sympathetic audience seemed to deepen her arousal. She gave a long series of cries. As her chest filled for each, her breasts threatened to break through the leotard.

'I will need the use of your pussy later,' the colonel declared in a soft voice, squeezing Dolores's arm.

'And I will need your cock,' Dolores replied.

Zellie seemed to hear. She gave a smile that was swallowed immediately by another orgasm.

'You take what you need, dear,' Dolores called to her. 'We will wait in the conservatory.'

Zellie half-nodded, then another great wave seized her. Her back arched and she began to pant. The colonel and Dolores withdrew. They walked back to the conservatory in silent awe.

12

Bedtime Therapy

Zellie's bedroom was dark. Only the light from the hallway showed her bed and the gold of her hair as it spread across her pillow. The colonel pushed the door open fully then stood watching the gentle rise and fall of the bedclothes. Satisfied that Zellie was absolutely fast asleep, the colonel stepped over the threshold. Tucked under his arm was a baby monitor. Hanging from one of his hands were the ties he would use, in the other was a long heavy cylinder of moulded plastic. Zellie shifted in her sleep as he approached and for a moment the colonel hesitated as if he were having second thoughts.

When she had quieted, the colonel set out the baby monitor on the bedside table and laid the ties and cylinder beside it. Then he leant across the bed and, taking the corner of the duvet, pulled it carefully away from the sleeping figure.

Golden skin was revealed – the sensitive, downy skin of long slender arms wrapped around the pillow, the shining smooth skin of legs tucked up to a perfect behind, the great plain of skin sculpted by muscle and bone that covered heart and lungs and womb.

Leaning over the sleeping figure, the colonel ran his hand lightly down that fabulous exterior, grazing shoulder blades, skipping lightly over vertebrae, ending in the curled tail of the coccyx. Zellie murmured and stretched out. Her lips parting revealed a moist opening – an entrance to the equally fabulous interior. The colonel let his fingers glide along the inside of her thighs until she twitched and opened them wide. A bare pussy was exposed, another entrance.

The colonel let the duvet fall at the foot of the bed and knelt to study his victim. Her face, in sleep, was as innocent as any infant's but her pussy still bore the bruises of the previous night's bike sex.

It was the astonishing – arousing – sight of Zellie acquiring those bruises that had driven the colonel to undertake regular nocturnal visits to Zellie's bedroom. He laid out the ties on the bed – ties that the captain had once used on Dolores – then gently turned the girl over, lifted her wrists and carried them to the corners of the bed. When he did the same with her ankles, lifting her long legs and opening them, she groaned softly and her eyelids flickered.

'Shh, sleep, baby,' he murmured.

The ties were an easy modern type – comfortable, padded, plastic straps with Velcro fasteners. The colonel looped them around the hooks he had installed in the wall a few days previously. Zellie groaned again and her legs edged closed. The colonel finished securing her wrists before returning to her ankles and pulling them wide again. He picked up two more ties and looped them through the bed's footboard.

When she was absolutely secure, he stepped back and looked at the beautiful vision stretched before him. No girl had ever had finer skin than Zellie. No girl had ever been touched by a finer dusting of suntan and pink good health. Even the shadows cast by her breasts had a golden richness. The lips of her pussy were stretched and narrow, pushed out by the stretched legs. The colonel might have been forgiven if he had forgotten his vows of faithfulness to Dolores.

144

The colonel sighed and took the plastic cylinder from the bedside table, laying it between Zellie's bulging thighs. Sitting down on the bed, feeling the heat from Zellie's belly and breasts, he reached across and began to slowly caress the girl's hair, smoothing it so that it didn't fall across her face and irritate her.

On the first night he had used a lubricant before inserting the vibrator but Zellie didn't need lubrication. She needed only a gentle fingertip to caress her clitoris and the moisture would flow.

The colonel was reaching over to perform this service when a tiny sound from the hallway caught his attention. He turned to see Dolores standing in the doorway. She was holding a towel – the previous night, after giving Zellie her treatment, the bed had been soaked and they needed to change the sheets. Tonight she was clearly intending to take precautions.

The colonel gestured for her to come in but to be quiet.

Dolores entered on tiptoe then stood and watched as the colonel prepared Zellie for the insertion. His finger – large and powerful as it was – was as delicate as a fly's tongue as it teased Zellie's clitoris from its hood. The girl quickly began to pant. Her breasts quivered, her head began moving from side to side.

The colonel lifted his hand to Dolores's lips. She licked the tip of his forefinger, moistening it lovingly, and watched as the colonel slipped the glistening digit inside Zellie's pussy lips. Zellie had quietened as soon as the colonel had left her clitoris alone but this new touch brought a strong reaction, a great groan. Muscular waves passed through the broad flat belly.

She was ready.

The colonel picked up the vibrator and began to work the pointed end into the now wet opening. It was impossible that Zellie wasn't awake now but she betrayed no sign of it. It was part of the game that saved her and the colonel embarrassment. In his mind he tried to remain as detached as a doctor treating an unconscious patient, or a parent attending to a feverish child. In return, Zellie pretended that this was all a delicious dream that she could surrender to without consequences.

Once the vibrator was fully embedded, snug against Zellie's womb, the colonel picked up a large sticking plaster and peeled off the plastic backing. Without some securing, the vibrator would soon slip out. He applied the tape dextrously and flicked the vibrator's switch.

Dolores leant over and tucked the towel under Zellie's bottom, making sure that it was smooth and comfortable.

Zellie was soon moaning and struggling against her bonds. After only a few minutes there was a note of desperation in the moans.

'Poor girl,' Dolores murmured.

'She'll feel better afterwards,' the colonel replied resolutely. He switched on the baby intercom set out on Zellie's bedside table.

On the first two nights of this treatment, the colonel and Dolores had sat and watched for the full hour of its application. They had watched the endless orgasms sweep through the girl, they had listened to the pleas to be released, they watched mucus and sweat flow. Reassured that Zellie had come to no harm – and with the receiver for the baby alarm set out in their bedroom – they decided that tonight they could leave her. They could allow her a measure of privacy. They retired to their bedroom where Zellie's moans made an arousing backdrop for their own sexual rituals.

An hour later, the colonel returned. The vibrator was the only sound in the bedroom. Zellie lay still, exhausted by the long purging of sexual desires. He stripped the plaster away in a single ripping movement. Even this violence brought no reaction from Zellie. The vibrator eased itself out of the motionless girl, plopping onto the white sheet like a birth.

These nocturnal visits became a regular feature of Zellie's life. Often, if the bearer of the dildo was Dolores, there would be cosy chats whilst bonds were adjusted and lubricants applied.

It was during one of these chats that Dolores suggested Zellie try to develop a more spiritual dimension. 'Your attachment to carnal pleasures is truly impressive,' she told her, 'but life has many facets.'

Zellie had developed great respect for the older woman and, as the cool plastic was driven home, she agreed to visit the Church of Acacia Heights and consult the legendary (in Acacia at least) Reverend Forty.

'The Reverend Forty is a Shelby you know, though some say he has wandered from his true flock.'

Zellie was far from concerned about flocks or reverends as the vibrations began and her belly convulsed.

13

Jimmy Jumps Aboard

Zellie did not hear from Jimmy for at least a month after she had run away. Then one evening she was walking in the gardens just before dark when she became aware of a shadow. It was a shadow that moved. It was definitely not her own shadow.

She had been gazing at the light reflected from the little ornamental pond behind the swimming pool when the shadow first appeared. All around the pond were tall spikes of nipa palms. Great clusters of red flowers hung from the scaly trunks. The shadow was wedged between two thick trunks, below the crowns of green spikes, at a level with the flower clusters.

When Zellie stopped and stared, the shadow stopped. When Zellie moved on, the shadow moved on too. Suddenly there was a sound – a low whistle. Zellie almost ran.

'Who is it?' she hissed.

There was a moment's silence before the low answer.

'Is there anyone about? I mean like grown-ups.' The voice was very, very familiar.

'Is that you, Jimmy?'

'Of course it is. Just tell me – is there anyone about?'

Zellie knew that she should have lied but it was not her way. No matter how many times honesty had betrayed into the hands of bad boys, it was a virtue she did not seem able to shed.

'No,' she replied in a weary, resigned tone.

The shadow stepped out of the nipa palms. It was Jimmy looking worried, and pleased to see her in the same moment. 'Hi,' he called.

Before her nightly treatments at the hands of the colonel, Zellie would certainly have been moistening and enlarging at the first hint of boy. Even Jimmy counted as boy when she had not fucked for a whole week. Her pussy though was resolutely dry. It stayed dry as Jimmy skirted the pond looking as jumpy as a stoat in someone's headlamps.

'Are you a prisoner?' he asked.

Zellie burst out laughing. 'A prisoner?'

'What are you doing here, then?'

'I'm staying with relatives.'

Jimmy crept forward towards the house. He peeked across the pool towards the glassed-in patio with its recliners and potted plants.

'Nice. Any relatives about?'

Zellie shook her head. The men were still at the base. Dolores was in her office working on *stuff*.

Jimmy relaxed. 'I was worried about you.'

'That's sweet.'

'You disappeared without warning.'

'It wasn't planned, much. Everything happened in a rush.'

'Some people said that you ran away.'

'I did sort of.'

Jimmy nodded in sympathy. 'I don't blame you. That aunt of yours is poison.'

He looked as caring and considerate as he had always been. Yet, all the time that he was taking such a kind interest in her welfare, his eyes were taking an interest in her body.

He began to circle. He circled her in the way that a hyena circles an antelope. He was sniffing the air. He was getting downwind.

149

Zellie knew immediately that she would not get rid of him easily. Certainly, pussy and behind were going to have to be shown. Who knew what else might be on his mind?

'I know what you came for, Jimmy.'

Jimmy stopped circling. He looked guilty. He was learning how to behave like a Rodrigo or an Eduardo but he still cared. Caring was his Achilles heel.

'I might just as well get it over with,' she said in a hurt voice, reaching for the belt that held up her jeans.

'No . . .' Jimmy began, the guilt flaring up into a deep, red blush.

Zellie gazed at him with big appealing eyes. 'No? You mean I don't have to show you my pussy?'

He started to shake his head. Perhaps he was not a monster after all. Perhaps he was still her friend! Yet, before he had completed a one-quarter turn of his head, he stopped himself. He stared hard at his feet.

'Well?' she asked.

He looked up intently. 'I have to see it.'

Her heart sank. She could see in his eyes that there was no hope. They were inflamed with boyishness. Testosterone boiled from every feature. He was a haze of longing.

'Jimmy . . .' Her plaintive tone hit his Achilles heel.

'I suppose we could talk first,' he declared, mournfully.

Zellie let go of the belt. Her hand fell to her side. 'I'd like that,' she said. 'I want us still to be friends.'

'Yeah.' Jimmy was staring at the hand that had so nearly undone the belt. Zellie could feel his disappointment.

'So, are we going to talk?' she asked gently.

He looked up. There was the same urgency in his eyes. 'Couldn't I talk and ogle at the same time?' he asked.

Zellie let out a long, low groan of disappointment. 'How can we treat each other with respect,' she began sadly, 'how can we be sensitive caring human beings, how can we share a moment of beauty in a universe of loneliness, if I'm holding open my pussy and you are staring at my pee hole?'

Jimmy seemed unable to see any contradiction. 'Your pussy is a moment of beauty in *my* lonely universe,' he declared with conviction.

Zellie sighed and reached for the belt.

'But you don't have to show me,' he said.

'Truly?'

He thrust his hands into his pockets. 'Truly – I can find a truck to jump in front of or a rope to hang from or a cliff to jump off or a –'

'Enough!' Zellie declared.

She undid the belt and found the zipper. A deft pull and her jeans were inching down her thighs.

'As long as you don't say that I forced you!' he said abruptly.

She sighed and lowered. Soon, the waistband of her jeans was round her knees. Jimmy was beginning to sweat. Hormones fought with pheromones fought with half-suppressed moans of lust.

She kicked off her shoes.

'Tell me that we're still friends,' Jimmy insisted.

'People don't force their friends to do stuff.'

'I didn't really force you. It's not like I have a gun,' Jimmy said, in as reasonable a voice as he could manage.

'No, but you did say you would kill yourself if I didn't.'

'You wanted me to force you.'

She stared at him in amazement.

'You wanted me to force you because it turns you on,' he concluded.

'It does not turn me on!'

'If it's wet, we'll know.'

Zellie looked at him archly. 'I can tell you now that it is *not* wet.'

'OK. We'll see.'

'Right!' Zellie pulled the jeans down abruptly and stepped out of them. She gazed down at her neat, un-swollen, un-leaky, definitely un-aroused pussy. 'Look!' she said emphatically. 'I have never been less turned on!'

Jimmy slipped to his knees. 'Open it up.'

'You are a complete pervert!'

'I'm a pervert? You are the one who screws every student who asks except for the one who actually cares about you!'

'You really think you care about me?' Zellie asked.

'Of course. I'm saving myself for you!'

Zellie let out a cry of frustration then took hold of her pussy lips and pulled them wide.

'There! Absolutely dry!'

Jimmy squinted at the spread lips. 'Is there somewhere private? With some light?'

Darkness was falling fast.

'There's the summer house.'

'Cool.'

They headed for the summer house. Zellie was in a hurry to show Jimmy just how dry she was. It was important that he realised she was being forced, that she was not turned on. Maybe if he understood that, the emotional blackmail would finally end. Yet as she walked through the darkening gardens, naked below the waist, her shaven pussy tinged red by the last rays of the setting sun, little tingles began to spread from her belly.

'Your bottom is so cute,' Jimmy told her as they crossed the lawn near the guest house. 'It really hurts me to think of all those guy getting ... inside you. Especially guys who don't respect you, or know who you are, or care what you think.'

'Jimmy, you didn't come all this way just to say hello or to ask what I think. You haven't looked me in the eye since I dropped my panties.'

Jimmy looked hurt. 'I know the way it seems but ever since I knew you were screwing around, I can't get the images out of my mind. I keep seeing you lying on your back with your legs open and some guy –'

'Jimmy!'

'I can't help seeing it! You should hear the way people talk about you!'

Zellie groaned. She did not like to think of people talking about her – not when it entailed her lying on her back, or having her legs wide open, or any other kind of thing that she could not help.

'If you let me fuck you,' Jimmy continued, the words flying out of him in a torrent, 'and I got it out of my system, I honestly think we could go back to being friends.'

She stopped abruptly and looked at him. 'You said you only wanted to look.'

'I do only want to look.'

'But now you say if you could fuck me we could be friends the way we used to be.'

'If I fucked you I might be able to look at you again without feeling so ... charged up. Every time I think about you, I get this feeling in my balls and in my head – it's like they are both going to explode. And if I fucked you I think those feelings would go away and we could just talk again. The way we used to.'

Zellie studied him carefully. He seemed absolutely sincere. He seemed to really believe that fucking could restore their friendship. She gave a decisive – and derisive – snort.

As she walked on, Zellie was struck by just how many men she knew who were completely insane. Rodrigo had never been stable. Eduardo was absolutely crazy. Jimmy was going downhill fast. If she hadn't believed in her own essential goodness she would have put it down to an evil power in her pussy.

'Think about it!' Jimmy insisted as he struggled to keep up with her.

'If you don't stop I won't even show you my pussy,' Zellie called over her shoulder.

'You promised to show me your pussy any time. Your pussy is mine.'

Zellie snorted again. She flounced across the grass, her head held high in as superior an attitude as a girl naked below the waist could expect to get away with.

Jimmy had to run to keep up.

The summer house was at the top of a slope at the seaward end of the garden. It was a simple wooden and glass structure with cane chairs and a table. Double doors stood open to the warm evening.

Zellie strode inside and threw herself into a chair. She immediately opened her legs wide and showed off her pussy. Her expression was blank. This was obviously just a chore, an irritating activity to keep someone else happy.

'Dry enough?' she asked in a bored voice.

'Don't be like that.'

She shot him a look of astonishment. 'Like what?'

'Angry.'

'Jimmy, come closer, look at my pussy, tell if you think it's wet. Then tell me if you think that I'm enjoying this.'

It was obvious that Jimmy couldn't resist. He was pulled to the wide-spread legs like a ball bearing to a magnet.

'That is the most beautiful thing I have ever seen,' he breathed in awe. 'I think I'm going to faint.'

Jimmy was never going to be a tough guy.

'Is it wet?' she asked, then answered herself, 'no, it is not wet.'

'Open it up.'

'If I was turned on, Jimmy, it would be all over my thighs.'

When lust seized Zellie, she was a fountain. It was one of Zellie's weaknesses.

'Let me look inside anyway.'

Zellie took told of her lower lips and pulled. She pulled hard. The lips stretched as wide as the wings of a sparrow. A whole new world was revealed – a world where babies grew, a world where men suffocated from inexpressible pleasures.

Jimmy had to sit or perhaps he fell. Either way, he ended in a squat between Zellie's knees gazing deep into a coral-pink underworld.

'Is this the way you hold yourself open for Rodrigo?'

The question came from nowhere. For a moment, it threw her. There was the hurt and jealousy again. There was an indifference to her feelings. Jimmy was getting more and more like the boys he despised.

'I can't tell you that,' she said finally, but not before the thought of Rodrigo gazing at her in this posture had fired a cluster of nerves somewhere deep inside her clitoris. (What was it about Rodrigo?)

'Why not?' Jimmy wanted to know. 'We promised once that we would never hide anything from each other.'

Every promise she had ever made was being wheeled out to defeat her. Making promises was one of Zellie's weaknesses. Honouring them was, perhaps, her biggest weakness.

'That was a long time ago,' she said in a quiet, dignified voice. She hoped that dignity would remind Jimmy of the sanctity of trust such a promise entailed. It did not.

'Do promises have a cut-off date?' he asked, looking into her eyes for the first time since she had made wings of her pussy lips.

'No, but . . .'

'Well, then.'

Things were going from bad to worse.

'Jimmy . . .'

Jimmy ignored the plea for kindness and squatted lower between her legs. Now, he could gaze at her pussy eye to eye. A shudder passed through her belly. Something about being looked at always turned her on.

Jimmy responded with a strange groan.

Zellie recognised the sound. It was the sound that boys made when they could not speak what they needed to speak. Jimmy needed to say something like – I want to spend my life in your pussy, I want to wake up every morning with your pussy sucking on my dick, and one hundred similar things, but all that would come out of his throat was that strangled, hopeless groan. It was one of those sounds that Zellie could not ignore. More nerves fired up in her clitoris.

Jimmy pulled back. He forced himself to look at her face.

'So, this is what you've been doing for everybody else all these months.'

It was his turn to be plaintive. It was his turn to show hurt in a voice shorn of all subterfuge.

At any other time, Zellie would have responded to that hurt with an open heart. This time, however, perhaps because Jimmy was so close to her spread pussy that she could feel the heat of his cheeks, something hardened in her heart.

'Not everybody.' Her voice was cold.

'Just the boys you fancy?'

'I suppose.'

'What else do you do?' Jimmy managed to ask.

'You really want to know?'

Zellie could taste his jealousy.

'Yes.'

Moisture flooded his eyes. Soon he would cry.

'I suck. I suck Rodrigo. I suck his friends.'

Jimmy winced. 'His friends?'

'His friends.'

A tear ran from the corner of his eye.

'I suck them deep. I suck them until they come. Or until they are hard enough to fuck me.' This was the cruellest thing Zellie had ever said to anybody. The feeling was a revelation – dizzying, wrong, also strangely grown-up. Zellie was suddenly learning to be bad.

Perhaps being bad would be Zellie's new weakness.

'Do you like sucking them?' Jimmy asked in a shaky voice.

'Yes.' As she said this, she felt a change between her legs. It felt as if something had switched on. A wheel seemed to be turning in her uterus. Gates were opening. Moisture began to flow. She let go of her pussy lips but it was too late. Jimmy had seen.

'You are getting *wet*!'

'Jimmy, it's time for you to go home.'

'You're wet and you're trying to hide it!'

'The colonel will be home soon.'

'And your clitoris is huge!'

Zellie looked down her half-naked body. Peeping above the parapet of her sweetly curving belly was the head of an aroused clitoris. It was as undeniable a fact as the moisture that was oozing from her pussy and running into the crack of her behind.

'You're soaking! Let me see properly!' Jimmy's voice had risen to a pitch of excitement. He sounded the way he used to sound when he was twelve years old and someone had stolen his football.

'Shh!' she hissed. Sound carries a long way on a quiet evening and Zellie did not want to be found like this.

'Open!' Jimmy cried, ignoring her.

Reluctantly, Zellie reached for her pussy lips again and began to open them. Jimmy wanted to see more though. He made her slip forward in the seat so that her behind was right on the edge. Then he made her throw her legs over the arms of the chair. Now he could see everything that a girl has to show a boy below the waist. These further degradations made her feel even more mean spirited.

'You know this wetness isn't for you,' she said, in a low tone.

His eyes flicked up to meet hers. She saw that he was insanely turned on. She realised that it was more than just her pussy that was affecting him. It was being hurt too. This was a new thing between them – a new playground.

'You know that it was thinking about Rodrigo that made me wet,' she continued.

Her stomach lurched again. She realised that hurting Jimmy was exciting. The wheels turned more rapidly. Guilt and lust contended more fiercely. Her body started to take its own measures. Her legs opened wider. Without being told, her finger flicked across her clitoris. She groaned, half in desire, half in surprise.

'Rodrigo fucks you the way you need to be fucked,' Jimmy said suddenly.

'You don't know how we fuck.'

'I know what the whole school knows.' His face was still pale but his voice was no longer shaky. Suddenly she was off balance. How much did he really know?

She tried to wriggle away from him but he pressed his hand onto her belly and held her in place.

'Rodrigo doesn't take no for an answer,' Jimmy hissed.

Something in his tone made her finger flick out again. Something in his eye said that he finally saw who she was. He knew now that there was an invisible ring through her clitoris. Whoever seized it could take her anywhere.

'He tells you to strip. He puts his hand in your pussy . . .' Jimmy stared at her with hot, strong eyes. With control had come confidence. Her finger flicked out again, she was beginning to pant.

'He fingers your clit.'

More flicks.

'He pushes his dick into your mouth.'

Soon she would come. The colonel's regime had failed. Little hopeless Jimmy had finally understood her. He had broken her discipline as easily as Rodrigo did.

'He pushes his wet dick into your pussy.'

The come broke deep in her belly. It came slowly. It pushed blindly through the deep membranes. It was looking for an out. It struggled like a baby trying to escape its womb.

It hurt. So much feeling couldn't stay inside a girl for so long.

'He turns you over so he can have you doggy-style. He makes you beg for it.'

Zellie's mouth opened wide. Part of the come would exit through her throat. Her legs kicked out further. Part of the come would exit through her pussy. She straightened her feet like a ballet dancer, her calves flexed, her thighs stretched. As an echo, her anus flexed, stretched, blinked. Part of the come would exit from that lowest of mouths.

Jimmy seemed to see it all. 'Eduardo likes to fuck your ass,' he said, gazing at the o-shaped pout. 'He takes his time. He's a big guy. He leaves you sore for a week.'

Unfucked for a month, Zellie exploded. She screamed, she writhed. Neither throat nor anus nor pussy were wide enough to let the come out quickly enough. It tore her. It felt as if her chest and belly would explode.

She was too shocked by the come to be shocked by Jimmy's words. They were not the words he would have chosen himself. They had come from someone else. She realised dimly that they must have come from Eduardo. Eduardo must have told Jimmy about the sex they shared. He must have revealed details.

Then there was another sound. A sound of boyish orgasm. Then another sensation – a wetness spraying across her foot. Through glazed eyes – and still buffeted by the aftershocks of her own profound and lingering pleasure – Zellie saw that Jimmy was pumping his cock with the fury of a storm demon. More, he was very deliberately coating her foot where it hung in midair. The sight prolonged her orgasm. The orgasm was prolonged even more when Jimmy took her ankle and bent her foot towards her head. It was exactly what Eduardo had done. Eduardo had betrayed their secret ritual, and now Jimmy was betraying Eduardo's betrayal. Come dripped onto her still-clad breasts as the foot passed over. Come dipped onto her neck as the sticky whiteness ran between her toes and oozed from beneath the sole. Then the toes were descending. Then Zellie's behind was twisting and opening as she was pushed and stretched. Then the toes were pushing past her lips and into her mouth. A new orgasm broke deep in her belly. It pushed through membranes already vibrating from earlier passages. It lodged in the bottle-necks of womb and throat. It was amplified in these places. Soon the feelings were more than any girl should be asked to bear.

'No more, please!'

No sooner had she spoken than Jimmy gave notice that he wanted more – much more. His hand slipped inside her pussy. It pushed into a deep wetness. It broke all their agreements. He had promised that he would only look! Now his forefinger was pushing at the entrance to her womb. She groaned and writhed. He had her as securely in his power as Rodrigo or Eduardo did when they seized her womb.

Still his semen was seeping into her mouth, dribbling from toe and heel. Then she felt a column of flesh bobbing against her behind. He was already hard again. His finger was pressing through the neck of her womb, painfully distending cartilage and connective tissue. His penis was scorching her thighs. His balls slipped across her buttocks.

'No! Jimmy!'

She was shouting her protests but still lay wide-limbed, open to hands and eyes. Worse, she found herself obeying his commands. When he told her to play with her breasts, she played with her breasts. When he told her to lick her lips, she licked her lips.

It was getting hard to pretend that she didn't want him.

'Hold my dick,' he told her.

She reached for it, even as she said no.

'Play with it.'

She played as she protested. He was hot and hard. Her tears were hot and hard.

'Put it in.'

'I can't. You are like a brother to me!'

'Put it in.'

'Don't rape me,' she pleaded.

His hand pulled out of her. He was making room for something else.

'I don't want it! Please Jimmy.'

'Put it in.'

She slipped the head into the wet opening.

'Tell me to fuck you.'

'Jimmy! You're my friend.'

'And you are mine. My fuck friend.'

She gazed at him in horror. She felt his sex edge forward, half an inch, three quarters . . .

'No!' she told him.

He began to move back and forth but he was clumsy. He was still a virgin. He still did not know how a girl's pussy joined onto a girl's legs.

His ineptitude teased her. Perhaps it was deliberate. She wriggled in the seat and he slipped a fraction deeper.

He grinned. 'You want it.'

'No!'

He grinned again. 'Lying is a sin.'

She blushed.

'Work your way down the seat,' he told her.

She worked her way down the seat. Slowly her pussy swallowed him. There was a sense of fullness. The colonel's vibrator could not give her that feeling. Cold plastic cannot fill. Cold plastic can only open.

Fullness made her belly feel warm. Fullness made her gaze at Jimmy with something close to love. It didn't end her resistance.

'More,' he demanded. He wanted her even further down the seat. He wanted to be deep.

'No more!'

'Further!'

She had to bring her feet onto the ground. Now she could work herself all the way. Finally, the lips of her pussy came to a kiss against his pubic bone.

'Now thank me.'

'What for?'

'For raping you.'

It was almost rape. Except that, in the end she wanted it, almost.

'Jimmy, I can't say that.'

'Say it.' He began to thrust. Soon, he had the hang of it. She was panting again.

'Thank me for raping you,' he insisted.

Through her grunts of pleasure she thanked him in a thick, hardly comprehensible voice.

'Now, ask me to come in your pussy. Ask me nicely as a friend.'

'Please come in my pussy.'

'Tell me that I can rape you any time.'

She had no more strength to resist.

'You can rape me any time.'

'Tell me I can come in your pussy any time.'

'You can come in my pussy any time.'

'Tell me we will always be friends.'

'We will always be friends.'

'And we will never have secrets.'

'We will never have secrets.'

All pacts made, words fled. Then, there was only grunting and toil.

It was a sad defeated Zellie that Jimmy finally abandoned in the summer house. She had slipped one more level. In her own mind at least, she was heading for complete slutdom. She wept, she berated herself. Then after half an hour she stood up and headed back to the house. She was hungry. Jimmy was forgotten by the time she reached the kitchen.

Forgetting bad things was one of Zellie's weaknesses . . . or strengths.

14

The Church of Acacia Heights

The Church of Acacia Heights clung to the side of the precipice like a spider. It was a high-tech structure of spikes and wedges held together by tensile steel. The failing violet light of evening gave it eyes. The figures in its stained-glass windows – which had gazed inwards during the day – gazed outwards now. Jesus and the Apostles gazed at the mountains above and down towards the sea beyond Acacia. Their straitjackets of tall slender glass created reflections that played across the surrounding car park. A car might drive through a benediction or stop over a benign smile.

Sirius L. Hampton, thirty-one years old, matured beyond his years, a master of his feelings and a good portion of what he surveyed, was watching the sun set from the broad sweep of the church balcony. Ferro-concrete legs stretched out into the void supporting the structure where he stood. Cantilevered arms reached high in the air and back to the plateau anchoring it in bolts as thick as ships' masts. The main bulk of the church – angles, arms and high-tension steel hawsers – seemed tightly wound as if ready to pounce on anything that passed, in a moment. A cool breeze blew on the balcony. There was the scent of mountain sage.

Sirius was enjoying an allowed indulgence, a cigarette. His mind was a calm and thoughtless void. He had made a hundred decisions that day, any one of which could cost or make millions. The memory of them was gone, temporarily at least. He had the capacity to forget anything that could weigh him down. Stress was inefficient. Guilt was inadmissible. Regret was more than regrettable. All negative feelings were simply unacceptable. He drew on his cigarette and allowed his eyes to roam without conscious direction.

Stretched out below was the Baraka, a shanty town of unplanned development held on three sides by the grip of the mountains. Only to the south did the land open out – and there lay Acacia, a wall of money and well-policed avenues. If a drop of blue blood had spilt from Sirius's veins, it might have burnt through the concrete floor and fallen two hundred metres onto a sticky upturned face of a Baraka dweller way below. Hampton blood was secure though. None had been spilt for two hundred years, and certainly none would be spilt tonight.

Sirius took another lungful of smoke and glanced into the pit. Lights were coming on across the ragged gorge. *Down there* it was already dark. He turned to the vision of the Aldahar Club – lit by a brilliant confection of neon tubes on the very edge of the Baraka. These lights had been burning all day and would burn all night. They promised every earthly pleasure. A rich man could waste a life and several fortunes inside its seductive walls. Sirius was heading that way soon. He was picking up a toy from the valley below first, a warm, soft toy with breasts of milk and honey and an opening between her legs that was never closed to Sirius and would soon be open to all.

The Baraka was a *resource*.

Above him, the tall cross of the church was blinking into life. Its builder had wanted to make the church the most visible symbol of the Baraka. The towering neon-lined cross soared thirty metres into the air. It could probably be seen from space.

The cigarette in Sirius's mouth was nearly finished. An irresponsible man might have tossed it over the wall and watched it fall. In the Baraka with its dry wood-walled buildings that could have been disaster. Sirius dropped the butt onto the floor and extinguished it with a meticulous heel. He gave a measured sigh. There were still tasks to be accomplished. He needed to find the Reverend Forty. He needed to deliver his father's instructions.

There was a click of heels. His shoes like everything else he wore were hand-measured and handmade. They would last a generation if they were maintained – and there were always people to maintain a Hampton shoe – but he would probably only wear them for a week. Objects aged quickly for Sirius. He had bored through the world twice before his teens had ended. The only things left were things he had already had, with the subtlest of variations.

These shoes were special because they were buckled with onyx – though even onyx could only be special for moments in Sirius's life. He headed for the glass doors of the nave. The click of heels let people know that he was coming, as discreetly as his Brook Row suit and the platinum of his Rolex.

A boy opened the doors and smiled. Sirius smiled back. It was as easy as signing a cheque but smiles were free. In the main body of the church they were preparing for a ceremony. Figures in white silk were running through a gospel song. The soaring angular walls – an algebraic vision of the Gothic – focused attention skyward. The click of Sirius's shoes turned focused attention earthwards.

A small army of women were polishing the acres of mahogany seating. Most looked up at the click and watched him pass. They smiled at him like so many mothers. He was still the Hampton baby.

'Where's the reverend?' he asked a pretty girl of fifteen or so, her eyes dark, her smile shy. Sirius used a voice of velvet and glass.

'In the yard.'

The 'yard' was the vast show arena that covered the plateau outside.

'Thanks, keep up the good work.'

'I will and bless you, sir.'

'Bless you.' Sirius had an easy way with people, especially church people. He had been around them all his life.

He clicked his way comfortably down the wide aisle. A bronze door carved with angels and demons opened to the deepening darkness. He passed through it and contemplated his mortality. It brought a smile. His mortality was distant. His corporality was good.

It was a warm night but there was a steady cooling mountain breeze. Tonight was a night for charitable works and spread out before him was an encampment of stalls. Food was being sold amongst clouds of steam. There was a throng around the samba band near the road.

Sirius moved into the mêlée. In the first row of stalls, Baraka dwellers were buying used trousers lovingly pressed by the good women of Acacia. A row down, they were buying used shoes, cheap. Women in shawls haggled and joked. Young men drew on hand-rolled cigarettes and glowered at the church volunteers behind their piles. Older men wandered sadly into the night clutching creased plastic bags.

Moving amongst the crowd were agents of the Lord. They could be distinguished by their careful grooming, cropped hair, and by their wide, unvarying smiles. Under their arms was *the book*. In their hands were

167

saving texts. The agents whispered in the ears of sinners. They too had once sinned. They took the arms of alcoholics. They too had once been sunk beneath the waves. They murmured prayers for all. Once, *they too* had needed prayer. They were an army of redemption, circling and mixing, poking and prodding.

Sirius had pushed beyond jackets and coats. He had entered soft toys. He was still smiling. It had been a good day. Deals had been signed. A leakage in the press office had been sealed. The right people had been hired, the wrong people had been dismissed (those wrong people might soon be here). He had nearly reached the end of his duties. He was nearing the time of play.

His eyes caught sight of the reverend.

Reverend Forty was carving a line as straight as his jaw through the ragged and the grubby. He was an imposing man, standing out amongst the crowd as a lion stands out amongst lambs. His broad chest was encased in a black button-less shirt. A golden crucifix protected his heart. His hat was broad-rimmed and high so that neither sun nor rain might smite him. His pale intelligent face promised the knowledge of evil. His intense gaze promised the certainty of its inevitable defeat. Reverend Forty was a rock that any sinner could cling to in surety but perhaps not in comfort.

Sirius changed course to intercept him.

The reverend was issuing encouragement on all sides. His strange, intense eyes told all they fell on that there was no place too deep that a hand might not reach, no place so obscure that a light (welcome or otherwise) might not fall. Sirius and the reverend met at the junction of underwear and kitchen goods.

'Reverend Forty!'

For the reverend, Sirius had a voice of sonorous brass.

'Mr Sirius! Well met, sir,' the reverend boomed.

'Well met,' Sirius agreed.

'I think that you have some business with me?'

'I do indeed.'

They cut through the lines of used underwear and broke out into the open space beyond.

'Before you raise your business, sir, may I ask about my request for minibuses for the children of the Baraka?' Transporting the teenage element to the sea beyond Acacia was the latest project to seize the imagination of the reverend. Teenagers were the most difficult section of the Baraka to reach and so sunk in sin that a shark could barely reach them. Separated from bad influences, lulled by nature's beauty, they might be more approachable.

'My father is sympathetic. He has handed the matter to Slip and Slide.' (Slip and Slide were the Hamptons' advertising agency.)

'I don't understand.'

'If we can sell space on the sides of the minibuses, we can defray the costs.'

'With Slip and Slide involved you may be able to make a profit,' the reverend observed.

His eyes had a glint that Sirius felt was disrespectful and he injected a note from an achromatic scale into his reply. 'A profit would be no bad thing.'

The reverend deferred. 'Quite so.'

'They have encountered difficulties with the most likely sponsors. Many companies consider themselves overstretched.'

The reverend looked disappointed.

'But rest assure we are a long way from failure yet.'

'I thank you for your efforts.'

Sirius took the reverend's arm. 'The matter that I most wanted to discuss is a request from my father for an angel of mercy.'

The reverend moved from disappointment to concern. 'For himself?'

'No, for an old friend of his, Magus Reach.'

'I don't believe I know the gentleman.'

'He lives in the Baraka though he was once a well-known scholar. My father went to school with him. He is aged now. His spirits have fallen low.'

'Your father thinks of all men.'

'Indeed. And he thinks that this man needs a visitor. He has become a recluse.'

'Well, we have many worthy volunteers.'

'My father has asked for a girl who is a good listener. He says that the girl should not be preachy, that she should never, in fact, even raise the subject of the Lord. He believes that if you can send the right girl, Magus will, in time, come to the fold of his own free will.'

'Mr Reach is perhaps a difficult man?'

'I guessed as much from what my father said.'

The reverend cast his eyes skyward. After only a moment an answer came. 'There is a girl. She has come to us recently as a volunteer. Any man might open his heart to her. She is milk and honey of the sweetest kind, though she too needs to find the Lord.'

'She is not *of* the Lord at present?'

'She is of good heart which is always *of* the Lord. But she is not yet, I fear, of the *Word*.'

'Perhaps I could meet her.'

The reverend motioned to a man of good grooming with a book beneath his arm. He whispered in the man's ear and the man hurried away. The reverend and Sirius walked on and returned to the subject of minibuses. Having hinted previously at disappointment, Sirius was now ready to deliver a pitch. His voice was unadorned plainsong.

'We had a fine offer from Wassen, reverend. They offered to sponsor three buses in their entirety – purchase, maintenance, diesel.'

170

'Wassen Personal Security?'

'Indeed.'

'They would cover my minibuses in handguns.'

'And assault rifles.'

'I don't think that would be appropriate.'

'That was my first thought too but then I thought what better way to enrol disaffected teenagers with a predilection for drugs and gang warfare? What could be more cool than driving through the Baraka in a minibus emblazoned with an AK-47?'

The reverend's eyes shot heavenwards.

'Will there be a cross rising from a rock of crack cocaine, too?'

Sirius had him on the back foot but he would clearly take some convincing. But before he could launch another assault, a vision broke from the crowd. The vision was wrapped in golden hair and such regular features that all around her seemed suddenly deformed. Sirius gazed. His eyes opened a fraction wider than was normal. They were a degree darker than usual.

The vision hesitated.

'Zellie,' called the reverend. 'Join us, please.'

Zellie came forward slowly. Her curiosity was palpable. It wasn't every day that a girl met the second most powerful man in Acacia.

'This is Griselda Stanton Shelby, daughter of Mathew Petrach Shelby and Mary Boccaccio Bose.' The reverend liked names to be given in full. In a perfect world he would have related her lineage back to the flood.

'Everybody calls me Zellie,' she told Sirius.

'You recognise Mr Sirius Hampton?'

'I've seen his photograph,' Zellie said.

'You're a Shelby?' Sirius's voice was mellifluous woodwind.

'It's my name,' she said with a depreciative smile.

Sirius held out his hand.

Zellie reached out slowly. Her grip took hold carefully. She was respectful but not awed. When she looked into his eyes, there was warmth and a question. The question seemed to be 'What would you like to tell me?'

He squeezed her hand. It was a squeeze that he usually reserved for powerful men. The question came back amplified. He looked harder into her eyes. They were as innocent as water. They had no history that could not be unmade. The question fell through him slowly. Sirius found that there were many things he would like to tell her.

He was surprised by the contact. He was surprised that he was surprised. He had bored through the world twice but remembered no handshake like this.

'We have a man who is in need of comfort,' the reverend began.

Sirius finally let go of Zellie's hand. She flushed as a young girl should flush after such a searching examination. 'He needs a good listener,' he said.

'Is he sick?'

'I haven't met him. My father says that he has dried up somehow. Become a recluse.'

Zellie looked at the floor for a moment. 'That must be very sad.'

'We think that a visitor might help,' Sirius told her.

'I don't have any special training. Or experience.'

'It is probably better that you don't. He might resent anything too formal. Apparently he is a clever man and difficult.'

'Difficult?'

'Difficult to get to know, but if he likes you he'll talk.'

'He just needs a friend?'

'Yes, and I think you would be perfect.'

Zellie smiled broadly. It seemed an unusual pleasure for her to find trust. Someone somewhere had sowed doubts in the mind.

172

'What prompted you to volunteer for the church?'

'I wanted to give,' she said. 'It helps me to feel OK.'

'Your reasons were selfish?'

'Is that bad?' She looked as if she would accept any opinion. She looked as if no opinion could change her.

Sirius shook his head. 'Not bad.' He turned to the reverend. 'I think you are right, friend. I think Zellie would make a very good visitor.'

'The gentleman lives in the Baraka,' the reverend cautioned.

'We can make arrangements for the girl's safety.'

'If she is willing to go.'

Sirius turned to Zellie. 'Are you willing to help this poor man?'

'I'll try.'

'Then it's settled. Someone will call you.'

Zellie found herself being dismissed. She said goodbye but neither man seemed to hear. The crowd swallowed her.

'And now you must excuse me, friend.' Sirius turned from the reverend abruptly. He plucked his mobile from his pocket and walked away, punching keys. He listened to the phone ring. A girl's voice answered. 'Are you ready?' he asked.

'Yes.' She sounded nervous.

'Start walking down the road. I'll pick you up.' He clicked off the phone. In another part of the arena, a girl hurried into the darkness. Sirius headed for his car. The Aldahar was waiting. Harry needed flesh for the show. Sirius needed another allowed indulgence. Angelina was waiting in the shadow of a cypress tree on the third corner. Sirius pulled the Jaguar over and flashed his lights. She ran, her legs pale in the beam, her dress dark. Sirius leant across and pushed the passenger door open. She was a parcel of excitement dropping into the leather seat.

'I worried you forget,' she said in her imperfect English.

He smiled his easy smile. 'Business.'

'Always business.'

She was a small woman but perfect. Her face was as regular as the silver chronometer in the walnut dashboard. It shone. The light in her eyes was as genuine as the Rolex on Sirius's wrist. She pulled the door to and the car spat gravel before regaining the road.

'I have a surprise for you,' Sirius told her.

'Every time is a surprise. I like surprises.' Her dark eyes beamed.

'We're going to the Aldahar.'

'People will see.'

Usually, Sirius took her out of town. He didn't like gossip. It was bad for business. It was bad for his father's moral outrage. 'We can work around that,' he told her.

'And I have only these clothes!'

He looked at her garish skirt, only a month old and already opening down one of the seams. He looked at the tight polyester top that made bad shapes of her breasts. 'We can work around that too.'

She looked over her seat. Her eyes scanned the back of the car. She was looking for boxes. Often he brought her clothes to wear – rich women's clothes to camouflage the Baraka girl. There was nothing and she settled back into her seat looking puzzled.

Sirius smiled his easy smile. 'You won't be needing clothes tonight,' he told her.

'In the Aldahar?' she asked in surprise.

He laughed softly. 'You are going to be a star.'

'Stop teasing me.'

'I'm not teasing.'

'You tease me every time. Sometimes I think you only want me to go places so that I will look a fool.' She was smiling as she said this but it was close to the truth. Sirius liked to take her to places where she didn't fit.

When he was a child, he liked to take frogs from the ornamental lake and carry them to the avenue of trees that was the driveway. Some hopped their way back to the water. He was glad. Some hopped the wrong way. He followed them to see where they would die. In the same way, he liked to take Angelina to expensive restaurants along the coast. He liked to watch as she dealt with waiters and flunkeys. He enjoyed seeing her wrestle with unfamiliar knives and spoons. There was a fascination that he couldn't explain.

'I have never thought you looked like a fool,' he lied.

'And when you make love to me, you make fun of me too.'

'I make you come,' he reminded her.

'Like no one else,' she agreed.

Sirius had skills. Sirius had skills like tigers have stripes.

The car was spinning around hairpin bends as they descended from the mountain. She braced her feet against the floor.

'You should wear a seat belt,' he said.

'If I thought a seat belt was a good idea, I would never come with you.'

He laughed softly again. 'So are you going to trust me?' he asked.

She shook her head.

'Are you going to do as I tell you?'

She looked at him with soft eyes. 'I always do what you tell me.'

'That's right,' he agreed. 'And because you do, you will come hard tonight. So hard you will never forget.'

It should have been a warning but Angelina was listening with innocent ears. 'I don't care if I come,' she said. 'I just want to be with you.'

For a moment, Sirius lost his easy smile. His foot eased off the accelerator. He thought of taking her to the shack that she called home.

These aberrations only lasted a moment.

The road flattened out. He punched the pedal. They sped through the badlands that separated Acacia from the Baraka – a place of flash floods and dust devils. At the junction of Route 13, he turned left towards the Baraka. A mile further on he turned towards the Aldahar. There were long untidy streets lined with broken-down shops and windowless houses. Breakers' yards nuzzled up to unsanitary-looking food retailers, women washed naked children at standpipes on un-paved corners. At regular intervals there were knots of men sitting out on boxes and old car seats. Some turned from their drinking and smoking to wave as the Jaguar slid past.

Angelina smiled at the familiar scenes. She reached out and rested her hand on Sirius's leg. He brushed it off. Tonight, she was just meat. She would be fed to the machine called Harry.

The Aldahar loomed up in front of them like a break in the wall of hell. Neon fires burnt across its façade. The damned swirled around its openings. Demons in bow ties broke heads that didn't fit.

Sirius swept past. A man in his position needed to be discreet.

The Aldahar was not a single building. It had not been purpose-made. It was an amalgamation of an old sugar refinery and several smaller confectionary workshops, unneeded now that outsourcing stretched beyond the Baraka. There were side ways and back ways into the Aldahar. Only a few people knew all of them and Sirius was one. By a tortuous chain of anonymous companies, he controlled it. The deeds were in his safe. His safe was in another city. The city was in another country.

He swung the Jaguar down a dark access road. He negotiated parked trucks and abandoned cars. Angelina's eyes were glittering. She had never been to the Aldahar. Perhaps she thought that Sirius was going to introduce her to his friends. Perhaps she thought that the days of discretion were coming to an end.

He pulled up outside a steel-barred gate. The remote that opened it was in the glove compartment. As Sirius leant over to get it, he allowed his hand to run up the inside of Angelina's thigh.

'You're wearing underwear.'

'Of course I'm wearing underwear.'

'Then take it off.'

She looked at him with *kiss me* eyes.

He ignored them and plucked the remote from the glove box. 'Take off everything under that skirt,' he told her.

Sulkily, she reached under her skirt and worked a thong down her legs.

'That's better.' The steel gate opened and the Jaguar slipped into a dark yard.

Sirius had re-found his easy smile.

They got out of the car and he led her through a dark alleyway and up a fire escape. The door at the top opened with a card. They passed wheeled laundry baskets and maids in short black uniforms. A security guard avoided looking at them as they crossed the floor of a control room. Sirius inspired discretion wherever he went. The more grubby his activity the less visible he became.

Angelina caught glimpses of gaming tables and crowded bars in the flickering screens of TV monitors set around the control room. Another corridor led them to a set of doors. Sirius unlocked the largest and ushered Angelina into a huge office.

'Wow,' she sighed. Angelina was impressed. It was a hellish version of palatial. Black satin lined the walls.

Muted gold covered chairs and pillars. Silver mirrors reflected mystery. The desk was like a command bunker for Mephistopheles – massive, convoluted, protective.

Sirius picked up a phone. 'She's here,' he said. 'I *know* I'm late. So hurry.' He turned to Angelina. 'In a few moments, you will meet Harry. Do as he tells you. Exactly as he tells you. He will hurt you but he will also make you come. You are absolutely safe with him. He is a professional.'

Angelina blinked. 'I don't understand.'

'It's a test.'

'A test?'

'You say that you love me?'

'Yes.'

'So prove it.'

She rushed towards him. Her look said that she wanted to be held.

His hand came up abruptly but it was the coldness in his eyes that halted her. 'Wait in that chair.' He pointed to a high-backed chair glittering with gilt. 'Don't move until Harry tells you to.'

He turned on his heel. A moment later, the door closed behind him.

Angelina was trying hard to breathe. She was trying hard not to cry.

15

Harry Shears

At the back of the Aldahar, behind the gaming rooms and bars, away from the gaze of all but the invited few, was the Top's Club. Sirius was already in place, occupying one of the special private boxes jutting from the walls in front of the stage. Smoked glass guaranteed his privacy. A beautiful and expert whore was kneeling between his thighs readying his cock for the night's entertainment.

The curtain was opening and a man of fifty or so, tall, overweight, balding, could be seen busying himself with equipment at the back of the stage. He glanced into the wings with an expression of disgust.

'Anyone expecting a professional show should leave now,' he muttered sardonically.

The voice was exotic, as out of place in Acacia as a toad at a banquet. For those who knew these things it was a voice heavy with menace. It was pure East London – Plaistow or Bow, Romford or Ham.

A radio mike was pinned to his black leather overalls and transmitted his words around the room. The volume kicked up and down as a sound man – hidden away somewhere – struggled to get the level. In Harry's ear was a radio receiver, a little piece of technology that allowed Harry's boss, Sirius, to send instructions from his box.

It was hard not to dislike Harry immediately. It was hard not to be repelled by his greyness. His lank hair was grey, his skin was grey, even his lips were grey. Worse, he looked and sounded like an old-time gangster, someone who had done time with one of the Krays or had run grim errands for the Richardsons.

'Just give me a few minutes please, ladies and gentlemen,' he said in a louder voice. 'My friends like to start the show on time – to the blinkin' minute, whether I am ready or not . . .' His broad, lined face twisted into a show of arch indignation. 'But there is no show until I'm ready.'

He stomped over to a rusty steel table at the side of the stage and began to arrange the array of instruments there with slow deliberation, apparently forgetting the audience. From time to time he would make a comment – 'That's nice' or 'She was supposed to have cleaned that' – remarks that no one could be expected to understand. The audience could have been peeping into the private life of a bad-tempered and obsessive monster.

His leather overalls had a pouch and from time to time he would hold something up to the light, examine it and then drop it back into the dark opening. A layman would have recognised chains, clips, whips and clamps but most of the items were alien, unidentifiable. When the table was the way he wanted it, he stopped and looked around at the various shelves that lined the stage.

'Wax,' he muttered. 'Better start the wax, I think.'

He pulled a large black electrical device from under the table and, with a grunt, lifted it onto one of the shelves. He fussed with it for a while, lifting lids, poking the contents, muttering before plugging it into the wall. Then, opening a brown paper packet, he produced half a dozen large candles – each the thickness of a man's

180

arm and about a foot in length. He cut them crudely with a serrated knife on the table top and dropped as much as he could into various openings in the machine.

'I feel like a waxy night tonight.' He went back to the table, stooped and pulled out a second machine, identical to the first. 'Feel free to talk amongst yourselves,' he told the audience. 'If you want your money back it's too late.'

Eventually, the second machine was in operation and a strong smell of hot wax filled the tiny auditorium. He picked up a long-handled ladle and, smiling wickedly at the audience, mimed filling it from the machine then pouring it across his arm.

'Ouch!' he yelled theatrically. 'That's going to hurt.'

He checked the machines again and made sure the plugs were secure, frowning with concentration. Then he stepped to the front of the stage and a grim smile stretched his thin lips. 'It looks like we have a full house . . .' He flicked his microphone experimentally and continued. 'Some of you know me. For those who don't, my name is Harry Shears.'

There was a smattering of applause.

Despite this, he surveyed the audience with narrowed, suspicious eyes. 'I recognise a few faces.' He followed his survey with a profound scan of the cheap seats rising beyond the tables and finished with a pointed stare at the smoked glass of Sirius's box.

Harry did not seem like the kind of man who liked bosses much.

'I'm glad to say I don't recognise anyone with a special grievance,' he continued, eventually. 'So I think we can begin.' He paused for a moment. 'We should have music when I say that.' He paused for another moment. 'But that would cost money. Now . . . what are we doing tonight?' He stared at the floor as if he had genuinely forgotten, then looked up with a wide grin –

his first show of any pleasure. 'Punishments! How could I forget? My favourite.' He stepped forward a little and shaded his eyes. 'Somewhere in this audience we should have two volunteers.'

The two women in the seats at the front of house started to fidget. One of them was Angelina. She had not volunteered but she had not refused to perform. Her eyes were red from crying.

'Ah yes. The volunteers. Step up here please.'

Angelina rose uncertainly and followed the other woman. They filed onto the stage awkwardly on high-heeled shoes, black and shining.

'Well,' said Harry. 'Not bad, I suppose.' The women stood self-consciously centrestage and he walked behind them, examining each in turn. 'Not bad at all. I could fuck either of them,' he told the audience. 'But fucking isn't what we're here for. Not tonight. Tonight is punishment night.'

His manner had changed now that he had the two girls in his power. He had switched on his charm. His hooded eyes had an avuncular warmth. He gazed into the eyes of the girls like a stage hypnotist. 'Tell us your names.'

'I am Marta,' said the tall voluptuous girl.

Angelina gave her name in a small frightened voice.

'So you want to be whipped?'

'Yes,' said Marta immediately.

Harry's eyebrows shot upwards in surprise. This was not the answer that he had expected. 'You *want* me to punish you?'

The girl smiled.

'Yes.'

'Good.'

He looked at her suspiciously for a moment then turned to Angelina.

'What about you?' he asked.

The girl was staring at her feet and didn't reply. Harry stepped closer. Taking hold of her hair, he raised her head.

'Angelina is it?'

'Yes.'

'Look at the audience and tell us why you are here.'

Angelina blinked into the lights. 'My boyfriend wants to watch me ...' Her voice trailed off to nothing.

'He wants to watch you suffer?'

'Yes.'

'How unkind of him,' Harry said with grim satisfaction. He turned to the audience again. 'So we have one girl who wants to suffer and one who is reluctant. Which to choose?' He shook his head. 'I like to punish the ones who don't like it. But that's just me.' His hand lashed out across Marta's backside. Her beautiful brown eyes opened wide. 'Face the front,' Harry shouted. 'Don't look at me. Look at the punters. Both of you. This is supposed to be a show.'

The girls dutifully faced front and raised their heads.

'Now, I can't be expected to punish both girls,' he said slowly. 'The management seem to think that I am some kind of machine. But I am not. If I punish a girl, I like to be thorough and that takes time. So who to choose?' He stopped for a moment. 'I think we need some audience participation. Girls, step back please. Don't fall over!' he barked when Marta, in turning, stumbled. 'That's it. Come to the back of the stage.'

He waited until they were motionless then turned to the audience again. 'I'm going to tell each girl to take a turn around the stage and I want you all to give her a hand. Whoever gets the most applause will be punished. OK? DO YOU UNDERSTAND?' he shouted, settling on a stool beside the table.

There were a few catcalls.

183

Harry gazed at the audience stonily for a moment then pointed at Angelina. 'You go first, love. Just walk around the stage a bit. Make sure everyone sees you.' Angelina began to do as he'd instructed but he suddenly changed his mind. 'Wait. I think you should strip first. How can the audience make up its mind if you are wearing all that stuff.'

The girl froze, incomprehension twisting her features.

'Strip! Take your clothes off!' He made the gestures of someone undressing.

As soon as the girl understood, she reached behind and undid the zipper on her dress. There was absolute silence as her dress slipped to the floor revealing well-formed breasts but exceptionally slender arms and legs. Her pubis was clean shaven and there was a tattoo of a star on her left hip.

'Come here,' Harry told her.

She stood in front of him. He reached out his hand lazily and fingered her pussy. Her eyes slipped to the ground.

'Dry as a bone,' he announced. 'This isn't your cup of tea, is it?'

The girl said nothing, refusing to even meet his eye. For a moment, Harry seemed to pity her. Then, he gave a deep sigh and turned to Marta. 'You as well,' he said. 'Strip. We haven't got all night.' Looking bored, Harry continued to finger the hapless Angelina.

Marta stripped gracefully. There was a murmur of appreciation from the audience as she stepped from her clothes. She was the material that goddesses were made from – tall, strong, voluptuous. When she faced the audience naked, her face was calm, her breathing even, her eyes modest but confident.

'Yes,' said Harry with a note of uncharacteristic wonder. 'Undoubtedly female.' He allowed the audience a few moments to savour the vision before pulling his hand from between Angelina's thighs and telling her to walk around the stage.

Angelina tottered forward, uncertainly. A spotlight came up, belatedly, and followed her. Marta sat at Harry's command and all attention came to focus on Angelina. She looked frightened and disorientated. Her pubis was red from the fingering but her sex lips were closed so that her pussy looked immature, almost juvenile.

Angelina came to a halt midstage. Her head slipped down and she was the perfect image of shame. Harry jumped from his stool and pulled her hair into a tight wad behind her neck. 'Don't hide,' he barked. 'Keep your head up. We want to see you.' He released her hair and then slapped her behind, hissing 'walk'.

She walked slowly across the stage with her head held high but with tears forming in the corners of her eyes. There was loud applause.

It was Marta's turn next. She needed no directions. She walked onstage like a professional. Her long muscled legs gleamed in the lights, her full firm breasts shook seductively, her sultry smile made her a star.

Again there was loud applause.

'A draw, I think,' Harry said gloomily. 'Never expect an audience to help.'

Someone shouted – an American voice: 'Do them both, you lazy fuck!'

'Hey, enough of that,' Harry shouted back, stepping centrestage and striking an aggressive pose. There were more demands for both girls to suffer. Harry began to grin at the faces around him. They were cruel, excited, expectant. He strutted from one side of the stage to the other, relishing the bearpit hubbub; the showman was finally happy. He let the noise rise to a fever pitch then raised his hands for silence.

'That's enough. OK, by popular demand we will punish both girls.' He turned to Angelina with a cruel

185

grin. 'For you, my dear, the punishment will be the humiliation of staying. And for you,' he turned to Marta, 'it will be the whip.'

There was loud applause.

Harry pointed out a stool at the back of the stage, a hefty item with a broad seat covered in brown leather. He told Angelina to fetch it.

Angelina moved as quickly as the shoes would allow her, dragging the stool slowly across the uneven stage planking whilst Harry watched impatiently. Finally, she had the stool set out as he wished, resting on a slightly raised circular platform stage left but still in the full glare of the foot lights. Harry fetched an electric screwdriver and screws. Crouching, he drove the screws through the legs of the stool and into the platform. He tested it for stability with a meaty paw.

'That isn't going anywhere.' He gestured to Angelina. 'Kneel up.'

It took a while for the girl to catch on. Finally, she knelt on the leather surface and balanced herself precariously, looking more frightened with every passing moment.

'Now, this isn't an ordinary stool,' Harry told them, bringing from the back of the stage a frame also covered in brown leather. 'This is a show stool. It lets me show off women and all their best features. And we all know what the best features of a woman are.'

The frame fitted to the sides of the stool, extending its surface forwards.

'Open your legs, love.'

Angelina edged her knees apart. Harry reached under the stool and pulled out some leather straps. 'Clever, isn't it? I had it made by a Turkish dwarf who lived in Limehouse. Well, he was almost a dwarf.' He strapped her calves down, pulling hard and tight, then took her wrists. 'Lean forward, don't be frightened. I've got you.'

186

Angelina let out a little shriek as she was obliged to tip forward.

'You are a scaredy cat, aren't you?' he murmured, resting her forearms on the extensions to the stool. He used small straps to secure her, winding them from wrist to elbow. Now, she was bent almost double, with her behind high in the air. Her head hung between pinioned arms in an attitude of despair.

Harry looked at her. 'We can't have you hiding your face like that, can we?' He rubbed his chin for a moment. 'I know. A little piece of equipment that I stole from a gentleman in New York, a place where they take this sort of thing very seriously.' He went over to the table and rummaged through some boxes. Finally, he pulled out a length of rope with a large thick round-ended hook at the end. It gleamed silver in the stage lights like a Christmas bauble no child should ever see. 'This will do the trick,' he said. He picked up a small plastic bottle and headed back to Angelina.

He squirted a clear liquid into the parting of Angelina's buttocks and rubbed it deep into her anus with banana-thick fingers. 'This may be a little cold,' he warned, then took the hook and worked its bulbous end into the lubricated opening.

Angelina wriggled in an attempt to prevent the entry but Harry barked at her to be still.

'It's like pushing a matchstick up an ant's ass,' he told the audience with satisfaction. When the hook was in place it fitted the curve of her behind perfectly, the roped end resting on her coccyx. Harry took Angelina's hair and pulled her head back. 'Stay like that,' he told her. Then he began to tie the rope through her hair.

It took several attempts for Harry to achieve his objective. When, eventually, he stepped back to admire his handiwork there was a round of applause. Angelina's face was now fully presented to the audience, held up by the taut rope that ran from her hair to the hook buried deep in her anus.

'No escape for you,' Harry said, with what might have been a chuckle, but from another man would have been a death rattle. He crouched and fiddled with the platform beneath her. There was a loud click and the platform was suddenly free to turn. Harry stood and gave a gentle push. Angelina began to turn in a slow smooth circle like a figurine in a music box.

'This is automated. Now where is the switch?' He found it low on the wall behind the platform. 'Who designs these things?' he asked, glancing around with a mock frown. He flicked the switch and there was the quiet whirr of a motor. Angelina continued in her steady circle.

'Very nice. Get a spot on her,' Harry called.

A moment later, she was lit fully and the house lights gradually dimmed. Soon there was darkness but for the brilliantly-lit figure.

'Shall I help her a little?' Harry asked, rhetorically. He stepped onto the platform so that he was turning slowly with the tied figure. The plastic bottle delivered more lube, this time to the girl's pussy. Harry's fingers were kinder, gentler this time. They circled her clitoris mechanically but effectively. Angelina began to groan. Her mouth opened, drool flowed, her eyes slipped backwards, became lost for a moment, her tongue flickered across her lips.

'What is it about the ladies? The more it hurts the more they like it. You do like it, don't you?'

Angelina gurgled.

'Is that a yes?'

Angelina gurgled again.

'Should I stop fingering you? Let the pain come back?'

Angelina shook her head as much as she could.

Harry carried on with his mission of mercy until Angelina began to come. He let her scream once, then stopped abruptly, cruelly, before her full due of pleasure, and stepped back onto the stage.

'That's enough of that,' he announced. 'Lights!'

The girl groaned in disappointment.

The lights came up to reveal a Harry well pleased with himself. He accepted his applause with good grace then walked over to Marta. 'How about you? Would you like a go on the wagon wheel?'

Marta nodded enthusiastically.

'I bet you would. But for you there will only be pain, because you, I reckon, have done this kind of thing before and you are too twisted to get off so lightly.'

Marta was unperturbed, her smile undimmed.

'I think we will start with a general whipping. Get some proper seriousness into proceedings. We need to take that smile off your face. Nobody came here for a beauty pageant.' He took her hand and led her to the centre of the stage. 'Stand here,' he told her, looking up into the shadows above her head, judging her position against an object invisible to the audience. 'A little to the left, back a bit, that's it.' Finally, he had her in position. 'Hands on head, legs apart,' he barked. 'I thought you were experienced!'

She did as she was bid, revealing her shaven pussy and the redness of her swollen lips. The inside of her thighs gleamed in the lights, wet from knee to groin.

Harry reached out and ran his finger through the succulence of her cunt. 'No need to ask if it's your cup of tea,' he muttered. He stepped to the side and unhooked a control box from the wall. A thick electrical wire trailed from its lower end. Two large buttons projected from its face, one red, one white. Harry's thumb came down on the red one and there was a whirring sound. A moment later, a horizontal wooden bar appeared, slowly descending towards the spread figure of Marta. It was the sort of bar circus performers use to swing through the air but at each end were leather straps and cuffs. Harry watched carefully, keeping his thumb on the control until the bar was very nearly touching Marta's head.

'Good. It works,' Harry said to no one in particular. He replaced the control box and stood behind Marta. There were thick leather cuffs descending from each end of the bar and he used these to secure Marta's wrists.

'Open your legs wider,' he told her.

Her feet edged out a little more so that her knees were bent and her pussy even more exposed.

'If you move those feet I will tie them,' he told her, 'and I'll tie them a lot wider than they are now. OK?'

Marta nodded and Harry stepped back to the wall.

He took the box down again and pressed the white button. This time the bar ascended. Marta's arms were slowly pulled straight. She had to shift a little to keep her balance and Harry barked at her again. 'Keep still, woman!'

She was still smiling, still had the look of a woman fulfilled, simultaneously at peace with her situation and excited.

Harry stepped in front of her and used his feet to widen her stance still further. The first signs of discomfort appeared on Marta's face. 'Now we are getting somewhere,' Harry declared. He walked to the back of the room and searched through the racks of floggers. 'Something heavy for you, I think,' he said, looking at Marta's straining back. 'Yes. Real leather, square cut. I have just the one, somewhere.'

His fingers ran across the neatly stacked instruments of torture, caressed each in turn, a look of something close to love in his eyes. When he found what he was looking for, he smiled and held it high for the audience to see. The handle was black and long, the thongs brown and even longer. All in all, it was as tall as the tiny Angelina who still revolved in her place, eyes wide. 'I use this one for special occasions. If this doesn't wipe the smile off her face, nothing will.'

He took a position behind the marvellous figure centrestage and flicked the flogger back and forth experimentally. 'I used it on a girl in Kensington once but it was too much for her. The poor thing fainted. She thought she was tough. A captain of hockey at Roedean, I think she said. Anyway, let's see what Marta makes of it.'

He laid the whip out on the floor behind him. The spread strands might have been the train of a wedding dress. Then he turned on his heel and launched them through the air. They fell with a heavy thud across Marta's back.

She gave a tiny yelp and her gaze fell to the floor.

Harry stepped up beside her. 'Face the audience! How many times do I have to say "face the audience"?'

'Sorry,' Marta murmured, raising her eyes.

'And call me Master.'

'Sorry, Master.'

'And speak up.'

'Yes, Master!'

'Good. Now I like to work in twelves. There is something about the number twelve that is very satisfying.'

'Yes, Master.'

'I want you to count them. I don't see why I should do all the work.'

'Yes, Master.'

'I see that you're still smiling.'

'Yes, Master.' Her smile was even wider than before, her eyes even softer, even more accommodating after the first blow of the whip.

Harry let his whip arm relax for a moment. His face creased with a sudden curiosity. 'Tell me why you volunteered. But make it quick. I don't want your life story.'

For a moment, Marta appeared nonplussed. 'I think that everything for me is too good,' she said after a moment. Her voice was shaky. 'Sometimes, I need to feel bad.'

'You need to feel bad like the rest of us?' Harry offered helpfully.

She nodded.

Harry shrugged.

'When I was at school I enjoyed pulling little girls' hair. I never felt bad about it. Except when one of the teachers caught me.'

The non sequitur ended his interest in Marta's motivation and he stepped behind her again. He laid out the whip. 'Start counting from one.'

'Yes, Master.'

The whip flew through the air. Marta yelped again, stumbled a little.

'One, Master.'

'Keep those feet wide. Let everyone see that pussy. Let them see what a dirty girl you are, dripping on the stage while an old man whips you.'

'Yes, Master.'

'And if you behave yourself, I might let you suck my cock afterwards.'

'Yes, Master.'

Harry proceeded with the whipping.

Marta gave her characteristic yelp after each blow. The audience was absolutely silent.

There was something in Harry's expression that rendered the act of whipping mundane. He never hurried. He didn't sweat. His eyes, hooded by the large venous lids, remained detached, suspicious, bored. The rhythm of the whipping remained unchanged from the first to the last. He proceeded relentlessly, pausing only to check the skin on Marta's back from time to time, looking for cuts perhaps.

Maybe it was this quality which made it all bearable. Perhaps it was Harry's passionless control that allowed his audience to sit through the spectacle of Marta slowly breaking before their eyes. Because Marta did break. The smile quickly disappeared from her face. Her eyes lost their calmness. After only half the blows had been delivered, she had the look of someone hunted. Between the blows, as she waited for the pain, anxiety etched lines around her eyes. Soon anxiety gave way to dread. Dread shaded into panic. Her voice grew higher and higher as she shouted out the numbers. Her chest heaved as she tried to breathe through the pain.

Finally, Harry stopped. He checked the whip for damage before replacing it carefully on the wall. 'Now that is a nice red back,' he announced in an even tone. He stepped closer to admire it. 'Turn around,' he told her. 'Let everyone see.'

It was awkward for her. Harry made it more difficult by shouting if she brought her legs together even a fraction. He sat back on his stool to watch her struggle. It was a slow, pitiful performance and more than once she slipped from the precarious perch of her high-heeled shoes and hung from her wrists, breathing heavily.

Slowly, though, she managed to turn and slowly her back, glowing red like a harvest moon, was revealed to the audience. Harry had judged the twelve strokes perfectly, using every nerve on her back but leaving her intact, reusable.

'Arch your back. Show them your pussy,' Harry told her, when she had completed her arduous semi-circle.

'Yes, Master.'

She arched her back as much as the cuffs and her stance would allow. It was enough to tip her bald pussy to face the audience. It seemed larger from behind: a broad white V. The lips that split it were as red as her back.

Harry stood and inspected her. 'Hot, I expect,' he said, reaching out and running his hand appreciatively from neck to coccyx. 'Lovely. Like jam on toast.' He slipped his hand between her legs. 'The triangle. I have a friend who says we are all crucified and this is where they do it.' He pinched on the sex lips above her still-hidden clitoris and pulled down. 'He drinks too much.' He pulled harder and Marta groaned. 'I suppose we should do the ass next. Make a match. What do you think, Marta?'

The girl stammered a bald 'Yes.'

'Yes *Master*!' Harry snapped.

'Yes, Master.'

'Good.' He let go of her pussy and the lips gradually retracted. He fetched a cane, exceptionally long and as thick as his fingers. 'I think another twelve.' He was about to deliver the first blow when he stopped himself. 'I have a better idea.' He reached for the control box. 'I'm going to let the bar down,' he told her. 'I want you to edge backwards so that you are leaning over. OK?'

Marta looked at him in confusion. It seemed that the whipping had taken her to a place far away.

Harry began to lower the bar and then rested his hand on her shoulders, pushing so that she bent over. 'That's it. Keep those legs apart.' As the bar descended and Marta edged backwards, her buttocks parted, Harry ran his fingers around the opening of her anus. 'Do you like anal?' he asked, almost derisively.

'Yes, Master.'

'Very tempting.'

Soon her head was lower than her behind and she could look between her legs.

'Look at the audience. Can you see them?'

'Yes, Master.' Upside down her face fell out of shape and lost its beauty.

Standing almost against the side wall Harry began to lay strokes across Marta's buttocks and thighs. This time she screamed as each blow fell. This time the audience could see the blows fall. They could see the shock waves passing through her muscles and the almost instant reddening of her skin.

'In England this would be a crime,' Harry told them conversationally.

He laid on a stroke.

'These ladies who volunteered –' he gazed at Angelina, with an ironic smile '– reluctantly maybe – would be the victims.'

He laid on a stroke.

'I would be the master villain.'

Another stroke.

'And you,' he said, looking at the audience, 'would be the accomplices. Perhaps more than accomplices.' He smiled in a self-deprecating way. 'After all, I am just a humble artisan and you have paid me to beat these simple-minded girls – who you have also paid, a little.'

He gave Marta another stroke.

'That should be a secret. Our volunteers get expenses.'

Another stroke.

'The thing I like about crime,' said Harry, 'is that it opens the mind. You commit one crime and you question all laws. And that makes you think. It's good to think.'

Another stroke.

'Or maybe it isn't. I had a girlfriend from Vietnam once. Whenever my eyes got that faraway look she would say, "No think!" ' He chuckled. 'Very Buddhist!'

He laid on another stroke.

'No think! I should be so lucky!'

Another stroke.

'How are we doing here?' He stepped forward and examined the bruised flesh, running his fingers across each darkening line in turn. 'Hmm. Those are coming up nicely.' He pinched her hard then stepped back in surprise when Marta gave a sudden deep-throated roar of rage. 'Does it hurt?' he asked in mock surprise.

'Yes, Master.'

'Good, it's supposed to hurt.'

He pinched her again. This time Marta only whimpered.

'Do you know why you deserve to be whipped?'

'No, Master.'

'We had better carry on then.'

He stepped back to his place. 'I'll give you a clue. If you weren't bent over showing everyone your pussy and asshole you wouldn't deserve this.'

He laid on another stroke.

Marta screamed. He examined her again.

'I have to be careful with this cane,' he told the audience. 'It can leave a nasty bite. And you should hear the complaints I get then!' He poked and prodded the snivelling girl.

'Seems to be all right. Some women make you go too far no matter how hard you try.' He took Marta's behind in his hands and pulled the cheeks open. 'Have you worked out why you deserve this yet?' he asked.

'No, Master,' she sobbed.

He pushed a finger brusquely into her anus. 'Compliance. Charming in children, in grown-ups it can be fatal. Compliance is a sin because it's too easy. Life isn't meant to be easy.' He pulled out and stepped back then laid on another stroke. 'Of course, if you don't comply, if you don't keep those beautiful legs wide open, I would have to tie them open and I have enough to do!'

He looked at the audience with a blaze of pure hatred then collected himself. His eyes re-hooded themselves, his unnatural calm returned, gathering like a chill cloud around re-frozen features. 'Two more will be twelve, I think. Quick and hard. Perhaps.' He raised his voice. 'Quick and hard?'

There was approval from the audience but it was muted, as if they dare not disagree.

Harry stepped back and laid them on, one after the other. Marta screamed and collapsed. Harry let her hang from her wrists for a few minutes. There was absolute silence. Everyone, it seemed, was taking in the arched, reddened back, the broad heaving chest, the long slender arms, the exposed dripping pussy. Everyone was listening to the sobs and gasps. Everyone was in a 'somewhere else'.

'Yes, well, that was very good,' Harry said softly. 'Very good.' He walked to the back of the stage and replaced the cane in its housing. 'We can't rest on our laurels though. There is always more to be done.' He lifted the lids of the wax machines and, taking the ladle, gave a little stir to each in turn. 'Well, *they* are ready.' A frown creased his brow. 'But I'm getting ahead of myself. Breasts next.'

He chose a flogger. The fronds were round in section and no longer than the length of his forearm, but they were heavy. Returning to the hanging woman he knelt and lifted her face. 'Have you had a nice rest?' he asked conversationally. 'Ready for some more?'

Marta didn't reply.

'Well, ready or not, we have to get on. Open that lovely mouth.'

Marta complied and Harry slipped the handle of the whip between her teeth. 'Don't you dare drop it,' he told her sternly. Standing, he used the control box to lift the bar and pull the exhausted girl upright. The stripes on her buttocks and thighs had been laid on at crazy angles. The lines intersected like the display of a tube map. It was a theatrical gesture. It ensured that every one of the twelve strokes could be seen from the back of the hall.

'Behold the painted lady,' Harry intoned mournfully. He stood with his hand outstretched and his chin tilted back, a performer from Dickens. His sinister features could only have been improved by gaslight. Then a wicked grin split his ashen lips. 'I use the same line every time,' he confessed, then turned to the object of his description. 'OK, turn around.'

Marta turned slowly. The flogger was still gripped between her teeth. Her eyes were wet with tears. Black lines smudged her cheeks where her make-up had run. She was no longer beautiful.

Harry plucked the flogger from her mouth. 'Ready for some more?' he asked.

'Yes, Master,' she replied, after a moment. Her voice was thin and small. Her eyes had glazed over. She had the look of a fish on a hook.

'That's the spirit.' He swung the flogger through empty air and Marta flinched. 'Tell us about the first time someone beat you,' Harry said suddenly.

Marta seemed unable to speak.

'Come on, don't be shy,' Harry told her.

'It was a man I knew at work.'

'A "man at work"? Hmm. How did he get around to beating you?'

'He liked to talk about the things he did to his girlfriend. Caning, spanking . . .'

'What? He came into work in the morning and told everyone that he had caned his girlfriend the night before?'

Marta managed a thin smile.

'He didn't tell everyone. Just me. I think he thought that he could shock me. I was very young. It was my first job.'

'And how old was he?'

'He was forty or fifty.'

'A dirty old man?'

'Yes. I think so.' Marta giggled. Conversation seemed to revive her. 'Though he was always very kind, when he wasn't spanking me.'

'And what happened?'

'I started to think about what he said and one lunchtime I asked him to take me to the storeroom.'

'Where he did what?'

'He gave me a spanking.'

'And that was it?'

'The first time.'

'And the second time?'

'Another spanking. I let him spank me once or twice a week.'

'No sex?'

'No. I was too shy.'

'Too shy!' Harry's voice rose incredulously. He turned to the audience, still not looking entirely convinced. 'Well, there you are. Just pick the prettiest, youngest girl in the office and tell her you spent the evening watching a show where a girl was whipped and who knows? She might say "take me to the storeroom".'

Harry examined the tips of his fingers for a moment. 'Anyway ... Breasts. We are going to work on your breasts.'

'Yes, Master.'

'Are you looking forward to this?'

'Yes, Master.'

'Hmmm.'

The flogger sliced through the air and fell across a perfect breast. Marta stiffened and her face twisted for a moment. The smile returned reluctantly after a reproachful glance in Harry's direction.

Harry ran his hand across the reddening breast. 'Harsher than you expected?'

'Yes, Master.' Her voice had climbed an octave.

'Good. Nobody wants to see you enjoy yourself.' Harry tweaked a nipple. 'Twelve on each. Let's see if we can take you from a C cup to a D cup.'

'Yes, Master.'

'Maybe, later, I'll give you a forced orgasm. Would you like that?'

'I don't know, Master.'

'You've never had an orgasm beaten out of you?'

'No, Master.'

'Think about it whilst I whip this tit.'

The whip fell. Once, twice, three times.

'What did you like about the spankings?'

Marta was struggling to get her breath. 'I liked the sneaking and the hiding. I liked the thought that we might get found. I liked the smell of paper and ink. I liked that he called me a slut . . .'

Harry pushed his hand between her thighs and toyed with her pussy. Her face became dreamy. 'What else?'

'I liked to feel him get hard when I lay across his knee. I liked that he could see my bottom.'

Harry slipped his fingers inside. 'If you come, you are going to be in such trouble,' he warned.

'Yes, Master.'

'And what do you like about this? Now.'

'I like your fingers, Master.'

'I know you like my fingers. You like my fingers because you are a slut . . .'

'Yes, Master.'

He pushed another finger into her so that there were three. 'Hmmm. Your pussy is as loose as any whore.'

'I'm sorry, Master.'

'I won't be fucking this. My dick wouldn't touch the sides.'

'Sorry, Master,' she said again, her voice breaking as she spoke, her hips starting to move from side to side.

'So what I was asking you is: what do you like about this treatment, *apart* from my fingers?'

She was struggling to control her breathing. Her words came in a series of gasps.

'I like that . . . so many people . . . are watching . . . It's like getting . . . caught.'

'Do you have friends in the audience?'

'No. I would never . . . tell anyone about this.'

'But what if someone here knows you? What if they tell everyone what a dirty little pain slut you are?'

'It would be terrible.'

'So you do feel shame?'

'Yes, Master.'

'You aren't a very bright girl, are you?'

'No, Master.'

Harry pulled his hand out of her pussy and took a nipple instead. He twisted hard. She shrieked.

'The terrible is my department.'

'Yes, Master.'

'You like to take risks?'

'Yes, Master.'

'So what if we just tore up our agreement? What if you said to me, "Harry, you can do whatever you like tonight."'

Her eyes came to a sudden focus.

'I don't know . . .'

Harry turned to the audience. 'I should let you in on a little secret. Marta and I had a talk earlier so that we could be sure exactly what she was volunteering for. But

I think Marta needs to go further than she agreed.' He turned back to the girl swaying on her wrists. He slipped his fingers into her pussy again. 'I think you need to tell me that we needn't worry about agreements. I think you need to know that anything could happen. I think that is what would really turn you on.' Harry's fingers pumped in and out, hard, as he said this, emphasising each word. 'And if you agree, I will let you come. I'll make it good.'

Her eyes were rolling up into her head. She was shuddering with excitement.

'Answer me,' he told her.

She looked as if she were in a world of her own. She seemed to have lost all sense of who and where she was. His fingers came out of her and she came back to the real world in a hurry.

'Tell me that you agree,' Harry said. 'Tell me that there are no limits.'

'No limits?' she said with a confused look.

'And I'll make you come and come. You want to come, don't you?'

'Yes.'

'So say it. Say no limits.'

With the reluctance of a lamb approaching the butcher's knife, she said the words.

'No limits.'

Harry pushed his hand back into her. She began to come immediately. He was rough, using his full strength. She twisted and screamed, wept and babbled. Finally, Harry pulled out. 'I have some needles for you,' he told her.

She groaned.

'You don't like needles?' he asked

'No.'

'All the better. But first we need to finish with these tits.'

* * *

202

A few metres away, protected from the gaze of the audience by smoked glass, Sirius was looking at his watch. It was time to finish up and go. His father was waiting. He glanced from his watch to the head of the girl in his lap.

'Make me come,' he told her.

The girl smiled and quickened her pace. She used tongue and lips, throat and hands in unison.

He watched as Harry laid on the final strokes. He saw Marta's breasts recoil from the sharp kisses. He watched Angelina turning in her restricted circle. He took hold of the girl's head and for the first time fucked. Her throat had glided like silk across his cock for almost an hour but now Sirius wanted friction. He adjusted his angle of attack, taking the line of most resistance. The girl's suffocating groans goaded him to cruel thrusts. Finally, he came, rising to his feet, fucking her throat as hard as he would fuck a whore's pussy.

Yet, as he came it was a vision of golden hair that he saw. He saw a girl whose history could be remade in any way that he liked. He heard a question in his ear – 'What can I do for you?' – and the beginning of an answer in his heart.

His scream filled the black box and coursed through the auditorium beyond.

Harry laid on the last stroke. Marta's breasts finally stopped shaking as the cry from the box died down. He turned towards the sound. 'Well, that hit the spot for someone, at least,' he declared and set the whip aside. 'We have other treats.' He shuffled to the back of the stage and pulled down a cardboard box from one of the shelves.

'Needles,' he murmured. 'All shapes and sizes. Big and small, sharp and blunt.' He wandered back to the front of the stage. 'We're going to have some fun tonight girls!'

He stopped abruptly and pressed his hand to his ear. It was Sirius.

'Let mine go. I don't care what you do with the other one.'

Harry let out a grunt of disappointment. He gazed at Angelina with an expression of loss, as if someone was taking away a toy. Then he told her the good news. 'Your suffering is no longer required.' He stopped the turntable and began to undo the straps. Angelina gave every appearance of shivering. Her muscles, bound into inflexibility, were twitching.

Before he had finished undoing the first strap though, Harry paused. 'We haven't used any of that wax yet, have we?' he murmured thoughtfully. 'That would warm you up.'

He looked at the audience. 'What do you think?'

No audience of Harry's had ever counselled mercy.

He grinned at the cruel suggestions shouted from the floor and then headed to the back of the stage. The wax was bubbling ferociously. The only man who might have protected Angelina had left the building. Harry was going to enjoy himself.

He picked up a large ladle and pushed aside the lids of the bubbling heaters. Stirring the first pot like a witch at a cauldron, Harry gurgled with pleasure.

'Enough to fill a couple of rectums,' he declared.

16

Hampton's

No sooner was Sirius through the front doors of the ancestral pile than Joshua – footman, valet, pimp and bodyguard – had informed Sirius that his father was expecting him in the Evening Room.

'Your father was very particular that you go to him immediately, sir.'

Sirius studied the demeanour of the broad-faced, broad-shouldered former soldier. Joshua was not an easy man to read. He would have worn the same expression to eat a boiled egg as the brains of his enemies.

'Is this going to be a bad experience?' Sirius asked, moving to inspect himself in a huge gilt-framed mirror.

'I hope not, sir.'

Sirius straightened his tie. 'Is my father alone?'

'I think you need to find that out for yourself, sir.'

Sirius looked at the man's reflection in the mirror. 'Don't fuck with me, Joshua.' Sirius did not like the servants to offer opinions.

'I would never do that, sir.'

'Remember that you aren't the only gorilla on hire.'

'No, sir, I would never forget that.'

Sirius turned on his heel and headed down the long corridor to the Evening Room. To left and right were the images of three generations of Hamptons.

Intermingled were images of Prime Ministers and Presidents, Hollywood stars and gangsters.

Unable to help himself, Sirius was still fiddling with his tie. Meeting his father was never a relaxed affair. Sparks would inevitably fly. Arriving with anything less than perfect grooming would have been a bad start. It would have conceded points in a game where points were very hard to come by. Hampton Senior had been grinding noses into the dust a lot longer than Hampton Junior and could still pull new humiliations from his trouser pockets at will.

With every echoing step down the broad, high-ceilinged corridor, Sirius could feel his shoulders tensing. He ran through the week's trading. He tried to identify any potential weaknesses in his dealings. He tried to decide if this meeting was a punishment or a reward.

The door to the Evening Room was closed when he arrived. He paused and listened. There seemed to be no sound within. With a final tug at his tie Sirius seized the door handle and wrenched it open. A timid entry would have sent the wrong message.

Inside there was darkness.

'Father,' he called.

Immediately, the lights went up. From every corner faces appeared. A drink was pushed into his hand. Men and women were calling out their congratulations. There was a sudden outbreak of 'For he's a jolly good fellow'. Then his father appeared and wrapped an arm around his son's shoulders.

'We have never celebrated you enough, my son,' he said with an expression of something close to tenderness.

After the initial surprise, Sirius was recovering himself. His smile was working again. His eyes were scanning the guests, gauging the meaning of the surprise

206

party. There was a heavy preponderance of business associates. The entire board of Hampton International Trading seemed to be present. There were CEOs from the major subsidiaries. There were bankers and lawyers.

After a few moments, Sirius realised that everyone who mattered was there.

Filling out the ranks of the grey suits, lightening the load of ageing white males, were the women of the tribe, picked for their beauty, their decorum and their discretion. They could always be relied upon to leave the room if their men wanted to use a whore or two. This was unlikely to be a service required this evening, however. Hampton Senior never allowed whores in his house without a marriage licence. He preferred to go out for paid flesh.

Beyond the wives and girlfriends, there were also the maids in black stockings and short black skirts, their ruffed shirts open enough to show some cleavage to anyone who was interested to look. A small fraction of Sirius's consciousness began sifting through these for fresh meat.

Gradually, Sirius was drawn through the crowd towards the podium set up near the windows overlooking the lake. He shook every hand that was offered and, by the time he arrived at the gaudy, streamer-decked stage, his hands were uncomfortably sticky.

As soon as they had mounted the stage and the microphone was in Hampton Senior's hand, the old man called for everyone to charge their glasses.

'We are going to have some toasts here, so fill those glasses and hold on tight to the bottles!'

There was universal laughter. No one needed to worry about holding a bottle while the maids outnumbered the guests.

'To my son, on the tenth anniversary of his joining our company.'

Sirius had missed it. He had missed that it was the tenth anniversary. Did it matter? Was it true? Something was going on. Something out of the ordinary.

Glasses were raised. There were more congratulations hurled at the stage. Kisses were blown by the women. Hampton Senior raised his hands and called for silence.

'Let's look at this man carefully. A good-looking boy, I would say, a chip off the old block. There is a shine to this face that doesn't come from cheap soap inexpertly applied. It comes from within. It comes from the certainty in this man's heart, the self-confidence, the certain knowledge of character that great expectations, routinely satisfied, produces. My son has never been asked to be anything less than brilliant in any area of his life and he has never disappointed.

'At school, his teachers expected straight As and he delivered. On the college playing field, his team mates expected power, speed, skill and professionalism. He excelled all of them. In business, we have expected strategy, efficiency and hard work. Sirius has helped take Hampton's forward as very few other men have. He has turned a fiefdom into a dukedom. Soon it will be a kingdom.' Hampton Senior paused then raised his glass. 'To kingdoms!'

The crowd boomed the words back and drank deep.

'But now I come to a plea,' Hampton Senior began. He took Sirius's hand and looked him in the eye. 'A plea from the heart,' he said with a seriousness that he usually reserved for the boardroom. 'A plea for an heir.'

Sirius stiffened. His father had come to the point.

The only area of life in which Sirius had disappointed Hampton's was the marital. He had shrunk from the very idea of marriage. He would squirm at the very mention of it. Like most men, he was only afraid of what had already hurt him. The Hampton matriarch, once his mother, now dead, had been cool in all things. Sirius had not learnt love at her knee.

So Sirius had not fallen in love in later life. He had not sealed the family future with aristocratic heirs or even bolstered it with dim-witted foot soldiers. He had been a warrior in the workplace but a dilettante outside of it. With women, he had toyed as a cat toys with mice, or as an anatomist toys with bodies. Yet there was no escaping his fate. His family demanded children. His maternal grandmother, who had renounced flesh and sided with money, begged. His paternal grandmother, according to reports, spun in her grave each time his childlessness was reported. His father had tried bullying. He had tried subterfuge, steering blue-blooded virgins in his son's direction like a zoo keeper with a prize panda. He would have used kidnapping and drugs to achieve the desired end. Nothing had worked, however.

Sirius's liegemen hinted that it was necessary for the image of the business. Sirius's friends, especially the most degenerate, said that it would cover a thousand transgressions, that it was the image of a wife standing stoically beside a husband that had staved off a thousand lawsuits.

This party was simply the latest gambit in a long, long game. Something had changed though. Sirius did not feel the usual rage bubbling to the surface when he was being shooed in the direction of the mating pen. Instead of rage it was an image of Zellie's face that surfaced.

He turned to the crowd. 'I'm glad that I have been of service to this company. I am proud of our achievements. I am happy to offer one more sacrifice, my bachelorhood.'

There was a sudden rush of cheering. Hampton Senior began to pump his hand enthusiastically.

'But,' Sirius began, booming into the microphone, 'if I am to marry, the bride will be my choice and no one else's.' He looked at his father as he said this.

His father nodded, reluctantly – Hampton Senior liked the last word in every matter.

'If that can be agreed,' Sirius continued, 'I promise that I will be married before the eleventh anniversary of my joining the finest firm in the world.'

There was wild applause around the room.

'That's good enough for me,' Hampton Senior declared. 'And now I am going to get very, very drunk.'

17

Magus Reach

Reach's place was down a side street near the big sprawling market. The limousine dropped her outside a bar. A group of young men drinking from bottles watched her step out. One of them called 'Hey, chica!' Zellie glanced nervously at his flat, tattooed belly – exposed to the blazing sun over shapeless jeans – and hurried down the little dirt track the chauffeur lazily indicated.

'Just keep straight. You'll see a blue door,' he called after her and then the car was gone.

There was a row of grimy houses with even grimier children playing outside. An elderly woman in a faded print dress was laying out chillis on a straw mat. When they had dried in the sun, they would be as wrinkled as her face.

The road ended at a wall overgrown with creepers. There was a single blue door. Zellie didn't know whether to knock or just push. When she looked back along the track, she saw the men from the bar standing in the main road watching her lazily. The one who had called to her laughed and his voice carried like a raucous invitation in the hot air.

She pushed. The door grated on the dry dusty ground and opened only enough for her to squeeze in. She found herself in an overgrown garden and had to stoop to pass under the branches of bushes and trees. The house was a one-storey affair with a raised veranda of bleached wood and windows open to the air.

Zellie stood nervously, for a moment, looking for signs of life. 'Hello!' she called.

Stepping onto the veranda she called again. 'Hello!'

A young woman appeared carrying a basket of washing. She was short but well built. Her breasts were high and heavy, her behind ample. Dark Latin eyes warmed the air around her smooth tranquil face.

'I was looking for Mr Reach,' Zellie said with a smile.

The woman looked her over in a leisurely way. 'He's busy,' she said. Her tone was friendly but not helpful. She waited for Zellie to leave.

'Mr Hampton sent me.'

The woman straightened up at the sound of the name. Hampton was a name with *reach*. 'Maybe he see you. I ask. You wait,' she said and set down the washing on a chair near the door, leaving it to steam in the sun.

Zellie peeped through the open door as the woman walked slowly away down the dark hallway. Once she was alone, she turned and examined the tangled garden. It must once have been very grand but overgrown paths and crumbling walls told a story of neglect. It was still very beautiful and alive with birds and insects. Large gold butterflies of a kind that Zellie had never seen before meandered amongst the low-growing, labial-petalled stands of acacia. Hummingbirds flitted amongst the groups of papai blooms, their feathers flashing, green and gold. More birds fought for space in a creeper-strangled, chipped terracotta birdbath. Their jostling wings raised a rainbow-lit mist.

It would have been a perfect place to dream away an afternoon or even a lifetime but, before Zellie could be completely seduced, Maria returned.

212

'Señor Reach says that he will see you but you will have to take him as you find him.'

'OK,' said Zellie.

The woman led her down the gloomy hallway smelling of dust and termites and out into another garden – this one a sort of cloister, enclosed on all sides by the low building. The shade here came from a single large balboa tree.

An S-shaped pathway led them through a patch of hibiscus to a man sprawled out on a rattan bed covered with rags. He was almost naked – a cloth seemed to have been draped across his groin as an afterthought. The shade of a canvas awning protected his fleshy body from the sun but he still had to squint to look at Zellie.

'Come into the shade,' he told her.

She stepped under the awning. There was a smell of something sickly. Close to, Magus was a big man. His body spread in all directions. It was a loose body, a body without tension, appearing almost boneless, no muscles defining its form.

'Maria was giving me my daily treatment,' Reach told her when her eyes flitted nervously across the huge expanse of pink skin.

'That's OK,' Zellie said as brightly as she could.

She had been expecting an elderly invalid. Reach was old and he didn't look too healthy but he certainly wasn't beyond the flesh.

He propped himself up on one elbow. It seemed a very great effort. 'So who are you and what can I do for you?' he asked.

'I'm Zellie. Reverend Forty at the Church of Acacia Heights thought you might like a visitor,' she said with a big but uncertain smile.

Reach's eyes narrowed. He examined Zellie's face with a mixture of contempt and pity. Zellie's smile faded to a ghost of itself. 'So you're one of God's agents sent to save me from sin?'

Zellie gave a little nervous laugh.

'I don't know about saving anyone from sin,' she said with absolute sincerity, thinking of her own weaknesses. 'Mr Hampton just thought you might like someone to talk to.'

Reach looked her up and down. 'And why should I talk to you?' He studied her breasts under the thin cotton of her top. He measured the breadth of her hips and the length of her legs, perhaps answering his own question by the end of that undisguised enquiry.

Used to male eyes, Zellie shrugged and smiled. 'I think I can be a good listener if you give me a chance.'

'You *think*?' he asked derisively. 'Well, I *think* the things that I would say to you would have you running from this house in a scream.'

Zellie frowned for a moment then stiffened her resolve. 'Maybe. But maybe not,' she said softly.

'So you think you are a good listener. To be a good listener you need understanding and acceptance. Do you think acceptance is a virtue, Zellie?'

Zellie thought of Dolores and the colonel. They seemed to accept all of Zellie's weaknesses. 'Yes,' she said with conviction.

'Do you think you could be understanding of a man who has more in common with the Devil than he has with Jesus?'

'I could try.'

'And how hard can you try?'

'*Quite* hard.'

Reach laughed then became suddenly serious. 'I'm imagining the shape of your breasts,' he said. 'How does that feel?'

Zellie blushed. 'It's OK. Every man does that,' she said wistfully.

'And I was wondering if you shave your pubic hair.'

Zellie looked at the ground, unsure of what to say.

'There,' Reach said, 'I've already offended you and I haven't even begun.'

'I came to talk,' Zellie told him regretfully. 'I didn't come for sex.'

'But sex is the only thing that I like to talk about. Sex is the only thing that matters to me.'

Zellie glanced at Maria. The girl seemed to be trying not to laugh. 'I suppose I don't mind *talking* about sex,' Zellie said bravely. 'As long as it is just talking.'

Reach turned to Maria. 'Maria, fetch the lady a seat.'

Maria disappeared towards the house.

'So tell me,' Reach resumed. 'Do you shave your pubic hair?'

'Yes,' said Zellie with a deep sigh.

'All of it?'

'Sometimes.'

Reach ran a fat tongue along his thick drooping lower lip. He seemed to be tasting her. Zellie felt a tingle inside her belly – a wrong tingle, the kind of tingle she shouldn't feel when a dirty old man (and Reach *really* was a dirty old man) looked at her with X-ray eyes. 'Is your pussy bare now?'

'Not completely.'

'So what is shaved and what is hairy?'

'The lower part is shaved.'

'The part below your clitoris?'

The word *clitoris* burrowed into Zellie's mind. It wormed down her spinal cord. It jumped into her groin and found the organ it referred to. There was heat. There was swelling. 'Yes,' she managed to say.

'I imagine that you have a very pretty clitoris.'

'Thank you.'

'I imagine that it is very fresh, as pink as your tongue.' His own tongue flicked across his lip again.

Not knowing how to react, she found herself gazing at her feet again.

'Is it so pink?' he persisted.

'I don't know.'

'Perhaps we should look . . .'

'No!'

He laughed hugely. The sound bounced around the closed garden. His belly rocked like a choppy sea.

'It's rude to laugh at me,' Zellie told him.

Reach brought himself under control. 'I'm sorry.' He allowed her a moment of peace before continuing his interrogation. 'Do you have a boyfriend?'

Zellie thought of Rodrigo. He was almost a boyfriend. 'Yes.'

'And does he like your clitoris?'

'Yes,' she said in a resigned tone.

'What does he like about it most?'

She thought for a moment. 'It's very sensitive.'

'You come easily?'

'Yes.'

'I like a woman who comes easily. Maria comes easily, if I let her – though usually I like to tease her. Does your boyfriend ever do that?'

All of the sexual predators in Zellie's life liked to do that. 'Yes,' she admitted.

'I would like to make you come. But I would tease you. I would make you wait. An hour, two hours, perhaps.'

Two hours! Rodrigo never had the patience to make her wait that long. When he was feeling cruel he would rouse her to a frenzy and then stop and make her finish herself off. One night, after forcing her to hold back while he fucked her mouth and fingered her until she was almost crazy, he had taken her into the street and made her masturbate under a street light while he laughed like a maniac.

216

Maria returned with a seat. She set it out in the shade, facing the prone figure of Reach.

'Zellie was saying that she comes very easily.'

The girl nodded as if she already knew.

'She has a very sensitive clitoris apparently.'

Maria smiled in Zellie's direction. 'I think you are embarrassing her,' she said softly.

'I like to see her blush.'

Zellie was indeed blushing. She waved her hand across her face in a futile attempt to generate a cooling breeze.

'Are you hot, my dear?' Reach asked.

'A little,' the flustered Zellie managed to say.

'Would you like to take off that dress?'

Zellie shook her head shyly while Reach grinned from ear to ear.

'Well, it's time for my treatment,' the old man continued, looking expectantly at Maria. The girl nodded and walked over to the head of the bed. 'If you wait, we will talk some more,' he told Zellie with a glint in his eye.

'OK,' said Zellie.

'It might test your capacity for understanding and acceptance. Think of it as a Christian trial. But I will do a deal. If you can show patience while Maria does her work, if you can see what it is that makes her so special, without flinching, we will talk as much as you like.'

Zellie didn't know how to react.

'Are you a prude about nudity?' Reach asked.

Zellie shifted uncomfortably. 'Not so much.'

Reach smiled. 'Good. Nudity is essential for my treatment.'

Zellie took a deep breath. 'OK,' she murmured with a sigh of resignation. This was not going at all as she had expected. The worst that she had imagined was

217

reading a very boring book to an old man who could hardly stay awake.

Reach turned to Maria. 'Just carry on as normal, as if we were completely alone,' he told her. 'Zellie is a Christian. Zellie understands that sins are committed so that good men can forgive them. And good women can enjoy them.' He directed the final remark at Zellie with an ironic smile.

Maria fetched a small earthenware bottle from the house and a bowl of ice water. A sponge floated amongst the bobbing ice cubes. She set the bowl on the ground and then poured oil across Reach's body with a slow steady motion. The sweet smell came again strongly. When she reached his groin Maria flicked back the covering cloth. His penis was semi-hard, resting on a bed of greying pubic hair. Its mouth was pointing directly at Zellie. He smiled when she took a sharp breath. 'What sort of things did you want to talk about?' he asked pleasantly as if nothing had happened.

'I don't know,' she stammered.

'Hampton must have said something.'

'He seemed to think that you don't go out very much.'

'I don't go out at all,' he told her in a heavy voice.

Maria placed the bottle on the ground and made Reach comfortable, rearranging the bedding, slipping a pillow under his head so that he could relax but still see Zellie. Then her hands began a slow, even massage of Reach's body.

'I have no need to go out,' Reach continued, stretching out his arms to the side.

There was silence as Maria worked her way around his body, beginning with his great fleshy legs, moving on to his Buddha-like belly, sweeping down his long arms and then beginning all over again. The girl's face was impassive, beautiful in the diffused sunlight. Reach seemed to sink a little deeper into the bed with each caress. His creased face with its wrinkles and lines seemed to fill with shadows. His eyes grew rounder and his mouth slack. He seemed to grow older but also more and more baby-like. His fat belly quivered as Maria worked on it. He gave gurgles of pleasure and Maria responded with soft, low sighs.

It was impossible for Zellie not to be drawn in. The languor of the enclosed garden, the slow repetition of caress and sigh, the heavy scents of the papai blooms – all these things slowed the mind and produced a dreamy torpor. Zellie felt her body slipping down in her seat as each of her muscles relaxed in sequence. The only dissonant note was provided by Reach's sex. As everything else relaxed and softened, it filled and hardened.

Zellie couldn't help but watch in fascination as it rose from his groin in a great arch, an arch that would have been shocking in any other place. The mouth breathed out a drop of liquid and Zellie's clitoris finally began its own steady swelling. Beads of sweat broke through the hot skin of her face. Her legs opened by infinitesimal degrees.

Maria glanced at her. She made sure than Zellie knew that the sweat had been seen. Then, her eyes flickered across Zellie's opened groin. Here only the thin cotton of a summer skirt protected Zellie's sex. From within the folds, a powerful new scent was rising. It was a scent that women knew. It was a scent that Zellie found herself happy to share with the gentle-eyed girl.

Looking into Zellie's eyes mischievously, Maria let her hands sweep down the sides of Reach's belly and, just for a moment, the fingertips grazed the bulging sex. Immediately, a low shuddering sigh spilt from the old man's throat.

'Water,' Reach groaned.

'Sorry, Mr Reach,' the girl murmured, still smiling in Zellie's direction.

She hurriedly leant over and picked the sponge from the bowl of ice. She squeezed out the excess liquid and laid the freezing sponge across his sex. He gave a high cry and Zellie realised how close he had come to orgasm from the simple touch of those fingertips. For a moment, Zellie imagined what it would be like to have her own body caressed by the quiet and beautiful girl – a girl who seemed to want only to give. Zellie slipped further in her seat, her legs opened a fraction more.

This time, Reach noticed. His eyes opened wide and gazed at her belly. They tried to slip beneath her skirt.

'Do you need ice?' he asked.

'Not yet,' Zellie replied, giggling sleepily.

Reach began to smile but Maria squeezed the sponge and a gentle flood of water coursed down his balls. His eyes closed and he gave another little cry. Maria leant forward and took his sex in her mouth – but only for a moment. It was a tease, a come-on.

Reach groaned again and his eyes opened. He had the expression of an infant on waking. He was calm once more. His breathing was deep and even. His hands and feet curled and uncurled with sensual satisfaction.

Maria replaced the sponge in the bowl and, now that the crisis was passed, resumed her massage in the gentle way that she had begun. A faint breeze filtered through the hot garden but not enough to dispel the sweet smell of the oil. There were sounds from the distant street but nothing to break the spell of deep and steady breathing, long loving caresses, burning swollen sexes.

Maria neither quickened nor slowed her pace but her focus shifted. She pulled Reach's legs wide and worked on the inside of his thighs, stretching and compressing the lined, old-man skin. She squatted on the bed and lifted his knees onto her shoulders. She worked into the folds of his buttocks as clear fluid dribbled from the side of his lax mouth. When she finally stopped and let Reach's legs back onto the ramshackle bed, Reach lay motionless. Wiping her hands, Maria gazed impassively across the flower-bright garden.

Zellie realised that the old man was asleep. As he slept, his penis gently bobbed as if in his dreams Maria was with him, and still caressed him.

'He sometimes comes like this,' Maria said over her shoulder in a soft voice. 'While he dreams. I catch his seed in my mouth and save it for him to see when he wakes.'

She walked over to Zellie and ran her hand down the side of Zellie's face. 'You are such a pretty girl,' she said.

Zellie didn't know what to say. She had no energy to resist the older girl. Neither did she want to. At the same time, Zellie felt that it was wrong somehow, that she should be strong.

Maria knelt and looked deep into Zellie's eyes. 'May I touch your skin?' she asked.

Uncertain, Zellie didn't react for a moment.

'I shall be respectful,' Maria promised.

'OK.'

Maria laid her hand on Zellie's bare ankle.

'I can feel your pulse,' she said. 'Such a slow steady beat!' Her hand ran slowly along the inside of Zellie's leg. 'It's as smooth as the side of a glass. Where do you feel my touch? In your chest or your belly?'

'Both,' breathed Zellie.

'Head, heart and pussy. When these three are joined, a woman is very powerful.'

'I don't believe that I have any power,' Zellie said softly. Maria's hand had reached her knee. It strayed beneath her skirt for a moment and there was a sudden

221

surge of excitement. She gasped and Maria sat back on her haunches with a broad smile.

'Was that a bad feeling or a good feeling?' Maria asked.

Zellie flushed. 'Both.'

'Both? Because I am a girl like you?'

Zellie smiled. 'I like men.'

'So do I,' Maria told her. She stood and walked back to Reach. 'He won't want to sleep long today. He won't want to come without seeing you again.' She picked up the bottle of oil and poured a thin stream into her hands. She started the long slow caresses again.

Reach stirred. His eyes opened with a little shudder and he examined Zellie with a languid expression. 'Do you think an old man deserves this?' he asked.

Zellie thought of the colonel. To Zellie, the colonel, too, was old. 'I think all happiness is good.'

Reach looked at her doubtfully. 'Even your own?'

Zellie smiled. 'Even my own, sometimes.'

'They will tell you that sex is a monster in that church of yours. But it is guilt that is the monster . . .' Reach's eyes turned to Maria as she moved around the bed. 'But let us forget theology,' he said softly. 'I am going to be fed.'

Maria undid the top of her blouse. Looking deep into Reach's eyes, she reached inside and took hold of her left breast. Reach licked his lips as Maria pulled out the large, perfect globe. When her hand came away, it lolled on her ribcage like a great pale moon. The nipple was broad and prominent. Its elongation was arresting.

Maria looked into Zellie's eyes again. Zellie sensed the girl's great desire to give. The sense of it slipped inside Zellie like a mist. She felt her throat open a little. She swallowed nervously. She had never wanted a girl, sexually. Even when she kissed a girl (to turn on Eduardo, to please Rodrigo), the arousal came from the lengthening of a boy's penis, not from the touch of a girl's skin. This was different. It wasn't to do with skin at all. It was something that Zellie did not understand. Something even closer to life somehow than pussies and penises, fucking and being fucked.

Maria smiled and sank onto the bed beside Reach. She stroked his head and then arranged herself so that her breast was in reach of his mouth. Reach gazed at the globe and the red flower that bloomed there. He licked his lips again. He had the look of an ancient addict – his eyes turning black as the pupils dilated, desire making his loins quiver, the light of reason fading from every feature until only longing remained.

Maria reached under the pillow that supported his head and pulled out a small jar. She unscrewed the top and a new scent filled the air – a scent like chocolate but not chocolate, a scent like milk but not milk, a scent so strong and so overwhelming that it made Zellie feel faint.

Maria dipped her finger into the jar and then ran her fingertip around her erect nipple.

Reach groaned. He gazed at the glistening nipple as if nothing else in the universe existed or had ever existed. His lips puckered. His head jerked forward. With a great sigh, he sucked in the red flesh and was connected.

The girl smiled widely and stroked his forehead.

Zellie felt the tension – a tension she had not even noticed until that moment – leave her body. As unnatural as the sight of an ageing man suckling from a young woman was, it seemed somehow right. The well-rehearsed routines, the harmony of man and girl, made it seem as if nothing else could happen in this garden.

Reach began a slow steady sucking. His penis seemed to grow even larger, strain even higher.

Maria began to hum a simple tune, a lazy sound with a hint of sadness. Her eyes turned to Zellie again. She had the inner peace of a Madonna. She had the patience of water. She seduced without movement, drew Zellie closer without invitation, enfolded her without using either arms or legs.

Zellie found her sex growing warmer. She felt herself settle even lower in her seat so that her pubis came to be more and more and more raised. In a dreamy way, she realised that she was offering herself to the girl. She realised that Maria expected it. It felt right. It felt exciting in a slow way. The arousal spread to her belly with the stealth of the sun slipping through the garden. It seeped into her thighs as a delicate heat. It took a long time for the need to become urgent. Maria watched Zellie with the same patience that she showed the old man. Each time Zellie's legs opened a little wider, each time her pubis reached a little higher, Maria acknowledged the movement with the faintest flicker of a smile. It felt to Zellie as if she were inching her way into the girl's arms. It felt as if she were edging her way into a store of boundless warmth, where the shelves were full to bursting with smiles and caresses, a place where perfect breasts could be offered.

Zellie felt that she too could suckle. Her mouth, too, could be filled with paradise. All she needed to do was ask – something that was so easy and so difficult.

Maria wriggled her leg a little so that her shoe fell off. A foot appeared. It was the colour of olive oil and as smooth and subtle. It gleamed in the diffused sunlight as it crept along Reach's belly. The toes flexed and tightened, stretched out to caress. A single slender tarsal dipped into Reach's belly button. He gurgled. The foot moved on. It hovered over his sex.

There was a sudden tension and Maria's smile grew wider. Reach was no longer breathing. He was waiting for the foot to descend.

Maria stroked his head, whispered into his ear. She was teasing him, making him wait. Then with only the slightest of movements there was the first contact of toe and sex. Reach's back arched. Maria gave a flurry of caresses to his forehead and chest, calming him, slowing him. He gave a deep groan and relaxed.

Now Maria's toes opened. They were as dextrous as any fingers. With reverence and grace, with the delicate touch of a mother, she took the quivering column between her toes and drew downwards. The foreskin pulled clear and the violently red head of the penis was exposed. At the same instance, with no bidding, with no deliberation, Zellie's legs fell open completely and she slipped even lower in her chair. The breeze caught the hem of her skirt and flicked it up. For the first time, Maria could gaze at Zellie's pussy clad only in the scantiest and thinnest of thongs. The engorged, near-bursting clitoris was as prominent and visible as the penis of an infant.

The girl froze. She seemed mesmerised.

Zellie was also stricken. She was staring at the taut penis. She had forgotten that it was an old man's. It was a thing on its own, a thing of itself. It was a column of flesh that she simply wanted because it was male and powerful and ready. It filled her vision. It created its own world – a world where Zellie was a series of openings, humming with the need to be filled.

Then a breath of wind flicked Zellie's skirt back into place.

Maria regained her composure and began to sing in Spanish. The words were soft and the tone low. It might have been a lullaby. Her foot began a steady up and down motion, so slow that each stroke seemed to take a full minute.

Zellie could hardly bear the tension. She knew that Reach must come soon. His chest was filling and emptying like a great set of bellows. Sweat was breaking from every part of his huge naked body and with every passing moment, he was sucking harder and harder on the girl's nipple.

From time to time, Maria winced and Zellie realised that he was biting. Strangely, after each nip she stroked his head as if to reassure him that she was OK, that she still loved him. Soon, though, the biting seemed to intensify. Maria gave little groans of pain, but even as her face contorted and she gave her little cries, she still caressed his head, still maintained the steady motion of her foot.

Then, when it seemed impossible that he would not come, Maria pulled away. Reach howled in frustration. The sound ricocheted around the garden like a bullet of pain.

Maria quickly swung around on the bed. Her foot found Reach's face, the big toe slipped into his mouth. He groaned with satisfaction and began to suck and gnaw. At the same time, Maria took his sex in her hand and worked it across her breast. Her nipple was red and distended from Reach's chewing. She worked the head of the penis slowly around the distended aureole. She opened the mouth of the penis with finger and thumb and worked her erect nipple into the opening. Reach was slobbering like an infant. His legs were twitching as he successively lost control.

Maria moved on to using her tongue on his balls. Reach writhed and bore it but when her lips slipped around the head of his sex it was too much.

'Water!' he cried immediately.

Maria reached for the sponge and applied it to his balls. Again the orgasm was averted.

Zellie's heart was pounding. She was sweating. She wondered how an old man could stand so much pleasure. She wondered if she would be forced to watch him die.

'I want to see the girl when I come,' he groaned.

Maria stood up and rearranged his bedding. She propped up his head so that he could see Zellie.

'You are an angel,' he told her. 'Sent to complete this paradise.'

Zellie blushed.

Suddenly, and without being instructed, Maria reached over and deftly flicked aside the hem of Zellie's dress. She gave a little laugh as Zellie's tight panties were revealed.

'So wet,' the girl breathed.

Zellie blushed even more deeply. She knew that she should cover herself, she knew that she should hide the dark stain of excitement that spread from the mouth of her pussy. At the same time, she knew that she had offered herself to the girl freely. She had offered herself and now she could not take it back.

'Is there more?' Maria whispered, leaning over so that her breath was soft and warm on Zellie's neck.

'More?' Zellie asked.

Maria's lips grazed the smooth, hot skin of Zellie's neck. 'Are you going to show us more?'

Zellie gave a little whimper. This had not been what she had come for. She had come to do good. She had come to be a listener. She had not volunteered to be an object of desire for an old man.

'I need to see her,' Reach said with sudden urgency. 'Completely.'

'Are we allowed to see you completely?' Maria whispered. Her lips sealed themselves around Zellie's earlobe and drew down in a moist sucking kiss.

Zellie whimpered again. There was a note of arousal this time and a note of surrender.

'Is that a yes?' Reach murmured.

'Can we look?' Maria asked again.

'If you want to,' Zellie told her, softly.

Maria knelt between Zellie's wide-flung thighs. Her hands took the sides of the stained panties. She smiled into Zellie's eyes as she drew them down.

A little gasp came from the girl's lips as Zellie's pussy was revealed.

'She is so big!' she said with excitement.

'Let me see!' called Reach.

Maria's body shielded Zellie's pussy from his view and she stood quickly so that Reach too could see the perfect sex. He too gasped.

Zellie had the overwhelming urge to close her legs but Maria left the panties around her ankles and used her hands to keep Zellie's knees wide.

'Like a boy,' he groaned in satisfaction, examining the engorged clitoris. 'Make it stand up.'

'I will not touch unless you ask me to,' Maria whispered. 'But I want so much to see all of you.'

Maria dipped her head and blew a stream of warm air across the pink glistening flesh of Zellie's sex. Zellie's belly expanded with breath and the clitoris popped from its hood. Another warm stream of air made Zellie groan with excitement and her clitoris rose proud and true.

'She should be fellated,' Reach declared.

Maria gave a soft low laugh. 'Would you like that?' she asked Zellie.

Zellie used her little remaining self-control to shake her head.

'She is shy,' murmured Maria.

'But she said that we could look,' Reach responded.

Maria slipped her hands under Zellie's knees and raised them high. Zellie's pelvis rotated so her pussy was upright. Maria pressed outwards until Zellie's buttocks parted and the pink rim of her anus was visible.

'She seems loose. Are you loose, dear?' Reach asked.

The words had a strange effect. Her pelvis seemed to relax completely, her pussy unzipped to reveal the red, blood-gorged interior, her anus pouted out, then opened.

Reach took a deep breath. 'She wants you,' he told Maria.

'Do you want me?'

Zellie blushed again. It was too much to admit to a strange girl.

'She is still shy, I think.'

'Her sex organs aren't shy. Her pussy is salivating, her anus is hungry.'

'Do you let boys into your bottom?' Maria asked.

'I think it is practised,' Reach interjected.

Zellie felt dizzy.

Reach's dark, rich, knowing voice, Maria's seductive smile and gentle but relentless questions were dissolving her defences. As the tide of words washed over her and drowned her in their pressure to disclose, as her own desire stripped her of restraint and dignity, she felt that she might pass out.

'Tell us,' Maria whispered, blowing air across Zellie's beautiful anus until it flickered and opened even further.

'If they want it that way,' Zellie murmured.

She glanced at Reach. She read in his eyes that the old man wanted her that way too. She wondered if she would be able to say no. If he were to stand and take that column of burning flesh and press it to her anus, would she even be able to murmur a feeble protest?

'I think that sometimes you can't say no,' Maria told her.

For a moment it seemed as if Reach were already inside her. Her bowels churned as the words penetrated.

'Is that true?' Reach asked the blushing, opened girl.

A tear squeezed from the side of Zellie's eye. 'Sometimes,' she admitted.

'Hold your legs like that,' Maria said softly. Zellie took hold of the backs of her thighs obediently and

Maria's hands came away. Zellie's pussy and anus remained open, like a pair of startled eyes.

'If you want to be touched, tell me,' Maria told her, stepping back to the bed.

Zellie hid her face in her shoulder. She was shy with strangers. She did not like to ask. Shyness was one of Zellie's weaknesses.

Reach brought his knees up and opened his legs wide, mimicking Zellie's posture. Maria knelt and took Reach's sex into her mouth. He groaned as the girl worked the sex deep. When her lips were pressed against his pubic bone, she stopped and kept absolutely still. Her fingers came to play with Reach's balls. They walked up and down his perineum with the delicacy of birds' feet. They tiptoed across the ancient rim of his anus.

Reach's eyes began to bulge, but still they darted from Zellie's blushing face to the widely stretched flesh of her groin.

Even as he came, he looked deep into the obscenely spread girl, deep into her pussy, deep into her anus, deep into her eyes.

He shuddered at the end, finally becoming still but for a panting chest and those large, scouring eyes.

Maria stroked his belly in slow circles for long minutes.

'You need something too, my darling,' Reach said to her after a while. His voice was dreamy now, as full of contentment as a cream-fed cat. It was Maria's turn to blush.

'I can wait,' she murmured softly.

'Wait? There is no need to wait. Zellie wouldn't want you to suffer.' He turned to Zellie. 'Would you?'

Zellie shook her head.

'I love Maria as I love myself,' Reach told her, his voice suddenly heavy with regret, 'but I cannot *make* love to her.'

Reach held out his hand and Maria took it with a smile.

'I can only watch as she makes herself come, or I can finger her or pay another man to fuck her as a young woman should be fucked but I cannot fuck her myself. It is painful to watch the woman that you love sucking another man, it is painful to watch her hold open her legs or her behind for another man to enter. It is even more painful to watch her come. But I never want Maria to go unsatisfied. That would be even more painful. Do you understand?'

Zellie nodded.

'And I know that at this moment, she is as wet as you are, and as aroused as you are.'

He pulled Maria closer and told her to raise her skirt. Slender fingers as brown as nuts pulled the fabric to her waist. Exceptionally slender thighs were revealed. A dark pubic region, impenetrable like a rainforest, occupied the space between. The belly was fuller than might be expected and broad, as if size was needed to contain such a slow-burning heat – and heat there was. As the skirt was raised it felt to Zellie as if a furnace door had been opened. A wave of desire scorched her face and belly. Zellie pulled her legs even wider – a jerky, involuntary movement that neither Reach nor Maria missed.

'Do you want to ask?' Maria said, gazing down at the flushed girl.

Zellie nodded then avoided her eye.

Reach's hand was beginning a slow ascent along the inside of Maria's thigh.

'I want you to ask, very much,' Maria said softly. 'I want to make you happy.'

Reach's fingers were probing the margins of the dark forest. There were little flashes of light as he rifled through the black pubic hairs.

Zellie summoned her courage. 'I want you to touch me,' she said in a soft, low tone. Overcoming shyness was one of Zellie's weaknesses.

Reach's fingers found a sensitive place and Maria groaned. 'She wants you to touch her,' he said. 'But I want you to touch you.'

'Will you touch me from behind?' Maria asked.

Reach nodded. 'Of course.'

Maria stepped closer to Zellie then knelt. Her behind was raised towards Reach, her head descended to bury itself between Zellie's thighs.

Reach slipped a gnarled finger into the dark purse of flesh. He pulled out moisture, carried it to his lips, tasted.

Maria, too, was tasting girl come. Her tongue was beginning a careful examination. She was unwrapping nerves, sucking membranes from their hiding places. She was seeking sensitivities.

Reach slipped in a second finger. He began to probe. His hand began to vibrate. Maria became less exploratory. She began to consume.

Zellie felt her whole pussy being sucked into the girl's mouth. She was being eaten in a way that no boy had ever eaten her. She realised that Maria, for all of her soft smiles, was a predator, as much as any boy.

Soon there were teeth, nipping and tugging, pulling and peeling. Zellie cried out.

'Gently,' Reach said softly. 'No forgetting who you are.'

Maria opened her mouth and Zellie's pussy, released, retracted into her belly.

The girl's eyes opened. Zellie was held by the fire of dark eyes. Tongue and lips were soon in play around Zellie's swollen finger of flesh, gentler now and more controlled.

Reach sat up heavily so that he could see better. He told Maria to tuck her hair behind her ears. He wanted to read her eyes. He wanted to taste what she tasted.

Zellie realised that he was hardening again already. His penis was semi-erect. She watched as he squeezed lubricant from the end and rubbed it around the prepuce. Then Maria's tongue found a place that was unbearably sensitive. Zellie was tipped into orgasm. She began to struggle.

Reach understood the problem immediately. He sent Maria for rope. They tied her open-thighed in the chair and began again.

It was going to be a long afternoon.

18

Sirius Swoops

A few days after her meeting with Magus Reach, Zellie was once more attending church.

The Reverend Forty had telephoned. He had thanked her, he had flattered her, he had begged her to help with the preparations for another fund-raising sale. So Zellie had come, dutifully and humbly, Dolores dropping her off in the vast car park surrounding the high-tech structure.

Male eyes watched as the girl with golden hair stepped from the car, but they were not the eyes of the Reverend Forty. It was Sirius who had been waiting for her, loitering in the bell tower like Quasimodo, smoking cigarette after cigarette like a nervous teenager. As soon as Zellie disappeared through the bronze doors beneath him, Sirius spun on his heel and flashed down the spiral staircase.

Reaching ground level, he surveyed the crowded concourse then, zeroing in on the blonde hair and perfect proportions, he swept directly towards his goal. Catching sight of the approaching whirlwind, Zellie smiled nervously. There were traces of guilt in her mind. She had no idea what Reach might have said, or to whom he might have spoken. Equally, she had no idea if Sirius had set her up, sending her as a sexual morsel for a dirty old man. If he had done that, he might want more from her.

As soon as she saw his expression, though, she realised that something new was in play. He was focused to a point that seemed almost painful. His eyes were locked on hers. A girl knows when a man is interested in her. Sirius was interested. Sirius was determined to show that he was interested.

'Zellie,' he said immediately. 'I've been looking for you.'

Zellie's hand went to her chest. 'For me?' She flushed.

'Do you think that's strange?'

'I don't know.' He was standing close. His extra height gave him power. His supreme self-confidence made him hard to resist. 'I need a date for the annual church dinner.'

The church dinner was quite an event. It was part of the season. It was the place where the great and the good mingled to bestow charity on lesser beings.

'Will you come?' he asked.

It was hard to say no. If he had asked to slip his fingers inside her womb it would have been even harder to say no. He moved a little closer, close enough to make Zellie feel faint – good-looking and rich was something new for Zellie.

The finger of flesh was twitching hugely – Sirius was more than boy, he was very definitely man.

'OK,' she said finally.

'OK?' He grinned. She was surprised. He was a measured man, even Zellie could see that, but the grin was wide. 'How did the thing with Reach go?' he asked.

It seemed a throwaway question, an excuse to study her lips and eyes while she talked. He seemed to be measuring her.

She gave a throwaway answer. 'It was fine. He seems OK.'

'Good.'

235

Zellie couldn't know it but Sirius was measuring her for a wedding dress.

Fate, standing a little to Sirius's left, was also in a measuring mood. He was measuring Sirius for a fall.

nexus

The leading publisher of fetish and adult fiction

TELL US WHAT YOU THINK!

Readers' ideas and opinions matter to us so please take a few minutes to fill in the questionnaire below.

1. Sex: Are you male ☐   female ☐   a couple ☐?

2. Age: Under 21 ☐   21–30 ☐   31–40 ☐   41–50 ☐   51–60 ☐   over 60 ☐

3. Where do you buy your Nexus books from?
☐ A chain book shop. If so, which one(s)?

_____

☐ An independent book shop. If so, which one(s)?

_____

☐ A used book shop/charity shop
☐ Online book store. If so, which one(s)?

_____

4. How did you find out about Nexus books?
☐ Browsing in a book shop
☐ A review in a magazine
☐ Online
☐ Recommendation
☐ Other _____

5. In terms of settings, which do you prefer? (Tick as many as you like.)
☐ Down to earth and as realistic as possible
☐ Historical settings. If so, which period do you prefer?

_____

☐ Fantasy settings – barbarian worlds
☐ Completely escapist/surreal fantasy
☐ Institutional or secret academy

- ☐ Futuristic/sci fi
- ☐ Escapist but still believable
- ☐ Any settings you dislike?

_____

- ☐ Where would you like to see an adult novel set?

_____

6. In terms of storylines, would you prefer:

- ☐ Simple stories that concentrate on adult interests?
- ☐ More plot and character-driven stories with less explicit adult activity?
- ☐ We value your ideas, so give us your opinion of this book:

_____

_____

_____

7. In terms of your adult interests, what do you like to read about? (Tick as many as you like.)

- ☐ Traditional corporal punishment (CP)
- ☐ Modern corporal punishment
- ☐ Spanking
- ☐ Restraint/bondage
- ☐ Rope bondage
- ☐ Latex/rubber
- ☐ Leather
- ☐ Female domination and male submission
- ☐ Female domination and female submission
- ☐ Male domination and female submission
- ☐ Willing captivity
- ☐ Uniforms
- ☐ Lingerie/underwear/hosiery/footwear (boots and high heels)
- ☐ Sex rituals
- ☐ Vanilla sex
- ☐ Swinging
- ☐ Cross-dressing/TV
- ☐ Enforced feminisation

☐ Others – tell us what you don't see enough of in adult fiction:

_____
_____
_____

8. Would you prefer books with a more specialised approach to your interests, i.e. a novel specifically about uniforms? If so, which subject(s) would you like to read a Nexus novel about?

_____
_____
_____

9. Would you like to read true stories in Nexus books? For instance, the true story of a submissive woman, or a male slave? Tell us which true revelations you would most like to read about:

_____
_____
_____

10. What do you like best about Nexus books?

_____
_____

11. What do you like least about Nexus books?

_____
_____

12. Which are your favourite titles?

_____
_____

13. Who are your favourite authors?

_____
_____

14. Which covers do you prefer? Those featuring:
(Tick as many as you like.)

- ☐ Fetish outfits
- ☐ More nudity
- ☐ Two models
- ☐ Unusual models or settings
- ☐ Classic erotic photography
- ☐ More contemporary images and poses
- ☐ A blank/non-erotic cover
- ☐ What would your ideal cover look like?

_____

15. Describe your ideal Nexus novel in the space provided:

_____

_____

_____

_____

16. Which celebrity would feature in one of your Nexus-style fantasies? We'll post the best suggestions on our website – anonymously!

_____

THANKS FOR YOUR TIME

Now simply write the title of this book in the space below and cut out the questionnaire pages. Post to: Nexus, Marketing Dept., Thames Wharf Studios, Rainville Rd, London W6 9HA

Book title: _____

NEXUS NEW BOOKS

To be published in December 2007

BUTTER WOULDN'T MELT
Penny Birch

When Pippa is accepted as a trainee at a city law firm, she fondly imagines a life both cultivated and intellectual, rather than the crew of sleazy ambulance chasers she ends up with. Worse still, they know rather more about her private life than she would have liked, leaving her little choice but to accept some deeply humiliating duties and help them out in areas which involve very little legal know-how and a great deal of having her knickers taken down. Then there's AJ, notorious diesel dyke and boss of a motorbike courier firm, who regards Pippa as her private property, and American businessman Hudson Staebler, who has his eye on Pippa's little sister.

£6.99   ISBN 978 0 352 34120 4

UNIFORM DOLLS
Aishling Morgan

This is a story straight from the heart of a lifelong uniform fetishist and conveys the sensual delight to be had from wearing uniforms and enjoying others in uniform. Whether it is the smartness and authority of military dress, the sassy temptation of a naughty schoolgirl, or the possibilities offered by an airhostess, policewoman or even a traffic warden, it is all described here in sumptuous and arousing detail, along with unabashed accounts of kinky sexual encounters.

£6.99   ISBN 978 0 352 34159 4

If you would like more information about Nexus titles, please visit our website at www.nexus-books.com, or send a large stamped addressed envelope to:

Nexus, Thames Wharf Studios,
Rainville Road, London W6 9HA

NEXUS BOOKLIST

Information is correct at time of printing. To avoid disappointment, check availability before ordering. Go to www.nexus-books.com.

All books are priced at £6.99 unless another price is given.

NEXUS

☐ ABANDONED ALICE	Adriana Arden	ISBN 978 0 352 33969 0
☐ ALICE IN CHAINS	Adriana Arden	ISBN 978 0 352 33908 9
☐ AQUA DOMINATION	William Doughty	ISBN 978 0 352 34020 7
☐ THE ART OF CORRECTION	Tara Black	ISBN 978 0 352 33895 2
☐ THE ART OF SURRENDER	Madeline Bastinado	ISBN 978 0 352 34013 9
☐ BEASTLY BEHAVIOUR	Aishling Morgan	ISBN 978 0 352 34095 5
☐ BEHIND THE CURTAIN	Primula Bond	ISBN 978 0 352 34111 2
☐ BEING A GIRL	Chloë Thurlow	ISBN 978 0 352 34139 6
☐ BELINDA BARES UP	Yolanda Celbridge	ISBN 978 0 352 33926 3
☐ BIDDING TO SIN	Rosita Varón	ISBN 978 0 352 34063 4
☐ THE BOOK OF PUNISHMENT	Cat Scarlett	ISBN 978 0 352 33975 1
☐ BRUSH STROKES	Penny Birch	ISBN 978 0 352 34072 6
☐ BUTTER WOULDN'T MELT	Penny Birch	ISBN 978 0 352 34120 4
☐ CALLED TO THE WILD	Angel Blake	ISBN 978 0 352 34067 2
☐ CAPTIVES OF CHEYNER CLOSE	Adriana Arden	ISBN 978 0 352 34028 3
☐ CARNAL POSSESSION	Yvonne Strickland	ISBN 978 0 352 34062 7
☐ CITY MAID	Amelia Evangeline	ISBN 978 0 352 34096 2
☐ COLLEGE GIRLS	Cat Scarlett	ISBN 978 0 352 33942 3
☐ CONCEIT AND CONSEQUENCE	Aishling Morgan	ISBN 978 0 352 33965 2

☐ CORRECTIVE THERAPY	Jacqueline Masterson	ISBN 978 0 352 33917 1
☐ CORRUPTION	Virginia Crowley	ISBN 978 0 352 34073 3
☐ CRUEL SHADOW	Aishling Morgan	ISBN 978 0 352 33886 0
☐ DARK MISCHIEF	Lady Alice McCloud	ISBN 978 0 352 33998 0
☐ DEPTHS OF DEPRAVATION	Ray Gordon	ISBN 978 0 352 33995 9
☐ DICE WITH DOMINATION	P.S. Brett	ISBN 978 0 352 34023 8
☐ DOMINANT	Felix Baron	ISBN 978 0 352 34044 3
☐ DOMINATION DOLLS	Lindsay Gordon	ISBN 978 0 352 33891 4
☐ EXPOSÉ	Laura Bowen	ISBN 978 0 352 34035 1
☐ FRESH FLESH	Wendy Swanscombe	ISBN 978 0 352 34041 2
☐ THE GIRLFLESH INSTITUTE	Adriana Arden	ISBN 978 0 352 34101 3
☐ HOT PURSUIT	Lisette Ashton	ISBN 978 0 352 33878 5
☐ THE INDECENCIES OF ISABELLE	Penny Birch (writing as Cruella)	ISBN 978 0 352 33989 8
☐ THE INDISCRETIONS OF ISABELLE	Penny Birch (writing as Cruella)	ISBN 978 0 352 33882 2
☐ IN DISGRACE	Penny Birch	ISBN 978 0 352 33922 5
☐ IN HER SERVICE	Lindsay Gordon	ISBN 978 0 352 33968 3
☐ INSTRUMENTS OF PLEASURE	Nicole Dere	ISBN 978 0 352 34098 6
☐ THE ISLAND OF DR SADE	Wendy Swanscombe	ISBN 978 0 352 34112 9
☐ JULIA C	Laura Bowen	ISBN 978 0 352 33852 5
☐ LACING LISBETH	Yolanda Celbridge	ISBN 978 0 352 33912 6
☐ LICKED CLEAN	Yolanda Celbridge	ISBN 978 0 352 33999 7
☐ LONGING FOR TOYS	Virginia Crowley	ISBN 978 0 352 34138 9
☐ LOVE JUICE	Donna Exeter	ISBN 978 0 352 33913 3
☐ LOVE SONG OF THE DOMINATRIX	Cat Scarlett	ISBN 978 0 352 34106 8
☐ LUST CALL	Ray Gordon	ISBN 978 0 352 34143 3
☐ MANSLAVE	J.D. Jensen	ISBN 978 0 352 34040 5
☐ MOST BUXOM	Aishling Morgan	ISBN 978 0 352 34121 1
☐ NIGHTS IN WHITE COTTON	Penny Birch	ISBN 978 0 352 34008 5

- - - - - ✂ -

Please send me the books I have ticked above.

Name   ....

Address   ....

              ....

              ....

              .... Post code ....

Send to: **Virgin Books Cash Sales, Thames Wharf Studios, Rainville Road, London W6 9HA**

US customers: for prices and details of how to order books for delivery by mail, call 888-330-8477.

Please enclose a cheque or postal order, made payable to **Nexus Books Ltd**, to the value of the books you have ordered plus postage and packing costs as follows:

UK and BFPO – £1.00 for the first book, 50p for each subsequent book.

Overseas (including Republic of Ireland) – £2.00 for the first book, £1.00 for each subsequent book.

If you would prefer to pay by VISA, ACCESS/MASTERCARD, AMEX, DINERS CLUB or SWITCH, please write your card number and expiry date here:

....

Please allow up to 28 days for delivery.

Signature ....

Our privacy policy

We will not disclose information you supply us to any other parties. We will not disclose any information which identifies you personally to any person without your express consent.

From time to time we may send out information about Nexus books and special offers. Please tick here if you do *not* wish to receive Nexus information.   □

- - - - - ✂ -